Men and women swept up in the turbulent currents of a nation's history . . . embraced by the irresistible forces of human desire

MICHAEL BRANT—Courageous son of the great Mohawk Aaron Brant, he must make a heartbreaking choice between family and country when betrayal forces him to join a rebel's cause.

CHARLES MILLER—Stern loyalist supporter of British rule, he willingly sacrificed his own son to further his ambitions . . . and to win a young girl's hand.

ELIZABETH MILLER—Adopted daughter of the Brants, her family mourned her as dead, while she faced a new life as an Indian priestess on the dangerous Northern Plains.

WILHELMINA MACKAY—Pixie-faced "Willie," she followed her father into a battle for Canadian freedom, but she feared she would always be a prisoner to her own secret love.

RAINBOW—Raven-haired Indian maiden, her dark eyes looked with adoration at the fair blond stranger, and so sealed a fate that would bring her face to face with terror . . . as well as desire.

JOSHUA MILLER—Defiant young patriot, he fearlessly fought for his dreams as he completed the path to glory begun by his forefathers in the dramatic saga of *Blackrobe*.

THE CANADIANS
A people ready to fulfill a promise
of greatness in a vast, towering land

Seal Books by Robert E. Wall
Ask your bookseller for the books you have missed

THE CANADIANS
by
Robert E. Wall

VI
DOMINION

SEAL BOOKS
McClelland and Stewart-Bantam Limited
Toronto

*For my sister, Barbara Wall Vachris,
and for her husband, James E. Vachris*

DOMINION: THE CANADIANS VI

A Seal Book / April 1984

ISBN 0-7704-1843-0

PRINTED IN THE UNITED STATES OF AMERICA

H   0 9 8 7 6 5 4 3 2 1

Acknowledgments

With the completion of this volume, the series *The Canadians* draws toward a close. I can honestly call it a labor of love, but there is no doubt in my mind that to write a series like this, one had also to be a lover of labor. I began *Blackrobe* in 1978 and completed it in 1979. It was published in January of 1981. The rest of the series, *Bloodbrothers, Birthright, Patriots, Inheritors,* and *Dominion* were written between 1980 and the date of this writing—two days after Armistice Day 1982.

Earlier in the series I thanked many of those who made *The Canadians* possible. I renew those thanks. In addition, I would like to thank Tanya Long of Seal Books and Beth Thompson of the Sterling Lord Agency for their patience. Also I would like to thank Jack McClelland for all his help and guidance.

I must thank my staff and the faculty at the Rutherford campus of Fairleigh Dickinson University for not assuming that the lights that burned in my office until 1:00 or 2:00 A.M. meant that the campus was in crisis. Also I must thank my doctors and nurses at the Hackensack Medical Center for pulling me through a ruptured appendix and giving me the "stuff" for the death of Stephen Nowell.

I must once again thank my typist, Nancy Traficante, and my editor, Jennifer Glossop, of Toronto. In addition, Robert Allen, Deputy Chief, Treaties and Historical Research, Department of Indian and Northern Affairs, Ottawa—military historian par excellence—saved me from many errors with his extraordinary knowledge of Canada's past. I thank him.

But most of all, I must thank my wife, Regina, for continuing to love me—"Through It All."

Robert E. Wall
Val David, QUEBEC
November 13, 1982

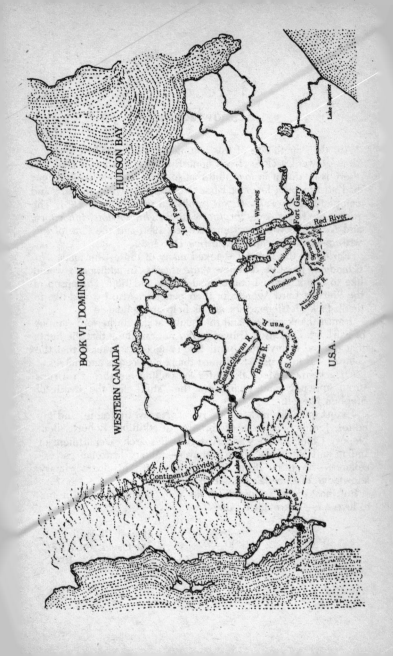

BOOK VI · DOMINION

WESTERN CANADA

HUDSON BAY

York Factory

L. Winnipeg

Fort Garry

Red River

L. Manitoba

Minnedosa R.

Spruce Fort

Assiniboine R.

Lake Superior

N. Saskatchewan R.

Battle R.

S. Saskatchewan R.

U.S.A.

Edmonton

Continental Divide

Lake

Fraser R.

Ft. Victoria

A GENEALOGY

BOOK VI - DOMINION

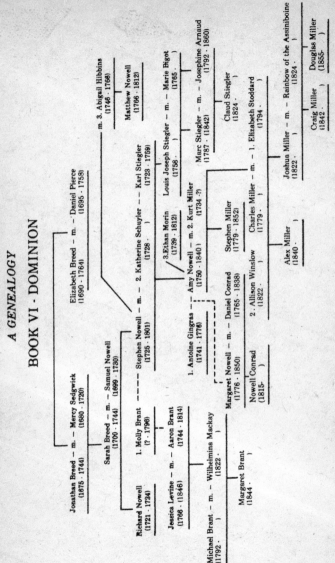

Prologue

1826

The magistrate twisted in his chair to relieve the pain in his foot. It was no use. His gout was acting up again, and the courtroom was packed with the curious. He hated these family disputes, especially with a family as powerful as this one. If he sided with Charles Miller, his career in York politics would run smack against the influence of the Honorable Michael Brant. But if he sided with Brant, he antagonized the richest man in all Upper Canada. He thanked his stars that the facts were clear-cut; all he had to do was stick to them.

"Mrs. Brant," he questioned Jessica, "you say that your grandson, Joshua Miller, was left to you for safekeeping and rearing by his uncle, Stephen Miller?"

"Yes," Jessica said firmly. "And with the concurrence of Mr. Charles Miller," she added for good measure.

"And how did his uncle come into possession of the boy?"

Jessica watched the magistrate warily. "Mr. Miller—Mr. Stephen Miller, that is—was traveling in company of my daughter, Elizabeth, when she gave birth to the child. After my daughter's death, Mr. Miller, Mr. Stephen Miller, took the child to England. He only recently returned Joshua to York on his way back to the Red River Settlement."

"What say you to that, Mr. Miller?" the magistrate asked.

Charles sat in his chair. He felt very weak. He had not yet totally recovered from the wounds he had received at the hand of his secretary, John Sutherland. He had just

ix

returned to his own home and had begun to look after his own business affairs. He was not sure why he had undertaken this legal battle except that he wanted the boy. He wanted Elizabeth's son. If he could not have her, the boy was the next best thing. He had restored the money to the Brants but he had kept Eli's portion. That belonged to Joshua now and Joshua belonged to him. He had given the Brants what he owed them. Now it was their turn to make restitution.

"Mr. Miller?" the magistrate interrupted Charles's reverie. "What say you to Mrs. Brant's assertion?"

"I have a question to ask her," Charles said, standing with the aid of a cane. He approached Jessica's chair on the far side of the magistrate's bench. "Am I or am I not the boy's father?"

Jessica did not respond. She knew that she could claim that Stephen was really Joshua's father. All York believed that anyway. But it would be a public admission of a guilt she knew her daughter had not deserved—an open and public admission that her innocent daughter had been an adulteress and the true cause of the split with Charles. Even if it might win her Joshua, she could not lie about Elizabeth.

"You are his father," she said in a soft voice.

"Please speak up," the magistrate interjected.

"Yes, Charles, you are his father. But I am his grandmother and that counts for something."

"Noble gesture, madam," Charles said. "But I am not noble, as you already know. The child's mother was your daughter, Elizabeth?"

"Correct," Jessica responded.

"Now, can you show me the evidence of Elizabeth's birth as a child of your body?"

"You know she was not."

"Ah, yes, she was your adopted daughter. Can you produce the legal evidence of that adoption?"

"I have adoption papers here, sir," said Michael Brant to the magistrate, and he presented the man the papers.

The magistrate placed his lenses on the tip of his nose and glanced at the papers. "These are all in good order except that they seem to award the child Elizabeth to the guardianship of one Mr. Eli Stoddard. I see no mention of the name Brant, either yours, Mrs. Brant, or the name of your late husband, Mr. Aaron Brant."

"And, sir," Charles spoke up, "the Mr. Stoddard mentioned in those papers is recently deceased. In fact, Mrs. Jessica Brant is no blood relation to Elizabeth Miller, who all agree is also deceased. Mrs. Brant has no blood or legal relationship to the boy, Joshua Miller, and therefore no right to keep him away from his lawful parent, his father."

"Mr. Brant," said the judge, "do you have a response to Mr. Miller's allegations?"

Michael rose to his feet. He looked over at Charles. He found the man despicable. Jessica had nursed him back to health and he repaid her by trying to take from her the only new joy that had entered her life since the death of her husband.

"There are other considerations beyond blood ties, sir," Michael began. "I am prepared to raise allegations about the moral fitness of Mr. Miller to raise the boy, Joshua."

Charles smiled at Michael, and the spectators commented to each other that the juicy parts would now start to be revealed.

"Mr. Miller," said Michael, "is known to have kept a housekeeper to whom he paid wages more suitable to the upkeep of a mistress."

"Michael, I never thought you would equate generosity with sinfulness," Charles interrupted.

There was some laughter in the room, and the magistrate called for silence.

"This woman," Michael continued, "this Virginia Meachum was known to be a woman of loose morals. Before her employment by Charles Miller she was a tavern wench and a practicing prostitute in her father's saloon on Front Street, which I am happy to say has since been closed by local ordinances that I myself sponsored."

Again there were murmurs in the courtroom.

"Are you prepared to bring this Meachum woman to court to testify, Mr. Brant?" the magistrate asked.

Michael shook his head. "I am sorry to say that we have

been unable to locate Miss Meachum anywhere since she jumped the bail set for her after her arrest at the time of the assault on Mr. Miller. She seems to have disappeared. But her character is known and her dwelling in the Miller household is an established fact."

"Mr. Brant, this is a justice-of-the-peace hearing. But even if it is not a formal trial, you are an attorney and therefore you must know that what you introduce here is not valid evidence without the presence of Miss Meachum."

Michael was prepared to bring in a host of witnesses who would testify that Ginny Meachum was a whore; some were even willing to testify that they had paid for her services. And he knew that he could establish her residence in the Miller house. But he had known, even before entering court, that without her actual testimony, he had little chance of success. Jessica had insisted on the fight and he would go through the exercise. He would call his witnesses.

Once the last testimony had been given, the gossips of York had enough grist to supply their mills for the coming year and beyond. But little had changed the basic facts. Joshua Miller was Charles and Elizabeth Miller's son. The Brants were not blood relations. The boy's other blood relative, the uncle who had raised him to this point, had deserted him and returned to the west. His paternal grandmother was old and lived off in Lower Canada somewhere. The boy had an aunt who lived in the United States but whom no one in the family had heard from in years.

"Do you have anything further to add, Mr. Brant?" the magistrate asked. Michael shook his head.

"Mr. Miller?"

"Just one further point on good character. I am a member of the Church of England here in York. I would like to ask Mr. Brant which church he attends?"

"I am an Anglican also," Michael responded.

"And your mother, the woman who proposes to raise my son, what church does she belong to?"

"My mother does not attend any church," Michael said rather defensively.

Jessica jumped from her chair. "Why don't you proceed, Charles Miller? My maiden name is Levine. My father's name was Moishe Levine. I am a Jewess. And therefore not fit parent for a Christian boy. That is where you're heading, isn't it? Why don't you ask me those questions?"

Charles smiled at her. "I don't have to. You've already answered them for me."

Jessica kissed Joshua atop his reddish-blond head. The nurse whom Charles had hired to care for his son waited impatiently in the hallway for the boy to be delivered. Joshua tried to throw his arms about his grandmother and cling to her.

"Go with her, son," Jessica said. She had no more tears left. Michael took the boy's hand and led him to the woman in the foyer.

The nurse took Joshua's hand and led him out the front door.

Jessica joined Michael at the door and watched Joshua disappear down Bay Street. Michael held his mother close to him to comfort her.

"I'm sorry, Mother," he said.

"You did your best. No need to be sorry. But Charles Miller is going to be sorry. I've only begun to wage this fight."

He looked into her face, but he did not see the expected determination there.

Part One

TORONTO

I

Toronto, Upper Canada, August 1837

Joshua Miller could not take his eyes off the tip of the choirmaster's nose. It was bulbous and warty. But its size and lumps were not the source of his fascination. He had seen Master Buckam's warts before. But now a drop of sweat hung precariously between two knobby protrusions as if thwarted by some invisible dam. Inevitably it would trickle through the obstacles and fall onto the white pages of his open psalter. But when? If Willie were here, Joshua was sure she would quote odds and place bets on the timing. But the very thought of Wilhelmina Mackay in St. James Church—the heart of Tory Upper Canada—was unthinkable.

The archdeacon's words droned on. The church was like an oven in August. The sweat soaked through Joshua's pants and cassock and the cloth made a peeling sound when he rose from the varnished pews for the Doxology.

The droplet fell with a splat onto the open book, startling Master Buckam. He raised his right arm to start the choir, and with the drooping sleeve of his surplice he discreetly brushed the sweat from his face. He looked about before his hand fell to see if any had seen his action. His eyes rested on Joshua.

Joshua quickly brought his hand to his mouth to hide his grin. Buckam would surely have something to say to his father if he displeased him, and Joshua wanted no further trouble with Charles Miller.

As he sang out in unison with the other choir members, his eyes sought out the tall frame of Charles Miller in the family pew. He knew his father's lips would be closed. Charles Miller offered no praise to the Father, the Son, and the Holy Ghost. Joshua knew that his father believed in no gods. He came to St. James only because he believed that the Church of England was a bulwark of conservative government and that conservative government was the salvation of Canada. Joshua knew that his father believed in nothing but Canada.

Heaven knew he did not believe in Joshua. He told the boy he was nothing but trouble. At times Joshua almost believed the stories that people whispered behind his back—that his real father was Stephen Miller, Charles Miller's twin brother. Only Master Buckam had had the nerve to say it, or rather to spit it into his face. Yet Charles Miller had fought his mother's family—the Brants—for control of him, and Charles Miller had won. Joshua had never dared ask his father why. He must love him, or maybe he just hated the Brants. No word had passed between the two families in ten years. He saw his uncle, Michael Brant, dark and swarthy-looking, on the opposite side of the church.

The hymn was suddenly over and Joshua was caught standing alone when the rest of the choir sat down. He hurriedly flopped back down onto his seat, again drawing the attention of old Buckam. For two full minutes he paid complete attention to the archdeacon and then again his eyes wandered. He focused on his unknown uncle. Brant was part Mohawk and part Jewish. Michael's dead father was Aaron Brant, the fabled Kenonranon, sachem of the Turtle clan and a hero of the battles of the Revolution and the War of 1812 against the Americans. Michael Brant's adopted sister was Joshua's mother, Elizabeth. She had drowned while he was a baby. Joshua's grandmother was the 70-year-old Jewish lady who no longer accompanied her son to church. Rumor had it that she had returned completely to her Hebrew ways and practices after years of token Christianity.

The sun poured through the leaves of the elm tree that stood next to the church. As a breeze parted clusters of leaves and branches, the light struck the stained-glass

4

windows, spraying the interior of the church with sudden splashes of red, yellow, and blue.

Joshua was startled when a streak of violet played on his Uncle Brant's dark features. All at once he knew what the great Kenonranon must have looked like when he entered battle, his face painted for war. In some ways Michael Brant was already at war, at war with Joshua's father, Charles. The two men stood at opposite ends of the political spectrum. All his life, Joshua had heard of how men like Michael Brant's own father, Aaron Brant, along with Archdeacon John Strachan and others, had protected them all after the American rebellion, protected them from the chaos and social revolution of mob rule that existed across the border in the United States. Men of property, of sober concern for justice under the law, sat in the seats of power in York. This, Charles Miller said, was how it must be.

Yet Michael Brant had joined the reformers like Robert Baldwin and occasionally even with radicals like William Lyon Mackenzie, who called for a broader franchise and responsible cabinet government along British reform lines. To Joshua, all that did not seem so bad, but his father denounced Michael Brant as "a Jewish traitor—a man who had deserted the cause of his own father and who would try to force on all of us an Americanized republican rabble."

Joshua was not sure what all this meant, but he knew it was bad.

Again he was jolted back to the ceremony as the congregation rose for the general thanksgiving. As his uncle stood, Joshua caught a glimpse of Allison Winslow. She had been hidden from his view by Brant. But his rising gave Joshua his one holy moment of the morning—the sight of Allison's golden face.

Her hair was a honey blond and her eyes were green, not hazel like some other girls', but actually green. Her nose was straight and perfect, and when she smiled, which she did not do often enough to suit Joshua, he felt himself captive. He did dumb, funny things to try to make her laugh just to see that smile, and when he succeeded he was driven to further absurdities to attempt to succeed

5

again. He knew she thought him a fool, but he could not help himself. Her father and his father were friends— well, not really friends. Charles Miller had no friends. Rather, they were business associates, and both were ardent followers of the gospel according to Archdeacon Strachan—loyal to the king and to the Church of England and the annual reelection of the right type of men—men of wealth and position.

Joshua had heard both Judge Winslow and his father argue on several different topics in his father's study but never did they differ on these basics. Nor was there any room given to Joshua to differ. He attended grammar school in the old blue schoolhouse. His instructors had been personally selected by the archdeacon for their religious and political orthodoxy.

They finished the final hymn and the archdeacon left the altar behind the procession of acolytes and choir members.

Once they were safely hidden from the view of the congregation, Buckam grabbed Joshua by the ear. The boy squealed with pain. The noise attracted the archdeacon's notice and he turned to face the choirmaster.

"Mr. Buckam," he said, "I think you should wait until we are out of range of sound as well as sight before you begin your punishment of the offspring of our congregation. Now, what did my friend Charles Miller's son do to earn your ire?"

"Nothing significant, sir. Just a wandering mind and wandering eyes—especially during your sermon."

Joshua tried to twist away from the pain but Buckam's fingers were like a vise gripping the lobe. Every twist produced shooting pains up the side of his head. He cried out again.

"Buckam, enough! It's bad enough his mind wanders; do you wish him a wandering ear as well? Let well enough alone. Let it remain attached to his head. Without an ear how is one to hear the word of God, even if, as I preach it, it does not seem to make much of an impression on Master Miller's mind."

The choirboys started to laugh. Buckam reluctantly let

go his grip. Joshua pulled away from the choirmaster and wiped the tears of pain from his eyes.

"I'll get you, Miller," Buckam whispered after the archdeacon left. "But next time I'll wait until His Nibs can't save you. He's too partial to the sons of 'The Family.'"

Joshua was out of his surplice as fast as he could pull it over his head. He scurried out the back door of the sacristy, out onto the corner at Church Street. The sun was still hot, but it had rained all day and muddy York still lived up to its reputation. Wagons moved slowly through the puddles in the road and splashed water onto the sidewalks.

Allison stood on the gravel path that led from the sacristy to the street. Joshua could not believe his good fortune: She was alone, her white frilly dress gleaming in the August sunlight. Her head was covered with a white bonnet but her blond curls escaped from it at the sides and in the back.

Joshua stopped running as soon as he caught sight of her. He started to walk down the path in her direction, whistling, his hands shoved into the back pockets of his trousers.

"Good morning, Miss Allison," he called to her.

"Why, it's Joshua Miller. My, you've just shot up since you went off to that school to study Latin."

"I guess I have growed a piece," he said, arching his whole body up a bit to appear even taller.

"My, I think you would be better off learning a bit of English," she responded slyly.

"Mr. Woodward, the schoolmaster, says that Latin can help you master any tongue if you learn the grammar well," he said, missing the point of her remark altogether.

But she was already bored with correct grammar. Her attention began to wander.

"Can I walk you home?" he asked.

"Goodness no. What would people say? They might begin to gossip about us—like we were spoken for."

Joshua wanted to say that fifteen-year-olds weren't spoken for, but he dared not contradict her for fear of losing his chance to speak with her.

"Besides," she continued, "my father's carriage is coming to fetch us home. He's still discussing politics on the church steps. I got tired of listening so I came down the street hoping to meet the carriage."

As she spoke, a wagon, clearly overloaded with lumber, came careering down the muddy avenue toward them. Its wheels sent a spray of mud high into the air. Allison saw it coming. A look of panic crept into her eyes. Joshua turned to see what it was that frightened her. He had no chance to step back. The spray of mud splattered against his Sunday suit. But Allison had time to duck behind him and use him as a shield. The wagon driver cursed at his horses, at the two children in the pathway, and at the world in general. The vehicle tilted first one way and then another, splashing all in its path.

The mud spray was warm but it might as well have been cold. It still shocked Joshua. It stuck to his body and his face. Even his hair was coated with mud.

Allison stamped her foot indignantly as she stared at the disappearing wagon. Then she turned to Joshua. Her indignation melted and gave way to an expression of concern.

"Oh, Josh," she said, "how brave you were! You protected me from the mud. I would kiss you if only I could find a spot on your cheek that wasn't slimy."

Now Joshua truly hated the wagon and he hoped the driver burned in the deepest fires of hell. A kiss from Allison Winslow was worth a mud bath. Losing that kiss was something not to be endured.

"Joshua, what in God's name?" He recognized his father's angry tone. Charles Miller, followed by Judge Winslow, Allison's father, came up the street toward them.

"Oh, Mr. Miller," Allison cried out. "Please don't be angry with Joshua. He was so gallant. He stepped right in the path of the mud. He absolutely saved me from mortal embarrassment. Imagine having to walk the streets of York with my dress completely ruined. I promised him a kiss as a reward but I can't find a clean place on him."

"None of that, child," Allison's father chuckled. He didn't take kindly to his daughter's forwardness. He had his hands full with her, or at least his wife did. But then again, if she kissed any mother's son it might as well be Miller's boy. The Nowell fortune, increased manifold by Miller's shrewdness, would all come to this mud-covered waif. He was the right choice for Allison.

Charles looked sourly at his son. He had little use for gallant gestures. They might be all right for boys or for fools like his twin brother, Stephen, but most men who indulged in them ended up dead, broken, or both.

"Go home and get yourself clean," he said. His annoyance was obvious in the clipped tone of the order.

Joshua did not know how to evade the horns of the dilemma. If he attempted to mollify his father and openly admit that he had not moved an inch to protect the girl, he would lose the adoring attention of Allison, whose sweet olive perfume even now enveloped his senses. He decided to remain silent.

"I'm driving your father home in my carriage, Joshua," said Judge Winslow. "I'd have offered you a lift also, but I am afraid we couldn't take you like that. The mud would be all over the seat. I'm afraid, boy, you walk. Come, Allison, your mother awaits us."

"Couldn't I walk with..." Allison turned to look at Joshua as she spoke, and her voice trailed off before she could complete the request. The brown-spotted face and clothes of the youth were reminiscent of the clown's in the traveling play troupes that often visited York in the summer months.

Joshua knew instantly that she thought he looked ridiculous. He began to wipe his jacket fruitlessly with his muddy hands. But her whole demeanor had changed. He knew that his chance of a walk home with Allison had slipped away with the last dart in his direction of those cool green eyes. Her own fiction of his gallantry had fallen before the cruel reality of the mud that dripped from the end of his own nose.

"Good-bye, Joshua," she said, taking her father's arm and walking with him toward the street, carefully keeping him between herself and the offending mud puddle.

Miller smirked at the boy. "Don't get messed up, Joshua,"

he remarked. "Remember those are your best Sunday clothes." He turned on his heel and followed Winslow toward their carriage.

Joshua followed Allison with his eyes. He didn't care how his father ridiculed him. Allison had offered to kiss him. He waited until they disappeared around the corner of the church, and then he gave a loud whoop of joy and leapt a good foot off the ground.

He turned to cut through the churchyard when he felt something hard bounce off the back of his head. He ran his muddy hand through the ooze that had soaked into his blond hair. He pulled his hand away and smelled it—apple. He looked off to the other side of the churchyard where the apple tree stood, its branches loaded down with its still green burden. He caught a motion in the highest branches. There was no breeze and Joshua had a good idea what caused it. He continued to walk across the yard in the direction of the cemetery. But as soon as he was out of sight of the apple tree, he stepped backward and pressed himself against the wall of the church. He had waited only a few brief seconds when a figure, clad in brown homespun and with a beaten-up felt hat pulled loosely over its head, came racing around the corner, arms loaded with hard green apples. Joshua stuck out his leg. Brown-and-green confusion resulted. Apples shattered against the walls of the church, and the felt hat went flying backward. The brown-clad figure fell in a heap at Joshua's feet, landing in apples and squashing them all over the jacket and pants.

"Son of a bitch," screamed the fallen assailant.

"Girls aren't supposed to curse, Willie," Joshua reproved her mockingly.

"Tell it to your mother, Miller."

Suddenly a frown replaced her anger. She had forgotten about Joshua's mother. Her retort had been instinctive.

"You're a little puke, Willie," Joshua responded angrily. "Why did you wait for me. Why the apple attack?"

"What difference did it make? You're already covered with scum anyway from saving the fair Allison. Oh, brave knight," Willie mocked, "you saved me from the mud

10

monster. How can I repay you? With a kiss perhaps. Kiss my ass."

Joshua moved toward the figure of the girl sprawled on the ground.

"Go ahead," she taunted him. "Hit me."

Joshua pulled back. "I don't hit girls."

"You bastard," Willie cursed him. "I ain't no prissy-assed whore like Allison Winslow."

"You watch your tongue, Willie. Allison is a real girl. Not some bedraggled orphan pretending she's something she's not, like you."

Now Joshua had touched on Willie's sore point. She didn't care about his feelings anymore.

"I ain't no orphan, Joshua Miller. I got me a daddy just like you. My mother may be dead, but at least she only slept with my daddy—not like yours."

The veins in Joshua's temples pounded with anger and his face turned a scarlet red.

"I'd kick your ass across Bay Street, Willie Mackay, if you were a boy," he spat out at her.

"Kiss my bum, Joshua Miller," she retorted. "It smells the same as Allison Winslow's mouth." Willie turned her rump toward Joshua and patted it with her hand.

The sight of the girl forcing the brown felt hat back down on her head with one hand and her ample rear turned awkwardly in his direction suddenly turned Joshua's anger off. He started to laugh. Deep rolling waves of laughter struck him. He leaned against the walls of the church for support, and still the laughter came.

"What's so funny?" Willie yelled, annoyed at his sudden change of mood. It left her feeling insecure. She was sure that he was laughing at the way she looked. But inevitably his laughter became contagious and Willie began to laugh in sympathy, not exactly sure what it was that was so funny.

"What is it, Joshua?"

"We're just so pitiful-looking, both of us, mud-covered, apple-covered," he said gasping for breath.

Willie stared down at herself, then she too began to laugh again.

11

Finally, Joshua sighed and his laughter started to subside.

"Why did you throw the apples at me?" he asked, still having trouble catching his breath.

Willie just shrugged. She would have preferred Allison, the sun-drenched golden Allison, as a target. But she dared hurl the apples only at muddy Joshua. Willie rose to her feet and tried to pick pieces of muddy apple off of her butternut-colored pants.

"Do you want to come with me?" she asked, looking up into his face.

He brushed the blond hair from his muddy forehead. The whole world seemed to be blond to mousy-brown Willie Mackay. He started to shake his head but she didn't wait for him to say no.

"Come on, Josh. Daddy's got a meeting going on."

"I've just come from church. Once a Sunday is enough. Besides, my pa's death on Baptists. If he heard I was stepping into a Baptist meeting, he'd whip my rear until it bled."

"I don't mean any kind of religious meeting. Daddy ain't much of a Baptist. He ain't much of anything, except a drinker. I 'spect you ask my dad what his religion is and he'd tell you he was a 'confirmed imbibist.'"

Joshua didn't know what she was talking about. Sometimes Willie scared him. He was the one who went to the Anglican Academy and Allison was being taught to be a young lady at Miss Upshaw's, but it was Willie who knew everything. His father had told him that Donald Mackay had been one of the first Presbyterian ministers in Upper Canada until he was expelled from the church as a drunk. He had broken his wife's heart and she had died within months of his excommunication. He had taken up Baptist revival meetings, although even that group was on the verge of breaking ties with him. One more drunken sermon and Mackay would be deprived of his platform. But he had a library in his run-down shanty off King Street and he had taught his motherless waif of a daughter to read—and read she did. Incessantly.

Joshua could parse the verb *ferre* and he had memo-

12

rized much of the *Anabasis*, but he knew very little compared to Willie.

"I don't care what kind of meeting you got going, Willie, my pa is not going to want me to be there."

"It's some meeting, Joshua. Politics. All the important politicians are there. Mackenzie, Baldwin."

"You mean all the troublemakers will be there. The radicals, atheists, like Ryerson."

"Ryerson ain't no atheist, he's a minister. A Methodist minister. Besides, he's in England."

"Same thing," said Joshua without flinching. He was sure of it. His father knew about politics, and his father had told him that all the Reformers were atheists. The Methodists had been Reformers too, although not so much in recent times—not since Mackenzie, the crazy Scotsman, and Egerton Ryerson had fallen out.

"Even your uncle, Michael Brant, is going to be there."

Joshua's interst was suddenly sparked by the mention of Brant's name.

"What's he doing there?"

"What are any of them doing there? They are plotting— what Daddy said they would be doing—plotting. And they got some sweet cider as well as hard. We could probably get some without even asking."

It was Brant, however, not the sweet cider, that lured Joshua down the back streets toward the wood-frame Mackay house. The picket fence around the yard needed painting and several of the wooden pickets were broken, the top portions tilted like arrows down the muddy streets toward the better part of town. A mongrel dog slept quietly on the wooden steps that led up to the kitchen door. He bared his broken yellow teeth at Joshua, but when he saw Willie his nose rose into the air. He sniffed at her legs and then went back to gnawing on a large rock he held snugly between his two front paws.

"Stupid shithead of a dog," Willie said, but in a tone so filled with affection that it caused the mongrel to wag its snakelike tail.

"Deacon, you're such a shithead," Willie said a second

time, bending down and patting his head. "Only dog in Canada that eats rocks."

"He doesn't really eat them?" Joshua asked.

"No, just chews them and breaks his damned teeth." She laughed. "He's so stupid that Daddy named him Deacon in honor of the Reverend Mr. Strachan."

Joshua was shocked by her remark about John Strachan, the name he most revered. At home his father spoke of the deacon with respect—perhaps the only man of whom Charles Miller ever spoke favorably. At school the master and the boys referred to the founder in whispered reverence. How many times had he heard Strachan praised as the Father of Upper Canada, the Loyalist of Loyalists—the framer of the policy of balanced government, the British tie, and the Anglican church, Father of the Family Compact, author of all that was right and holy. And the Mackays had named their stupid rock-eating mutt after him.

Willie pulled open the wooden kitchen door, and the boy and the girl stepped into the darkness of an unwashed pantry.

"Dog's bladder is going," Willie offered, to explain the acrid smell of urine that rose from the floor. "Going to have to keep him in the yard from now on."

They heard voices coming from the parlor. Willie found the pottery cider jug sitting on the wooden table in the center of the room. She sniffed it, then wrinkled her nose in distaste.

It was hard to see in the gloom of the airless kitchen. Willie moved to the sink and began to pull on the handle of the pump. The clanging of the pump mechanism was followed by the gush of cool water from the tap.

"Come over here and get the mud off your face and hair," she said.

Joshua stepped to her side. She smelled of green apples. It was not at all an unpleasant aroma, even if more common than Allison's sweet olive. He stuck his head under the water as she pumped. It felt deliciously cool in contrast to the heat of the day outside. He pulled his head away and swept his blond hair backwards, spraying water in several directions. He looked about for something to

14

dry his jace. Willie handed him a towel. It smelled of soap and the sun and fresh air. And he knew that she tried to keep this house from turning into a pigsty, but from the look and the smell of the kitchen he guessed she was losing the battle.

The voices continued to come from the parlor. When Joshua finished drying his face Willie handed him a clay mug of cool sweet cider. They pushed through the kitchen door into the hallway.

"I'm home, Daddy!" Willie called out.

The voices in the parlor stopped and then Donald Mackay's deep bass voice called out a greeting.

"Play outside or go up to your room, Willie. We're doing business in here."

The girl stepped onto a landing leading to a flight of steep, narrow steps. Joshua followed her. The two of them sat on the hard wooden steps and, unseen in the gloom, peered into the smoke-filled parlor.

"I am telling you now," said a voice from inside the parlor beyond Joshua's view, "the only reason I came to this meeting was Brant. I would never be so foolish as to trust you Methodists ever again. I said it in the old *Colonial Advocate* and I'll say it again in my new paper, the *Constitution*: You people are Jesuits in the garb of Methodist preachers."

The owner of the voice paced from the back of the room into full view of the landing. Joshua recognized the former mayor of Toronto, as York was now being called, William Lyon Mackenzie. He was shouting, and even from the gloom of the landing Joshua was quickly mesmerized by the steel blue of his eyes. His body, however, was tiny and crooked, almost malformed. He wore a disheveled red wig to cover his baldness. The wig occasionally slipped over his eyes and ears and gave him a totally lopsided look. But as he spoke Joshua soon forgot how silly he appeared.

"We are controlled, gentlemen, by a cruel and vindictive priesthood—the archdeacon and his Tory cronies have leeched this province of its lifeblood of liberty. I come from poverty in Scotland and I have made my way here in Upper Canada. There is no doubt that a man may thrive

15

and, aye, he may be able to support a wife and put some milk into his wee babes, but I'd rather be starving and free back in my old home in Scotland than have more money than Charles Miller and be a slave to a Tory Family Compact here in Toronto. The time to rise up and strike is upon us. You can't just sit there while Strachan and his new lieutenant governor, Sir Francis Bond Head, forge new chains for you. He is well named, this Bond Head. He'll have some bond feet and bond wrists for you as well."

The man in the minister's garb whom Mackenzie had attacked rose from his chair.

"I've heard all of this from you before, Mackenzie, and the Reverend Mr. Ryerson has warned us of you. He has revealed the true nature of your radicalism back in Britain. It's godless talk. Your British allies are all atheists. Not the type of people men of God should be allied with."

"It wasn't godless talk when the Anglicans had all the mission money tied up and you Methodists were starving. It wasn't until the British opened the purse and found a few pieces of silver in there for you that we Reformers became godless and not fit companions for Methodists. How many pieces were there? Thirty or so?"

"I don't have to listen to this," said the Methodist.

"Of course you don't," said another, calmer voice. "Mackenzie has his sights set on becoming a Canadian Andy Jackson. He'll bring democracy to all with a touch of American republicanism."

Mackenzie turned ferociously on this new voice.

"Baldwin, you are a bloodless one. What does the Family Compact have to do to you before you get your dander up?"

"All I want, William, is a democracy. I don't need any Yankee republic."

"It's democracy you want is it? Well, how is it that although I've been elected to the Assembly, I've been denied my rightful place by a spiteful Tory pack of wolves? And it has happened not once, but more times than our minister friend here could count on his fingers and toes," quipped Mackenzie. "Where's the democracy in that? Why, you yourself were appointed to the council and still the governor refused to be responsible to either house of our legislature. You resigned, and the bloody prime minister in England told us that responsible government, which they are getting over there so slowly in Britain, is not so good for the colonies. You'll wait a long time for your democracy, Robert Baldwin. You'll be an old man with a beard down to your navel, counseling the young men to patience and a British system fifty years from now, should you live so long. I've no such patience."

"I'll not have a Congress or a president, Mackenzie. I'll have a queen and a Parliament."

"I don't care if you have a monkey in the circus, man, so long as I have my freedom. The forms don't matter. It's only the results that count." Mackenzie stomped his foot as he shouted, and his wig almost fell off of his head.

Joshua and Willie started to giggle.

Willie's father turned sharply toward the stairs.

"Wilhelmina? I thought I told you to go upstairs."

"Leave the girl be," said Mackenzie. "She should be hearing every word. My fight is for the young ones rather than for the old has-beens like you, Donald Mackay."

A new voice broke into the discussion. Joshua recognized it. It was his Uncle Brant.

"I don't agree with your method, William. There are reports that you've got farmers making pikes and drilling in the back country. Are you planning an open rebellion? The rumors are all over the place, the back country up Yonge Street is rallying to you."

Mackenzie smiled. "I've got me a few friends in Hog's Hollow and Lansing and New Market and Holland's Landing." He pulled his wig back into position. "You don't think I'm damned fool enough to answer that question directly, do you? Not with a member of the governor's executive council sitting in front of me."

"A resigned member," corrected Baldwin.

"That's your trouble, Bobby, you're too resigned." Only William Lyon Mackenzie and Mrs. Baldwin could have

17

gotten away with calling the dignified leader of the moderate reformers Bobby. Even so, Baldwin's mouth pursed almost as if he were sucking a lemon.

"Responsible government is the answer, Mackenzie. A cabinet, an executive responsible to a Parliament. That is what we must have in Canada."

"Yet Lord John Asshole—I mean Russell," Mackenzie corrected himself, smiling and bowing toward the now totally silent reverend, "has just announced in London his ten resolutions denying us a responsible executive and an elected legislative council and attacking the basic principle that only a properly elected Assembly, the Commons, can vote money to the executive. In fact, he empowers the lieutenant governor to use what available funds they have even if the Assembly pulls the purse strings tight. Whether we approve it or not doesn't matter anymore. Next I suspect our beloved lieutenant governor will try to vote taxes without Assembly approval."

Again Brant interrupted. "What you're saying sounds an awful lot like what my grandfather told me Sam Adams said back in 1775 in Boston."

"Well, Sam Adams must have been right if he sounded like me," said Mackenzie. "And you mustn't forget that Strachan and his ilk were the very ones who tried to suppress freedom in the thirteen colonies. The Americans had the good sense to kick the bloody Tories out. Unfortunately for us, they kicked them into Canada."

"You go too far, Mackenzie," Brant said softly. "You forget that among his ilk were men like my father, Aaron Brant, and his uncle, Joseph Brant, and our family friend and physician, Eli Stoddard. They were men of courage and conviction. They fought the Americans for the right to disagree. They came to Canada to exercise that right. You and I are enjoying that freedom this very moment."

"Tell that to Mr. Robert Gourlay, who organized the convention of townships back in 1818," interrupted Mackay. "Strachan's bunch expelled him from Canada."

Mackenzie interrupted Mackay. "Tell that to the people of this county who have elected me to represent them in their Tory Assembly and who have been without a voice

18

because your Tory friends won't seat me. Tell that to those who have been bilked by the bank of Upper Canada and who have been robbed by the very proper Charles Miller and his Welland Canal bunch." Again Mackenzie was stamping his foot.

Willie leaned over and whispered in Joshua's ear. "This is boring. Let's go back to the kitchen and get some more cider."

Joshua shook his head. He had never before heard his father criticized. He had never heard ideas like those expressed by this fierce little man, certainly never spoken aloud. They were foreign ideas, ideas his father, Charles Miller, Tory of Tories, would have detested, but they were exciting ideas—partly because they defied his father's thinking, but also because Mackenzie spoke of freedom and freedom of expression and personal liberty to a boy who had known little of either.

"It is not much different in Quebec," continued Mackenzie. "My good associate Louis-Joseph Papineau has been in touch."

"A Papist," Mackay said sourly.

"William," said Baldwin, "how can you support Papineau and his crowd?"

"Because they fight the same tyranny in our sister province of Lower Canada."

"Mackenzie," Brant spoke out, "the French protesters argue against the very freedom you call for. If they rebel, they will rebel *against* reform, not for it. They want a return to the old ways. You and Papineau have very little in common."

"We have a common enemy: Lord Gosford, the governor-general, for him, and Sir Francis "Bone" Head, his lieutenant in this province of Upper Canada, for me."

"You might as well include the queen as an enemy, Mackenzie," said Baldwin angrily, "and if she's on your list then you had better add my name."

"And mine," said the minister.

There was silence in the room. All turned to look at Michael Brant.

"Mine too," he said, just above a whisper.

19

Mackay grabbed Mackenzie's shoulders. "Be of good heart, William. I am a true Highlander. I'll stay by your side."

"Aye," said Mackenzie, "but for the wrong reason. Would that you'd stay by me because you were a good Canadian. Well, I'm sorry, gentlemen, but I must do what I must do."

He turned abruptly from his listeners and walked out into the hallway. He did not even glance at Willie and Joshua. He opened the front door and slammed it behind him.

The minister and Baldwin spoke briefly to Brant. Mackay was clearly annoyed with his guests and no longer made any pretense of playing the gracious host. He left his own parlor and went alone into his kitchen looking for his jug of hard cider. The three remaining men started for the front door.

"Uncle Brant?" Joshua called out.

Michael stopped and stared at the gloomy landing. He removed his spectacles. He wore them normally only for reading, but in the parlor he had been glancing through the latest edition of Mackenzie's *Constitution* and he had forgotten to remove them.

"Is that you, Joshua?" he asked as a smile of recognition crossed his face.

"Yes, sir."

Brant started to laugh. "Good God, if Mackenzie had known that Charles Miller's son was listening to every word he said in there he would have had a stroke of apoplexy. It was bad enough that a Methodist minister was called to the meeting. What brings you to this den of sedition, young man?"

"The chance to speak with you, sir," the boy responded.

The softness that came into Brant's eyes had the startling effect of gentling his face. He was no longer the hard-nosed man of politics. Now he was Jessica Brant's son, lonely Jessica Brant, who longed for the opportunity to do what he did—to speak with her dear Elizabeth's child.

"Walk with me," he said to the boy. "We'll take the back

streets and cut through the yards—the long way around to Bay Street. I don't want too many prying eyes to see us together."

They walked through the hall together and out into the kitchen.

"Good-bye, Josh," Willie called after him, but not loud enough for him to hear. At this moment he gave no thought at all to the girl in baggy pants and the oversized felt hat.

"How is your father?" Brant asked, once they had stepped outside into Mackay's yard.

Joshua shrugged his shoulders to emphasize his indifference to the question. They walked along in silence together for some moments. Finally Brant broke the silence.

"Back inside you indicated you wanted to speak to me, boy. Now that you've got the chance you don't seem to have much to say."

"I don't know how to begin, sir."

"How about responding to my questions?"

"I guess . . . I guess he's fine. He rarely tells me how he feels or anything else about himself or about anything else."

"That doesn't surprise me," Michael said bitterly. "Does he ever mention your mother to you?"

"Not directly, sir."

"What does that mean?"

"He never mentions her name."

Michael looked at Joshua. "What do you want to know?"

"I want to know why he never speaks of her. Who was she? Why do others snicker when they mention her name?"

"Are these the things you wanted to talk to me about?" asked Michael.

"Yes, sir, and more. I'd like to know who I am and where I come from. And why you're my uncle, and why this is the very first time I have spoken to you despite the fact that we live only a few houses away from each other and go to the same church."

"It's a long story, Joshua, and I'm not the one to tell it all to you. You have a grandmother. Two, in fact—an old

21

lady who lives in Quebec, your father's mother, Amy Nowell Morin, and my mother, Jessica Brant. You should speak at least to her."

"My father never hears from his mother, and he has forbidden any communication with the Hebr—" Joshua stopped himself. He had almost called his grandmother by the epithet his father usually used. "I am sorry," he stammered.

"No offense," laughed Michael. "My mother was born a Jewess, and although my father gave up being a Mohawk to become an Anglican, he never quite won my mother to Jesus. In fact, as she grows older she reverts more and more to the way of her girlhood. 'That Hebrew woman' —is that how he refers to her?"

Joshua nodded, not wishing to burden him with the fact that the other children referred to her as the Hebrew witch.

"Well, I suppose he is right. She becomes more and more a Hebrew woman every day." He remained thoughtful for a few seconds and then he turned to Joshua. "We're almost to Bay Street and it will not do to be seen together. You stay behind for a few moments and let me make my way down the street. Tomorrow after school, instead of going straight home, stop off at my mother's home. Do you know where it is?"

Joshua nodded his head.

"After school tomorrow," Brant said, and he stepped briskly onto Bay Street toward his own house.

Joshua entered the front door of his father's home and started up the stairs toward his own room. His father's study door swung open and Charles Miller, book in hand, stepped into the hallway.

"Joshua," he called out.

The boy froze on the stairs and then turned around to face his father.

"Good God," the older man said angrily. "You're still in those filthy clothes. Where have you been?"

"I bumped into Willie Mackay and we walked together and had a talk."

"Can't keep away from the girls, eh? Is that it? First Allison Winslow and then Willie Mackay, although God and only perhaps her mother—if she had one—could recognize Willie as female. I want you keeping away from the girls, Joshua. I want you to stay away from Willie because her father is a drunk and probably a traitor. I want you to stay away from Allison because she is a very attractive girl and you've got your mother's bad blood for sure. I'll tell you when it is time to pay your respects to Allison Winslow. And you'll pay them when I tell you to pay them and only when I tell you."

Joshua stiffened at the insult to his mother's name. He had heard it all before. But as he grew older and began to understand the insults, he had become more and more resentful.

Charles smiled when he saw the boy's reaction.

"I think you're growing up on me, Joshua. So you see I am right. You are to keep away from Allison, unless of course the young lady is properly chaperoned and I arrange it."

Joshua nodded assent and turned to continue up the stairs.

"And, Joshua," his father called after him, "please wash your body so you don't quite look the pig in the sty."

"Yes, sir."

Joshua closed his door and kicked an upholstered ottoman clear across the room. The ottoman had served before as a release for his tensions. He pulled off his jacket and threw it in a heap in the corner. It was soon followed by his shirt and pants. He stood in his shorts, which came down to just above his knees. He walked to his dresser. He opened the drawer and touched the gold locket with the gothic *N* on it that he had received from his uncle, and that he kept hidden under his handkerchiefs, tucked way in the rear. It was really his only tie with his roots and with his past, and he enjoyed its secret presence.

There was a pitcher of water and a basin on the dresser. His face had been covered with mud until the pump in Willie's kitchen had cleared it, but there were still streaks of dried dirt. He sniffed at his armpits and wrinkled his nose. He had begun to grow tufts of fine blond hair there, but with the hair had come the pungent odor of manhood. He thought of Allison and his father's warning about staying away from her. As soon as he thought of her he felt a stirring in his groin. Some months ago that had happened; he had grabbed himself and reveled in the pleasure until he had frightened himself to death when the semen had spilled into his hands. He thought he had done some terrible injury to his body but he had been too terrified to tell anyone. Later, in school, the master had referred to self-pollution and several of the boys had snickered. From gestures and remarks on the way home from school Joshua realized he was not alone in the practice of "self-pollution." He was relieved and burdened at the same time—relieved that he had not done some terrible unique damage to himself and burdened to discover that what gave him such pleasure was a terrible sin and would eventually soften his brain. He vowed that he would never do it again. But the next morning as he awoke and felt the stiffness with his hands, he once again was unable to stop.

But now he profaned the beauty and virtue of the purest creature in all the world—Allison Winslow. His betraying member rose in all its full glory. Joshua shook his head back and forth as if to scatter the filthy thoughts that flooded into his mind and made him hate himself. He pushed his hand behind his back. He would not touch himself. This time he would win.

The door to his room swung open and Joshua's father stepped through. "Haven't you finished . . ."

Miller did not complete his question. Instead he stared as Joshua attempted to hide his erection.

"You filthy little pervert," the older man screamed out. "You've been up here touching yourself instead of dressing as I told you to do."

Joshua had not seen his father so angry before.

"What you're doing leads straight to hell, you filthy little beast," Miller screamed, spittle spraying from his mouth as he yelled. He picked up a leather razor strop that he had given Joshua when his first whiskers appeared on his chin. He struck the boy a crashing blow across the

24

back. A red ugly welt appeared immediately. Joshua cried out in pain.

"I'm sorry, I couldn't help myself," he called out.

"I know all about it," his father screamed, wild with rage. Again the strop fell, this time across the back of Joshua's thighs.

"Please, Father," he screamed, "don't hit me again!"

Miller paid no attention to him. The strop struck the boy across the chest. Joshua whimpered and fell to his knees. His eyes pleaded with his father to no avail. Again his father struck him, and again.

Miller's voice was a high-pitched whine.

"You begin by soiling your body and it grows and takes possession of you. It unmans you. It must be beaten out of you now, boy, for your own good, or else you'll be no man."

Joshua had fallen on his face now and pulled his knees up into his stomach. His hands covered his head. The strop struck him again and again across the buttocks, tearing the cotton shorts to shreds. Joshua shouted no more. His chest heaved with painful sobs and a terrible whimper came from his throat.

Finally Miller stopped. He looked down at the boy at his feet. He dropped the strop onto the boy's prone body. Joshua, in terror, did not dare look up. If he had, he would have noticed a bulge in his father's groin that made walking out of the room awkward.

The boy lay on the floor sobbing. Finally he pulled himself up on the ottoman. His legs and buttocks were numb but he knew he was hurt. He pulled himself over to his bed and dropped onto it. None of the maids dared enter his room and no one called him for the evening meal. He could not have answered the call even if it had come. He drifted off into a fitful sleep but he was awakened by every move of his bruised and bleeding backside. He covered his body with a light bedsheet but later that night he kicked it off. His body felt as if it were on fire. He could feel every blow of the strop and he resented every bruise and cut on his body. His father had no right to treat him so brutally. Never again, he vowed, would he lie there

25

and allow himself to be abused. He did not believe he was guilty of any wrongdoing, no matter what his father said, no matter what the schoolmaster said. He would run away before he would let it happen again. Then he felt a sinking feeling in his chest. Where would he run to? His boyhood dreams of a fair-haired uncle—a mirror image of a father—who lived in the far west with buffalos and Indians flooded into his mind. But how to find that man? No one, not even his father, knew where Stephen Miller was. He had returned to the Red River Settlements. That was all anyone remembered of him. Then he recalled his conversation with his other uncle, Michael Brant. He had a grandmother. He did not have to go to the west and to the wilds of Rupert's Land to find new friends. He had merely to walk down Bay Street. A smile broke across his face. He rose unsteadily from the bed. He walked to his dresser and fished in the drawer for the Nowell locket. He placed it around his throat. Tomorrow he would go see his grandmother. Finally, just before dawn, he fell into a deep sleep, and the flames that engulfed him subsided.

Jessica Brant sat in Eli Stoddard's old room. She had touched almost nothing in it since the day of his passing. Unlike the bedroom she had shared for years with her husband, Aaron, this room remained a monument to the man. Every afternoon for the last years of Eli's life as he grew weaker and more aged, Jessica had visited him, sitting in the same rocking chair. She sat and listened to him pontificate from the bed. She still came every afternoon. It was a good place to sit and remember. Normally the room was dark with the man's heavy, dark wooden furniture, but at this time of the day it came alive. The warm afternoon sun poured through the white organdy summer curtains.

She was alone now except for Michael, and she had resigned herself that he would never marry. He would produce no grandchildren to replace Elizabeth's son in her heart.

Aaron, her beloved, the strange Indian learning white ways who had wooed her and won her away from her

26

father's home in New Hampshire, had been gone for over twenty years. Elizabeth, her adopted daughter, and Eli, the girl's guardian, were dead almost as long.

Her black hair was now very gray, and her beautiful skin had given way to the dryness and scaliness of advancing age. She had arthritis in both knees, and if she sat too long she had difficulty in standing up. She liked the rocker. She could sit and yet continue to exercise her legs. She looked down at her hands, grabbing the armrests of the chair. She did not look in the mirror any longer. She didn't have to. Her hands told her that she was an old woman. But where had the years gone? How could her beloved have been gone so long? How could the young girl have turned into an old woman so soon?

The shadows lengthened in the room. She knew she had sat too long. In summer the shadows did not come until early evening. The servants had not called her to dinner, which meant that Michael had not yet returned from his office and the lazy cook was taking advantage of her lack of supervision. You couldn't get proper servants any longer. They were too independent. Chastise them, call them stupid, and they left the city and ran off into the country and became farmers' wives. That silly Irish girl, Mary, had done just that. Now she had four runny-nosed brats of exceedingly low intelligence. Jessica sent Christmas presents to them every year, to their farm north of the city. She chuckled. Little Irish wet-noses getting their only Christmas gifts from the crazy Hebrew lady in Toronto whom they had never seen. Mary had been such a stupid girl but she had not had a better maid since.

"Doesn't say much for the lot of them," she said aloud, "since that Irish wench was a total incompetent. Lillie?" she called out. "Where is everyone?"

She stood up slowly from the rocker. The pain shot toward her ankles and then up into her thighs. She would walk awkwardly now, straining her calf and thigh muscles. At night, when she lay in bed, the dull ache in those muscles kept her awake with throbbing reminders that she was now seventy-one.

"Lillie," she called out again to the cook.

27

She walked out into the broad hallway and opened the door to the back stairway that ran from the servants' attic floor down into the kitchen. She yelled into the landing, knowing that her voice would travel equally well up and down.

"Lillie, if you're between the sheets upstairs you should be in the kitchen cooking dinner. Where are you?"

She listened. Her hearing was not what it used to be. Well, there was only one thing to do. She gritted her teeth against the pain of the climb. The back stairs were steep, not like the gentle slope of the main stairs of the house. She reached the attic level. The narrow hallway was dark. Three unpainted wooden doors opened out into the hall. All three were closed. Jessica realized she didn't know which room Lillie occupied. She hadn't been up to this floor in years. Well, Mary had lived in the room at the end of the corridor. She would start there.

She threw open the door without knocking. Lillie was leaning on the sill of the small dormer window. Her generous rump was braced against it, her skirts pushed up over her shoulders. Phinias, the carriage man, was standing before her. His pants were below his knees and he was pushing up against Lillie with considerable effort.

"Good God!" Jessica yelled out.

Lillie screamed and pulled her skirt over her head to block out the sight of this angry angel of the Lord standing in the doorway, come to smite the wicked.

Phinias grabbed his trousers and pulled them up, trying to force his erection back into their confines but with no success.

Jessica picked up a broom that lay propped against the door. She moved rapidly. The pain in her knees was forgotten, and she swung the broom against Phinias's bulging crotch, which was only partially blocked by his hand.

"Get your filthy thing out of here. Is this what I pay you for?"

Phinias now had no trouble arranging himself. The next blow landed with a smack atop his head. Holding his pants with one hand to prevent them from falling and covering his damaged privates with the other, the carriage man dashed past the broom and out into the hallway.

Jessica turned to go after him but instead hurled the broom. It caught between his knees and sent him sprawling on his face. Phinias was terrified that the Hebrew witch would fall on him again. He scrambled to his feet. His trousers had fallen again, this time to his ankles. He turned to run, but his pants tangled in his feet and he could only take tiny, shuffling steps. He made it to the end of the black hallway at this gait. He tried to place his right foot on the first of the steps, but the pants prevented the foot from reaching. His eyes widened in fear. He pushed his foot down with all of his might. He heard a tearing as the pants seam gave way and his foot shot out of its bindings. He lost his balance and fell three steps onto the landing, where the steps turned to the right. He looked behind him in terror. She had not followed.

Phinias sighed deeply, disentangled his pants from his feet, and with all the dignity he could muster, pulled them up into position. He sniffed haughtily in the direction of Lillie's room and stepped elegantly down the remaining steps, the torn seat of his pants flopping.

"He tried to rape me, Mrs. Brant! You saw what that fiend was trying to do with his big ugly thing."

"Lillie Julien, you are a consummate fabricator," Jessica said in the best manner of Eli Stoddard. The realization of it made her smile.

Lillie was confused, and when she saw Jessica's smile she took the signal.

"I sure am, Mrs. Jessica," she nodded vigorously. "I am the consummatist fabric eater you ever did see."

"But," said Jessica, drawing herself up in anger, "if you had been in the kitchen cooking dinner as you should have been, then the attempted rape would have occurred there. I could have rescued your virtue just in time for you to serve the soup. Now get your bare ass covered and get it down into the kitchen and get me my soup."

Lillie raced past her to join Phinias on the lower level.

Jessica was angered, not by the no-longer-secret love affair within her household, but by her lack of dinner. As

29

she descended the stairs her pains returned and she cursed —something she did in private now very often. She reached the bedroom floor and walked out into the hallway toward the wide curved main stairway of the house. Just as she descended it, the front door of the house swung open and her son, Michael, stepped inside. As she opened her mouth to greet him, she saw a blond-haired boy step into the house behind him. The boy looked about nervously.

"Michael, who is this young fellow with mud on his shoes that you brought home with you?"

Joshua looked down at his feet. He had held Michael up at the doormat while he painstakingly removed the last trace of York's famous mud from himself. She hadn't even checked to see if he was muddy before she made her charge. He did not think he was going to get along with his lady.

"This, mother, is our . . . our Elizabeth's son."

Jessica stopped her descent down the curved stairway and stared at the towheaded young man. She brought the spectacles she wore about her neck up to her eyes to get a better look.

"You favor your father, child. Pity," she said as she continued her journey down to his level. She came very close to him, still peering through her spectacles.

"Yes, it is you, Joshua. I recognize you. I've seen you growing up and playing with the other children on Bay Street. Why has it taken you so long to come to pay your respects to your grandmother?"

"My father forbade it."

"Why didn't you disobey him?"

Joshua looked confused. "I don't know," he stammered.

"Mother," Michael interrupted, "that's hardly fair. The boy is barely fifteen. You can't expect young fellows like this to go about defying a parent."

"Nonsense," Jessica dismissed Michael. "Anyone with two pennies' worth of common sense could see right through the foul heart of Charles Miller and disregard the command of such an unworthy parent."

"Well, that's kind of what I just did," Joshua offered.

"Tell me about it," Jessica commanded.

"There's not much to tell," Joshua responded defensively. "I had the chance to meet with Mr. Brant."

"Uncle Michael," Brant corrected the boy.

"Uncle Michael," Joshua continued, "and he seemed not at all like my father always claimed he was, and he offered me the opportunity to come and meet with you."

"Well, what do you think?" she asked. "I'll bet just at this moment you were thinking that the old Jewess was every bit as bad as Daddy always claimed she was."

Joshua looked about the room with chagrin. His grandmother must be the witch the children of the neighborhood always called her. She had read his mind.

"No matter," she said finally. "At least you're not the coward your father is. You worked up the courage to come and see your grandmother and defy the man. Come into the parlor. You too, Michael. Despite the late hour," she shouted over her shoulder toward the kitchen, "dinner is not yet ready."

Jessica placed the man and the boy, her son and grandson, so unlike each other, on a divan opposite her favorite parlor chair. She watched as the boy lowered himself cautiously into the seat and she saw the look of pain fill his eyes. Then she sat in her own straight-back chair. She kicked aside the little footstool whose upholstered material matched that of the chair. Raising her knees aggravated the inflammation in them.

"Well," she sighed as she leaned back in her chair, "I have more than a decade's worth of history to counteract before dinner. Can you stay? Won't your father come looking for you?"

"He's late at the office tonight and the servants think I am at choir practice. Besides, they cover for me."

"Perhaps we could arrange a trade," Jessica commented sarcastically. "Let me start at the beginning. Your mother, Elizabeth, was my adopted daughter. She was a spoiled, willful, loving child who, despite Eli Stoddard's pampering, was a good daughter to me and to my husband, Michael's father. Then, God help her, she fell in love with your father. She fell for the seeming strength of the man, the aura of confidence and respectability, stability. So did all of

31

us. When we compared Charles Miller to his twin, who would have thought it was Charles who was the true scoundrel and disreputable Stevie who was the true noble man?"

"Master Buckam says my mother was a bad woman who ran away with my uncle and got killed for her sins."

"What is a Master Buckam?" Jessica yelled.

"He is the Anglican choirmaster," Michael interjected.

"Well, Charles Miller is your father," Jessica said more calmly. "Elizabeth loved him. He betrayed her love and drove her from his home even though she carried his child—that's you—in her belly. She knew he planned to destroy his brother, or at least she thought she did, and she ran to warn your Uncle Stephen. They both realized they loved each other—and so they did! What do you think of that, Joshua Miller?" She stared at him defiantly.

"What do you mean?"

"I mean I am telling you that your mother and your uncle lived as man and wife out in the Red River country and she gave birth to you and the two of them raised you until she died."

"I don't think anything about it. Maybe my uncle really is my father."

"If you think that," Jessica said, rising from the chair as her voice rose in anger, "you call your mother a whore!"

Joshua looked confused.

"I don't think the boy perceives the distinction, Mother," Michael interjected.

"I mean," she said, trying to summon up more patience, "Charles Miller betrayed her and she found a new love. She was justified. My Elizabeth was faithful to her husband until he destroyed her love. Then she sought out another. She was faithful to Stephen until she died. Then that nitwit came back here to bring you to me and allow your father to steal you away from me."

Lillie came cautiously into the parlor.

"Supper is ready," she announced, not daring to look at Jessica.

"How could it be?" Jessica asked, her black eyes flashing at her servant.

32

"We're having a cold supper, mistress. Some sliced roast beef and some fruit for dessert. I'm sorry, mistress."

Michael watched the interplay between the two women with some confusion. Then he rose.

"Come, Joshua. Join your grandmother and me for supper."

The boy rose and his uncle placed his arm about his shoulder. Jessica saw him wince in pain. She'd heard the stories about Charles. Her heart went out to her grandson and his sufferings.

"Michael," she interrupted his conversation with his nephew, "where are your manners? You usually take my arm."

"I'm sorry, Mother," he apologized. "You're right, I am forgetting myself."

"Never mind," Jessica said, contrarily. "I don't want you anyway. Not when I can be escorted by a fair and hand- some prince."

Michael bowed deeply toward his mother in mock deference. She turned her back to him and proceeded toward Joshua.

"Would you be my champion, noble prince?" She smiled at him.

Joshua picked up the change in her mood. He grinned at her and she saw Elizabeth in his smile. Her eyes filled instantly with tears, which then overflowed down her cheeks. She straightened up. "Oh, my boy," she gasped and reached out her arms to enfold him.

At first his body stiffened as she touched him. No one had ever hugged him before and he was not sure he liked the closeness of it—the invasion of his privacy that it represented. But he felt her need to touch him, this strange lady, so gruff and stern one minute and teary-eyed and loving the next.

She continued to hold him. Her head reached only to his shoulder and her tears wet his shirt. He looked over toward his uncle, a bit dismayed and not knowing how to respond. But he could see Michael Brant was looking away and up toward the high vaulted plaster ceilings, trying to control his own tears.

Joshua placed his arms tenderly at first about the frail frame of the old woman who clung to him. Her need for him amazed him. His arms pulled her closer to him, and from deep within him, its presence a mystery and unsuspected by him, came the overwhelming need to respond to her.

II

Toronto, Fall 1837

Joshua went frequently to the Brants from that day forward. His father worked late most weekday nights, and it was easy, with the support of his father's servants, to slip out for the visits. He and Jessica became close and the old woman became more cheerful with each passing month. But as the weather grew colder and the fall descended, it was difficult for anyone but Jessica to grow more cheerful. Word came upriver from Montreal of increased tensions. Louis-Joseph Papineau and his Patriotes were close to open rebellion against Lord Gosford, the governor-general. And in Toronto, William Lyon Mackenzie was all but issuing declarations of independence.

This night Joshua had left the Brants' house early. His father had warned him to be prepared to attend a party at Judge Winslow's home. It was the first time he had been allowed to attend such an affair and the first time in months that his father had acknowledged that it was appropriate for him to approach Allison Winslow. And despite the fact that it meant he had to leave his grandmother's early, he was still very excited. He had seen Allison on occasions since the summer, usually at St. James on Sunday morning. She seemed to have matured and grown more beautiful each time he saw her.

The Winslows lived on Queen Street, until recently called Lot Street, close enough to walk, despite the chilly winds coming off Lake Ontario. But a man of Charles Miller's wealth could not afford to be seen walking. A carriage, drawn by a chestnut horse, awaited father and son at the front steps of their Bay Street house. The driver, a retired canal man from one of Charles's projects, spoke softly to the mare when the wind, cutting through the space between the houses, forced her to quiver and then stamp her foot to register her displeasure at being forced from the warmth of her stable. Charles and Joshua came out of the front door together and climbed into the closed carriage compartment. The boy was wearing black formal attire for the first time in his life. He felt stupid and confined in the starched linen. He would have greatly preferred his father's red-coated militia officer's uniform. All the officers had agreed to wear the military uniforms to remind the population that there were loyal queen's men in the town who would fight to preserve order in the colony of Upper Canada.

"I want you to pay particular attention, Joshua, to Miss Allison," said Charles as they settled into the carriage.

"Yes, sir," Joshua said eagerly. His father had never given him an easier command.

"I know that both of you are very young, but the judge is a farsighted man. He wants his daughter to marry well. He has set aside a handsome sum to achieve that end. Knowing your propensities, I don't want you to ruin it. Behave like a gentleman to the girl. Keep your baser instincts to yourself until you bed the wench on your wedding night. After that I don't care what the two of you do to each other."

Joshua bit his tongue and remained silent. His grandmother had admonished him about replying to his father's constant criticisms. She had warned him to remain silent and not to retort. "The man can increase his own stature only by reducing the self-confidence of those surrounding him," she had advised, shaking her head sadly.

"What's the matter?" Charles demanded, interrupting his reverie.

"I was just thinking," replied Joshua.

"Good, let me record it as another first in the family Bible, like a first tooth or a first step or a first word. But then, none of those things are in the family record since you weren't with me when you did them. Well, it's not much of a family."

Joshua decided again to ignore the insults and change the subject.

"I'm a bit young to be considering marriage," he said.

"Of course. I expect your courtship to be several years in duration. But get this straight, Joshua: You are to control yourself. Even if the girl tries to lure you—and she is a hot little bitch—you keep your hands off. I saw the way you indulge yourself. I know you are prone to the sins of the flesh. But I warn you, ruin this arrangement and I'll take every ounce of skin off your hide. I want that dowry."

"Yes, Father," Joshua responded as the carriage drove up to the portico of the Winslow mansion.

The street in front of the house was filled with carriages. The servant opened the carriage door and dropped the folding steps down until they reached the top of the wooden footstool he had placed in position.

Charles descended first and Joshua followed. After the servants had taken their coats, Judge and Mrs. Winslow greeted their guests in the black-and-gray marble foyer of the house. Mrs. Winslow was a straight-backed gaunt woman whose blond hair was turning gray. She might once have been a beauty, thought Joshua. Then his attention was taken away completely from the older woman as Allison entered the foyer. She was dressed in a hooped dark-green velvet gown. It was cut very low and revealed far more than her father would have wished.

Joshua stared at her. The green of her eyes matched the color of her dress—or so it seemed to him. Her hair was piled high upon her head, revealing the gentle white curve of her neck. Joshua's eyes followed the course of her shoulders and then dropped to the beauty of her well-formed breasts. He realized that he was staring and broke eye contact. He looked around to see if anyone had noticed his boldness, but he saw that all eyes were on Allison. Her father and mother looked at her nervously. Even his own father was feasting on the beauty of the girl.

Joshua could not remove his eyes from his father's face.

37

The smile that parted Charles's lips was no different from the sneer that accompanied his verbal abuse, particularly when his venom was turned on Joshua.

The front door swung open once again, and Sir Francis Bond Head, lieutenant governor of Upper Canada, entered, escorted by two staff members in the red-and-gold uniforms of the regular army. One of the aides was a captain, the other a major. Mrs. Winslow and Allison curtsied, while the men bowed slightly from the neck.

"Judge Winslow, Mr. Miller, it's good to be among friends," Sir Francis said good-naturedly.

"Your Excellency," Mrs. Winslow offered, "is always welcome in our home."

"And in every God-fearing home in Toronto," continued Charles Miller.

"Toronto—what a name! I can't for the life of me figure out why you city fathers went to the trouble of changing the name of this place from a good English one like York to a heathen one."

"Perhaps it suits the place better," said Charles.

"Nonsense," said the judge.

"It's radicals like that fellow Mackenzie who do these things. He is still the mayor, isn't he?" Head interjected.

"Not any longer, and I try not to think about the time when he was," said Winslow. "Indeed, I try not to think about fools like that bold little dwarf at all."

"Hear, hear," applauded Head.

"I don't think it wise to ignore Mackenzie, no matter what the judge says. The man is dangerous and should not be taken lightly," said Charles.

"Nonsense, Miller," retorted Head. "The people of this province are loyal to our new Queen Victoria and Her Majesty's government. I'd have no hesitation in sending the regulars I have off to Montreal to help Lord Gosford handle the frogs. That's where the trouble will be, gentlemen, in Quebec, not in this province—not among loyal British subjects."

"Agreed," said the judge.

Charles was about to disagree most forcefully but changed his mind. He mumbled something about fools and offered

Allison his arm to lead her into the parlor to join the guests.

Joshua followed them with his eyes.

"Well, young man," said the judge, "if there is a fight, it's young fellows like you who will be in the thick of it—just as your father and I were back in the war against the Yanks."

"My God," said Head, "don't tell me I'm going to have to hear about Brock and Queenston Heights once again."

"No, sir," said the judge, "I was not there. I played my part in the gallant defense of this fair city."

"I thought the Yanks burned it," said Head's aide.

"Some buildings were fired, but thanks to the courage of the Reverend Mr. Strachan and the brave citizens of York, we drove the Yanks back into the lake."

The two aides looked at each other and smiled. They both knew that the American attack on Toronto had been a raid to destroy the shipyards and the craft being constructed there. The Yanks had planned to withdraw all along.

"How about you, Mr. Miller? Joshua, isn't it? Do you have a story to tell us about the war?" Head asked.

Joshua smiled. "No, sir. I wasn't even born then."

"Why let that stop you?" joked the major. "It has never stopped any other Canadian teller of tales."

Winslow ignored them. "The boy's family distinguished themselves in the war, sir. His father was a hero of Lake Erie."

"We lost that one, didn't we?" said the captain.

"A gallant fight, nevertheless," the judge countered.

"On my mother's side I'm a Brant. They were great fighters," Joshua blurted out.

Mrs. Winslow looked embarrassed, and the judge took the lieutenant governor's arm.

"Let's get out of the foyer and into the party, Your Excellency."

"Just a moment." Head resisted. "Are your father and Mr. Brant, the liberal reformer, related?"

"Not really," said Joshua, taking his cue from the Winslows.

The governor looked at the boy strangely, then he turned and started to walk into the party with his hosts.

"Too bad," he said to Winslow. "Men like Brant and Baldwin could be wooed from the enemy's camp. Miller would do us a real service if he would bring Brant around to his senses."

"I don't think Miller will have much influence on Michael Brant, Your Excellency."

"Well, again, it's too bad."

Joshua followed them into the parlor. There the candlelight played on the gilt furniture and mirrors. The Oriental rug had been rolled up to expose the highly polished dark-brown floorboards and a string orchestra—a violin, a viola, and cello—played a polka.

Since Allison was dancing with his father, Joshua went to the buffet table in the dining room. It was loaded with cold meat and fresh-baked bread. There were also peaches, apples, and plum preserves to spread on the bread if the crock of freshly churned butter was not attraction enough.

The captain who served as aide to the lieutenant governor reached the table at the same time as Joshua.

"Doesn't everything look good?" the boy said, his eyes wide as only a fifteen-year-old's eyes could be at the sight of a table full of goodies.

The captain looked over at the boy and realized he was serious. He sniffed some snuff from the back of his hand and made a snorting sound that Joshua found disgusting.

"In a pastoral way I suppose it is," the captain responded.

Allison came breathlessly into the dining room. The captain's eyes went from the table toward the girl and never left her.

"I say," he breathed.

"Joshua, your father has given out on me. Poor fellow claims he hasn't danced in years. Come join me in another polka."

"I am sorry," Joshua stumbled over the words, "I'm—" He did not want to admit he did not know how to do the polka.

"It's simple." The girl guessed his secret. "You just have to jump up and down and take wide steps, one, two, one—oh pooh, Joshua, you're no fun."

40

"May I be of assistance?" offered the captain. "I've done a few turns around the ballroom to this beat."

"Why, Captain . . . ?"

"Elliot, Miss Winslow."

"Captain Elliot, I thank you for your gracious offer."

She glanced scornfully at Joshua as she took the arm of the red-coated young man. Joshua's heart sank. He was angry with himself. First, for allowing his father to lead Allison off, and now for allowing Captain Elliot to be her escort. If only he weren't so shy. He placed some sliced beef on his buttered bread and walked slowly out into the parlor. His father was standing across the room. He gestured toward the captain and Allison with annoyance as he stared at Joshua. The boy was becoming more and more uncomfortable. He could almost feel his father's scorn from across the room. Later tonight he knew he would hear it. He turned and left the parlor. The dining room was crowded and he continued down the hall until he came to the cloakroom. It was deserted. Joshua looked around for a place to sit. The few chairs had been placed behind large wooden screens upon which were painted scenes of China. Behind the screens the chairs were draped with the guests' cloaks, laid there by the servants.

The boy shoved several aside and collapsed on a chair. Nothing was going well. Allison was so beautiful and he was so clumsy. He would not even get a chance to speak with her tonight. He was sure of it. He could barely hear the music from the parlor.

Joshua ate his meat and bread slowly, almost absent-mindedly. All he could think of was Allison—Allison being held by his father, Allison in the arms of Captain Elliot.

The cloakroom door was swung open, cautiously.

"In here." Joshua heard the voice of the English captain. "No one's in here."

Joshua rose to make his presence known but was stunned into silence when he heard Allison's voice.

"You are a naughty man, Captain."

"And you, my dear, are the most beautiful woman in all Canada."

41

"You flatter me!" she responded lightly.

"Not at all. If anything I belittle your beauty by limiting it to this region of ice and scrub pine."

Joshua sat down again, now sure how to get out of this predicament. He chose silence.

The officer and the girl stopped speaking also. Joshua could hear them kissing.

"My God, girl, you are beautiful. Just loosen the bodice and let me hold you. I don't think there are any more beautiful breasts on any continent."

"Now you do flatter me," Allison responded. But there was a wariness now in her tone.

"No, Captain. Please don't touch me there."

"What do you mean?"

"I mean I expect you to behave like a gentleman and treat me as I deserve. Don't!" Her voice became a bit more high-pitched.

"I am treating you exactly as you deserve to be treated. Why else would you accept my invitation to the cloakroom?"

"Captain Elliot, my father will speak to the lieutenant governor about your behavior."

But Elliot was too far gone in passion. He tugged at the front of her dress, but the heavy velvet resisted his efforts. Joshua stepped out from behind the screen and grabbed Elliot's arm.

"What the hell?" the captain exclaimed. "Where did you come from? What were you doing back there?"

Allison looked instantly relieved to see Joshua appear from nowhere.

"Leave her be," he said to the older man.

Elliot swung at Joshua, striking him in the mouth. His lip was pushed painfully into his lower teeth and blood gushed from it. But now the boy was angry. He feinted with his left hand. As the captain blocked the blow, the boy's right fist slammed home into the captain's nose. Joshua could feel the bone and cartilage give way beneath his knuckles.

"Stop it," Allison cried out. "Both of you, stop it. My parents will be furious. You'll ruin the party."

42

But Captain Elliot was not going to allow a boy to smash his face without receiving severe punishment in return.

"If you were a gentleman, or even a man, I'd call you out," he murmured, brushing away the blood that gushed from his nose. "But you're a cur, and like a dog you are about to be beaten."

He lashed with his knee and caught Joshua in the stomach. The wind went out of the boy. He grabbed his belly and gasped for air. The captain's fist went crashing down on the back of his head, sending Joshua sprawling onto the cloakroom floor. Again and again Elliot's hard-tipped boot went smashing into Joshua's ribs, belly, and groin. The boy was beginning to lose consciousness. He glimpsed Allison standing against the cloakroom door, her eyes wide with horror. He saw the black boot coming toward his face. He grabbed for it and stopped its progress. He twisted and jerked. Elliot lost his footing and came sprawling onto the floor. As he did, his head banged into the heavy wooden Chinese screen with a sickening crack.

The captain lay on the floor motionless, his face a distorted mass of blood and cartilage. Joshua got to his feet. He was gasping and he felt as if he was going to throw up. He gagged and forced the vomit back down into his throat. Allison rushed to the fallen captain. She dropped to her knees beside his body. Everything was silent now except for the distant music of the violins that floated down the hallway from the parlor and the sound of dishes rattling from the kitchen.

"Oh, no, Joshua," Allison called to him, "I think he's dead. I think you've killed him." She started to sob.

The boy looked at her in disbelief. The blood still poured from his cut lip. It had already fallen onto his starched white shirt. He knelt beside the girl and put his ear to the captain's chest. There was no heartbeat.

"I did it to protect you," he blurted out.

She looked at him in horror. "Don't drag me into this, Joshua Miller. You've killed a man, a queen's officer. There'll be no escaping them. They'll hunt you down and hang you for this."

Joshua could feel the panic rising. "But you'll tell them I was only trying to save you."

He could see the coldness coming into her green eyes. They narrowed almost to slits and her beautiful face turned hard, like that of a statue. He knew she would say nothing in his defense.

He rose to his feet again. He rushed to the cloakroom door and pushed it open. He stood facing the red-coated form of the captain's companion, the major whose name Joshua had failed to learn. The major's eyes darted to Joshua's blood-soaked shirt. Joshua raced past him out toward the kitchen. The major reached for him and missed.

Allison saw her chance and quietly stepped out of the cloakroom. She walked softly up the stairway to the second floor. She stepped into her bedroom.

"You can't panic now," she said aloud. "That stupid boy loves you. He'll cover for you. You don't have to be involved. You can't be involved. Your reputation. My God . . ." She stopped in the middle of her soliloquy. What did her reputation matter now? The boy her father had picked out, the heir to the greatest estate in Canada, had just killed a captain in the regular army. He was a fugitive, the heir to nothing. Her future had fled with Joshua Miller into the night.

Joshua had no trouble losing his pursuer. He knew the backyards of these Queen Street houses as well as he knew the backyards on Bay Street and Front Street. He didn't know where he would go at first. He just wanted to throw the major off his trail. His first thought was to return home, but then he realized that would be the first place they would look for him. He could feel the rope tightening around his neck, cutting off the precious air. Where to go? Then he remembered his grandmother. They would not think to look for him there right away. He might be safe for a while with her.

He traced his path through the back alleys and mews. The smell of horses was even stronger here than it was in the streets. He usually entered the Brant house from the mews to avoid being seen and so he knew the way. The

44

back door was locked and all the lights in the house were out. He knocked lightly on the back door but there was no answer.

He tried all the windows of the lower floor of the mews side of the house but to no avail. All were carefully locked and shuttered. He had to get inside somehow. He was afraid to go around the front to Bay Street; they might be looking for him already.

The old door to the cellar caught his eye. A rusty old lock held the bolt in place. It might give if forced. Joshua looked around for something to use. He picked up a rock the size of his fist and smashed it against the lock. It bent slightly. The noise, however, started a dog barking. He didn't care. One more solid blow and the lock would be gone. He struck again and the lock fell from the door and landed at his feet with a clank. This time the dog started to howl.

The door squeaked noisily on its rusty hinges as Joshua pushed it open. He stepped into the blackness. He had never been in the basement before and he had no idea where the stairway to the first floor was located.

He inched forward, his hands extended ahead of him. He touched what seemed to be a bookcase. He felt inside it and touched glass—a bottle, probably a wine bottle. He moved forward again. He thought he heard a noise off to his left. His eyes had not yet adjusted to the darkness. He remained still, trying to let his ears hear what his eyes could not see. Nothing. He started forward again, inch by inch. Now objects began to take shape before his eyes. Shadows loomed out of the blackness. He could see the steps directly in front of him. He felt more confident now. He stepped toward the stairway. Suddenly a pair of arms grabbed him from behind. He screamed in fright, but his shout was drowned out by a woman's piercing shriek. Then he didn't hear anything more.

Phinias proudly wrestled the groggy intruder to his feet. Lillie's scream had awakened Mrs. Brant and her son. They came down the wine cellar stairs, a lamp held high. Mr. Brant had his pistol in his hand.

"No need for that, sir," Phinias called out. "I've got the bastard. Conked him with a wine bottle, sir."

45

Michael came to the bottom of the stairs and raised the lamp. Despite the swollen lip and the wine-drenched hair and blood-soaked shirt, he had no trouble recognizing his nephew.

"Mother," he called out, "it's Joshua. I think he's hurt."

"Bring him upstairs," Jessica called out worriedly.

Phinias looked confused and suddenly deflated. He had fallen from protector of the household to assaulter of family.

"I had no idea, sir," he fussed. "Nor could I have."

"You're quite right, Phinias."

The carriage man let out a sigh. He glanced at Lillie, who had backed into the shadows hoping not to be seen.

"Let's help him upstairs," said Michael. "You, Lillie, take the lantern and lead the way," he ordered, dashing any hopes she might have had of not being detected.

They brought him into the Brant kitchen. Jessica took water from the pump and soaked a cloth while Michael propped Joshua in a chair. He took the boy's filthy dress jacket off of him and opened his shirt. He breathed a sigh of relief.

"The blood is from his lip, Mother. There is no other wound that I can find."

Jessica came to her grandson's side and wiped his dirty face with a cool cloth.

He began to regain full consciousness and he started to moan.

"Joshua," Jessica said to him, placing her face close to his. "What is it, boy? What has happened?"

The boy looked into her face, and tears came to his eyes.

"What is it, Joshua?" Jessica repeated. "Is it your father? Has he put his hands on you again?"

Joshua shook his head. The words came pouring out of him.

Phinias and Lillie stood wide-eyed as the boy told of his fight with Captain Elliot over Allison and how Elliot had been killed and how Joshua had run.

Michael Brant, always the lawyer, began a careful questioning of his nephew. When he had finished he leaned back in his chair.

"It strikes me as a solid case. The girl will have to testify that the officer put his hands on her and you rushed to her defense. His death was a pure accident."

Joshua covered his face with his hands. "But she said she wouldn't and I could see it in her eyes. She would rather I died than explain what she was doing in the cloakroom. She would never let the world know that the man, or any man, put his hands on her."

"Nonsense, boy," Jessica muttered. "She'll come around."

"It's my only chance, isn't it? I must make her talk."

Jessica turned to Michael. "What shall we do with him?"

"I think we should put him to bed. I'll get dressed and see if I can nose around and discover what the word is. See what the constables have to say. They know me. Phinias, you come with me."

"Yes, sir," said the servant.

"Before you go, Phinias," Jessica said, "I'd like to know what you and Lillie were doing together in the cellar."

"We heard noises, madam," Lillie offered.

"All the way from the third floor, Lillie? Perhaps Phinias could hear them from the carriage house, but the third floor, Lillie? Commendable hearing. I'm surprised that a girl with that talent can't hear my bell tinkle when the guests are awaiting the next course." Her voice grew gradually louder until she was shouting.

Phinias stepped out of the kitchen and waited for Michael to dress and join him in the hallway. The woman was a holy terror. Well, she could terrify Lillie—the girl was always getting him into trouble—but she could not terrify him.

Lillie and Jessica helped Joshua to the guest room on the second floor. Jessica took one of Michael's nightshirts and laid it on the bed while Lillie eased the boy back down onto the sheets. No sooner was he lying down than he fell into a deep sleep.

"Is he dead?" Lillie whispered in terror.

"Shut up, you stupid woman," Jessica hissed. "He's asleep and I don't want you waking him up. Help me get his clothes off. I doubt we can get the nightshirt on him,

47

but at least we can undress him and get him warm under the covers."

Jessica had Joshua's pants off before she finished her last sentence. Lillie started to giggle.

"He's cute," she said.

"Ah, I had forgotten you are especially attracted to the boys."

"Well, I'm no nun," said Lillie, forgetting herself and Jessica as she stared at the boy.

Jessica started to laugh and threw the sheet over Joshua, then covered him lovingly with a quilt. Her lightheartedness lasted only a few minutes. She looked down at the sleeping boy and his beautiful face and torn lip. She had only just found him again in the last few months. Was she going to lose him once more? Well, certainly not to the constables!

Lillie got no further than the door to the room when Michael came through it rapidly, almost knocking her over.

"It's all over town," he told his mother, "that Charles Miller's boy has murdered a regular army man. There are troops in the streets looking for Joshua and they are mean. If they catch him he'll never see a constable alive. I've decided to get him out of Toronto."

"Where can he go?"

"Phinias has the carriage ready. We have the horse hitched and ready out in the mews. I'll take him to Montgomery's Tavern outside the town."

"But—" Jessica looked at Michael in some confusion.

"I know," he said, "that's Mackenzie's headquarters. But it's the only place. The governor is never going to send troops there looking for Joshua Miller. Not to Mackenzie's tavern, not unless he wants to precipitate a rebellion." He grabbed the boy by the shoulders. "Joshua, wake up."

"He's just now fallen off to sleep."

"We've no time for sleep." He shook the boy.

Joshua awoke with a start. "What is it?" he called out.

"Here, grab your clothes. We've got to get you out of Toronto and right away. Mother, you and Lillie make him a basket of food and give him one of father's muskets. I can't send him empty-handed into the lion's den. The gun isn't much, but with it he is still likely to be the best-armed man in Mackenzie's army."

Jessica and Lillie disappeared from the bedroom. Joshua dressed with his uncle's help while the older man briefed him on his plans.

"After a few days with Mackenzie, I'll come back and speak to your father and the girl's father. I'm sure I can reason with them. Once they prevail on Allison to testify, then I'll bring you back and you can give yourself up. No jury will convict you if what you told me is true."

"Every word of it is true, Uncle."

"Fine," said Michael, patting the boy's shoulder.

Jessica returned carrying the old brown bess musket that Aaron, her husband, had carried to war. She handed it to Joshua.

"It was a Mohawk sachem's weapon, boy, your grandfather's. Do it proud and come back to me safe and sound." She grabbed him and hugged him. "Now be off with you."

Michael and Joshua descended the stairway and walked down the hall to the kitchen. Lillie jumped with fright when they entered the doorway to her domain.

"Where's the food?"

She handed the basket to Michael, but there was such fright in her eyes that he turned around to see if there was some intruder in the kitchen. There was none.

"Let's go," he said to Joshua. "Phinias is waiting for us."

They stepped out into the mews. The carriage stood empty. The black gelding, Michael's horse, was hitched to it.

"Phinias?"

The man was nowhere to be found.

"Get in," Michael whispered, pushing Joshua into the open coach. "And get down low."

Michael jumped into the front seat and hit the startled horse a stinging blow with the buggy whip. The gelding shot forward just as Phinias, leading two soldiers, entered the alley directly in front of them.

"The bastard has turned us in," Michael yelled over his shoulder. "Hold on. We're in for quite a ride."

49

He drove the carriage directly toward Phinias and his two companions.

"There they are," shouted the servant. "There are the traitors and murderers who pick on innocent working people."

He had no chance to say anything more. The muskets of both soldiers fired at once. One ball missed the horse and carriage altogether. The soldier was a bit too anxious to jump out of the way of the thundering horse. But the second ball whizzed past the shoulder of Brant and struck the carriage, splintering the highly polished wood. A flying splinter struck Joshua's cheek, gashing it open.

They were past the soldiers now and out into the street. Michael turned the horse toward Yonge Street and then north up the long trail out of the city toward safety.

Joshua pulled out his handkerchief and pressed it against his cheek to stop the bleeding. Then he climbed up into the driver's seat next to his uncle.

"The son of a bitch. I trusted the man. What a fool I am."

"Does this change things?" Joshua asked.

"Change? It does indeed. Phinias knew our plans. He knew I was taking you to Mackenzie. I think it wise if I stay a few days with you at my esteemed radical friend's headquarters. I might just be arrested myself if I return to Toronto." He started to laugh. "Well, William Lyon Mackenzie, you've been after me for years to join you but I never would. You argued, you shouted, you even tried bribery but I would never join you. But here I come and you didn't get me—a fifteen-year-old boy did."

The ride out Yonge Street was long. Once they passed the outskirts of the town, the road, although straight, was dark and rutted. But the horse was sure-footed and found its way among the potholes and wagon ruts. The carriage bounced them about but the gelding never lost its footing. They passed through the Bloor tollgate and out into the countryside. About a half a mile away from Mongomery's Tavern, they were stopped by a sentry. At least they thought he was a sentry. He had no weapon. He eyed Brant and Miller suspiciously, especially after he caught sight of the musket that Joshua carried across his lap.

"What are you doing coming out here this late at night? Don't you town folk have nothing better to do?" he called to them.

"I've come to see Mr. Mackenzie," Michael interrupted him.

"What makes you think he's here?"

"My good man, all Toronto knows he is here. They also know that you are here and that you farm folk spend the days carrying wooden pikes and parading up and down like an army."

"They know that in Toronto, do they? Some folks here have been talking too much. You'll find him at the tavern straight down the road."

Michael clucked at the gelding and flicked the rein. The horse pulled ahead again.

The lights from the tavern could be seen after they rounded a slight bend in the road. Michael urged his horse onward, and the gelding, seeing the light and sensing a rest and possibly food, moved rapidly toward it. The head of the horse was seized just as soon as Michael called out to it to halt and pulled in the reins.

Mackenzie, his wig fitting badly and worn carelessly, came onto the tavern porch.

"Who is it, Jack?" he called to an assistant.

"Two men—man and a boy really—one looks familiar."

"William," Michael called out.

"Well, I'll be damned. Michael Brant, you son of a gun, you've finally seen the light. Holy Jesus," Mackenzie shouted at no one in particular. "What a day. Now if only that blockhead Baldwin would come around, we might make ourselves quite a proper little rebellion."

He leapt up onto the carriage to grab Brant's hand and shake it. Michael could not help but laugh at the fiery little man's reaction to seeing him.

"Who's the boy and what happened to him?" Mackenzie asked.

"I'm Joshua Miller, sir," responded Joshua, returning the Scotsman's handshake. "I got cut."

"I can see. Next time you're shaving boy, which from the looks of you should be in about six months' time, try using a razor rather than a saber. The cuts don't bleed so much then."

It hurt Joshua to laugh but he could not help himself.

"The boy's a fugitive, William," Michael explained and told Joshua's whole story.

The reformed leader looked at Joshua with some concern on his face.

"So you are the first of us to raise his hand against the Crown. You won't be the last. Before the year is out, boy, I swear you'll not be alone, and for bringing Michael Brant to me I'll even forgive you if they send a troop looking for you and we have to begin this thing before I'm ready."

"You're going through with it then, William?"

"Unless Sir Francis 'Block' Head gives in to our demands and Papineau's in Quebec; yes, I intend to create a republic out of Upper Canada."

"You can't succeed."

"That's what your great-uncle Joseph Brant said to George Washington!"

"I don't think they ever met."

"Whatever. Now tell me, what did you say the boy's name was? Miller?"

"He's Charles Miller's son."

"Holy Jesus. Tory Charlie's son is with me. I know it's going to work. Come, lad, I've got me a sawbones who will stitch you up. He's not a proper physician, he's more like a barber, but he's a wizard with needle and thread."

Charles Miller had hoped never to confront Jessica again after the trial. Despite the proximity of their homes, he had managed to avoid her for eleven years. Yet when Francis Gregg, his secretary, had delivered her calling card to his inner study at his Front Street offices, he was not surprised. He had heard that Joshua had run straight to Michael Brant after the incident at the party. The old lady had stirred herself to call. He could not avoid her. He knew that she was stubborn enough to outwait him.

"All right, Francis, I'll see her."

The man merely stared at his employer.

"Now," Charles said in annoyance.

The secretary jumped. "Yes, sir," he responded and departed.

Charles shook his head. He had not had a competent secretary since John Sutherland, but considering Sutherland's actions, Charles had wanted no more brainy secretaries.

Jessica entered his office. He was startled by how she had aged. Her hair was now gray and her skin wrinkled, and she looked tired, very tired.

"Mother Brant," he greeted her with a sneer in his voice.

She looked at him wearily. The disgust on her face was obvious.

"I've no time for pleasantries, even surly ones," she said. "My son and your son are in deep trouble."

"I have no son," Charles responded. "He killed an officer of the Crown in cold blood. Then, rather than face the consequences, he fled with your rebel son to join the outlaw Mackenzie in the countryside."

"I've spoken to the boy, Charles. It was an accident. He tried to defend the young girl's honor."

"The young girl denies it," he responded, interrupting her. "She is a proper young thing who would not place herself in compromising circumstances."

"You don't believe that." She looked at him incredulously.

"It doesn't matter what I think. That is what Judge Winslow thinks and that is what the constables think."

"But you must help Joshua. We have to work together. Michael doesn't side with Mackenzie. He is with him because it was the only place where Joshua would be beyond the reach of the law."

"Precisely," said Charles. "They have both placed themselves beyond the reach of the law. They have become outlaws—traitors to the queen. If they and the little runt who protects them are captured, they will all swing on Gallows Hill."

"Your son? You would let them hang your own son?"

Charles merely stared at her.

"My God, man, you are cold."

53

"I am merely stating what will happen. My son and your son must face the consequences of their own actions. I'll not take Joshua's part."

"You are a sick man," Jessica said, taken aback by the calm in his voice. "You are really trying to punish them through the boy, aren't you? Elizabeth is dead. For all we know, so is your brother. You can't harm them. They are beyond your reach and so you take your anger out on the child. You beat him; I saw the scars." She raised her hand to silence his protests. "I see there is no gaining your support to get our sons back safely to town."

"I told you, I have no son. I tried to control the boy; to keep the wickedness of his heritage from emerging. But it was no use. He has shown his true nature by his actions."

Francis opened the door. "Colonel Fitzgibbons to see you, sir."

"Ask him to wait," Charles responded. "Mrs. Brant was just leaving."

There was a long embarrassed silence. Finally Jessica turned to go.

"I assumed you had your eyes set on the Winslow girl's dowry. The only good thing that has come from all of this is that Joshua will clearly not be forced into a union with that lying, scheming child and you will be denied her wealth."

She slammed the door behind her.

He stood quietly for some minutes after she left. The woman always got under his skin. He sat down at his desk. Then he smiled. Her parting shot was only partially true. Joshua would not be his instrument to claim the Winslow fortune but he would have the fortune nevertheless. Still smiling, he asked Francis to show Fitzgibbons in.

The colonel was very excited. His round Irish face was flushed and he could not remain still. He paced back and forth in Charles's study.

"The little bastard is ready to strike, Charles. I'm telling you, he's ready."

"Calm down, James. Mackenzie has little support in the city, and his country bumpkins are no match for the loyal militia."

54

"There are no regulars, you know. The lieutenant governor has sent the last of them to Montreal. I have gone to him, I've begged, I've pleaded, but he simply smiles and tells me there will be no rebellion."

"And he's right, James."

"Don't you think that Mackenzie is crazy enough to try anything?"

"I don't think he is crazy enough to put his head in a noose."

"Was Sam Adams or George Washington?"

"Now, James, I'm no lover of the American cause, but this little bewigged monkey is not in their class."

"I'm telling you, Charles Miller, as adjutant general I've had my spies out there in the country beyond the Bloor tollgate, out toward Montgomery's and then up the road to the farm villages. He's whipped them up. He's attacked you for the canal. He's attacked the archdeacon for almost everything, but especially for the bank. They're making bullets. They're drilling. They're practicing their marksmanship in competition—for the sport of it, they say. Some are just carrying pitchforks, but they're congregating out there somewhere to the north of us. I've arranged to ring the college bell once they appear. I've put a picket on the road north of the tollgate."

"His Excellency went so far as to agree to that? I'm surprised."

"I didn't ask him."

Charles sighed. "James, go home and get some sleep. All of this will pass."

"Damn it, Miller, you're as blind as Head. Will no one listen to reason?"

He turned away from Charles and looked about the study in frustration and then left, slamming the door behind him.

"My, my," Charles said aloud, "everyone seems to leave here in a temper." He walked to the door and stepped into the outer office.

Francis rushed to his side. "Mr. Charles, sir, I just heard the word about your son. I'm sure it is all a terrible mistake. I'm sure the boy is innocent."

"Oh, really," said Charles. "Francis, I've business in Kingston immediately. Please send my carriage to my home to pick up some belongings. I must catch the steamer before she leaves this afternoon."

"But, sir, we've had word there's been fighting down the St. Lawrence. The French have beaten Lord Gosford's troops at Saint-Denis. Kingston may be in danger if Montreal falls."

"I guess I'll have to take my chances."

"But what about your son?"

"I guess he'll have to take his also."

Joshua's cheek throbbed but the swelling seemed to be going down. He sat in the taproom of Montgomery's Tavern nursing a glass of ale.

"Landlord," William Mackenzie called, "you are to serve dinner to the army."

"My ass," said the fat man in the apron.

Mackenzie looked at him as if he had been struck in the face. The two men began to scream at each other.

"I'll hang your ass from the tree in the front yard, you piss-head."

"The only hanging that will take place is your own for raising your hand against your queen," said the landlord.

Michael Brant flopped into the chair next to Joshua. "What a mess," he said.

"I'm sorry, Uncle. I've dragged you into all of this. You had no desire to join this rebellion. If it hadn't been for my troubles you'd be safe home with Grandmother."

Brant touched Joshua's shoulder with his hand. "In our family we come to each other's aid. That was sufficient. Eventually I would have had to come to terms with this thing. I agree more with Baldwin and the moderates, but they seem to be getting nowhere. Maybe Will's call to violence is right. Besides, I wasn't referring to your mess. I was talking about Mackenzie's army."

"What do you mean?"

"Look about you. Armies need discipline, organization, food. Mackenzie is a talker but he is light on doing. More and more men are coming in from the north and he can't

56

even feed them. This was to be his supply depot. Montgomery was friendly enough but he sold out a while back. This new proprietor is not with us at all."

"Then it is *us*?" Joshua asked.

Michael nodded. "My head tells me to get as far away from this place as I can but I can't just dismiss it. Even if it took helping you to get me here, here I am."

Mackenzie came storming over to their table. His face was as red as his wig.

"Brant, can you do something with this imbecile who runs this tavern?"

Michael walked to the landlord.

"Innkeeper," said Michael in his softest voice, "we have several hundred men outside who are growing hungry."

"That's not my problem, rebel," said the landlord.

"It just might become your problem if Mr. Mackenzie turns them loose. God knows what will be left after they finish."

For the first time an uneasy look came into the landlord's eye.

"Why don't you see reason?" Brant continued. "Mr. Mackenzie has requisitioned your stores. Just as soon as he takes control of the treasury in Toronto you'll be compensated. That's certainly better than a looting of the tavern."

The landlord started to reply, then thought better of it. Within an hour the troops in the yard began to receive cold rations of beef and beer.

"Thank you, Brant," Mackenzie said wearily. "I'm glad you're one of us."

He sat down at the table with Joshua.

"Gentlemen," he said, "I know it is going to work. Papineau has beaten them in Quebec. Now it is our turn. The state of Upper Canada, with our own elected governor and our own elected Assembly, will soon be free at last."

"Not without a fight, Will, and you're no general."

"I've got me a general, a Dutchman, VanEgmond. Fought with Napoleon. Now I need more soldiers. I'm going out recruiting again. I'm leaving young Anderson in charge, Brant. He's a smarter man than Sam Lount, although you can't have a braver, more true fellow than Lount. I'd appreciate it, nevertheless, if you kept your eye out for all of them while I am gone."

"Is it safe for you to leave?"

"Don't worry." Mackenzie laughed. "Old 'Bone Head' will not dare leave Toronto to find me. He'll be there when I go in after him."

"And when will that be?"

"Seventh of December. In a week. I'll be back in plenty of time. In the meanwhile, see that my army eats." He rose from the table. His spirits and energy seemed to have been restored by the outlining of his plans to Michael.

Joshua rose when Mackenzie left. "I am going to find a place to sleep," he said to his uncle.

"I am sure you can handle the ground with the bedroll Mackenzie gave you. I am certainly happy he regards me as important enough to deserve a cot there in the tavern."

Joshua stepped outside into the brisk December night. There was some snow on the ground but most of it had melted as more and more campfires were lit and more and more feet trampled the campsite.

A small crowd had gathered around the largest campfire. Someone was shouting and haranguing the crowd. Joshua walked in the direction of the commotion. He recognized the speaker as Donald Mackay, Willie's father.

"I'll tell you, my lads, the true Scotsman's, the Highlander's day has come, thanks to Will Mackenzie. We'll drive out the high and mighty English and their vicious Orange Lodge henchmen."

Several men in the crowd clapped, perhaps more to keep their hands warm than to give approval to Mackay. Someone in the crowd yelled.

"Give old Donald another swig."

A cheer went up and a large jug was passed over the crowd around the fire until it reached the speaker.

His eyes sparkled in the firelight when he saw the jug.

"Aye, by God," he called out. "I have a terrible thirst. It was good of you to think of me."

"You've had a terrible thirst for thirty years," a bystander yelled.

Everyone laughed.

"Aye, a terrible thirst for freedom," Mackay slurred his words.

Joshua felt someone prod his ribs. He looked down at the familiar felt hat of Willie Mackay.

"My dad's really important now, ain't he, Josh?"

"Willie, how come he brought you out here?"

"He don't go nowhere without me. Hell, who'd put him to bed and sober him up in the morning? And Mackenzie is going to need him and need him sober."

Donald Mackay took another swig from the jug. This time he allowed the cider to pour into his open mouth, splashing some of the liquor on his face and whiskers as well. Again the crowd cheered. Makay staggered and tripped and fell into the fire.

Willie Mackay screamed and ran forward through the crowd. By the time she reached her father's side he had already risen to his feet and brushed the hot charcoal embers from his filthy clothes.

"Gentlemen," he said, weaving unsteadily and placing his hands on his daughter's shoulders to steady himself, "this fire grows too hot and too large. It is time to extinguish it."

He reached down and opened his pants. Soon the steady stream of urine fell onto the blaze and caused a hiss and then an acrid smoke.

"Daddy, don't shame yourself," Willie whispered to him.

"Don't give me no lip, brat," he said and swung around and directed the urine at the girl.

She backed off, a look of shock on her face, then she looked down on the wet stain on her pants leg where the stream had hit her. She ran from the fire out toward the blackened fringes.

"You had no call to do that, Mackay," a man in the crowd, soberer than most, called out.

"I certainly did," the drunk responded. "I had a call of

nature." He began to laugh and slap his thigh. "And I'll piss on the old archdeacon's altar over in Toronto once we get there. In fact, I'll piss on the archdeacon himself."

Joshua found Willie leaning against a tree in the tavern's yard. He could tell she had been weeping.

"Are you all right?" he asked her.

"Why shouldn't I be?" she said quietly.

"That was a rotten thing to do to you."

"Don't you start in on my daddy. He loves me and he treats me good. Sometimes when he is drunk...he forgets."

She started to weep again. Joshua didn't know what to do to try to soothe her. He stood there watching her cry until she again grew quiet.

"Want to find a spot to go to sleep?" he asked finally.

"I don't do that sort of thing."

She could not see him blush in the darkness but he could feel his face redden.

"I didn't mean to do anything," he said sheepishly. "I wouldn't do that sort of thing with you anyway."

"Why not?" she said turning to him. "What's wrong with me?"

"Well nothing, it's just that . . ."

"I'll bet you would have done it with Allison Winslow if she'd let you."

"She wouldn't do that sort of thing," Joshua said heatedly, defending the honor of the sacred Allison once again.

"She wouldn't tell the truth either, would she?"

Joshua frowned. "She would if I could only get to her and ask her."

"And what else would you ask her? You'd ask her to do it with you, wouldn't you? But not me. Why not me?"

"Hell, Willie," Joshua said. "To do it with you would be indecent. You're like a boy."

"Joshua Miller, if you want to see yourself when you ain't got a mirror, why don't you put your head between your legs and look up at your own asshole."

She fought back her tears and walked back toward the campfire where her father still held court.

III

Toronto, December 1837

On the evening of December 6, Joshua found himself marching through the dusk in the heart of the column advancing toward Toronto. All his companions were men with rifles and muskets, about sixty of them. They were to be the advance party—the shock troops.

No one knew for sure how the word got spread. Some said it came from Dr. Rolph, the mayor of Toronto, a secret sympathizer of Mackenzie's forces. But someone let it be known that the city lay open to anyone with the nerve to advance against it. In Mackenzie's absence, Sam Lount and the other officers decided on an attack. They sent word to Mackenzie, and the mercurial Scotsman rode at breakneck speed back to the tavern.

Yet on the sixth they had dallied all day long on the road south of the tavern until they came to the Bloor tollgate. At this point truce parties came out of Toronto to seek negotiations, or at least to delay. Mackenzie seemed in no hurry. But when no further negotiations took place, the Scotsman grew impatient again. Finally at dusk he gave the word for the final assault.

Joshua was edgy. He could barely see the back of the man ahead of him in the dusk. Captain Lount had drilled this group of farmers into a rifle company and it alone had any semblance of military bearing. Behind the rifle company marched two hundred pike men like specters from an earlier century, and behind them, ambling along without much discipline, were the mass of the farmers of York County.

Joshua felt privileged to join the rifle company, although the look on Uncle Brant's face when he learned of it was clear indication that he disapproved. Joshua was sure that he had gone to Mackenzie about it and had been turned away. He was almost sixteen years old, and he knew how to fire a musket. He had to get back into Toronto. He had to see Allison and make her tell what had really happened in the cloakroom. But he was sure of one thing. Now that he had tasted independence and now that he had found family who cared for him, he would never return to his father's home.

They continued to trudge forward. Captain Anderson, who was supposed to have been the leader of the whole army, had been killed earlier in a freak encounter with an alderman from the city. Most of the men regarded it as an ill omen. In addition, Colonel VanEgmond had not yet arrived from the north. Leadership had fallen to Samuel Lount, who rode his large horse at the van. By his side, on a diminutive pony, rode Mackenzie.

Mackenzie had behaved erratically all day. When he was overjoyed he removed his wig and tossed it into the air. Most of the men had cheered the first time, for he seemed so happy. But as he continued to waver from joy to despair to rage, the men became nervous. Now they marched on the capital. They had been told it was undefended and that the people would welcome them as heroes freeing them from a Tory bondage. Mackenzie had assured the men of their welcome. Joshua knew that most of the people among whom he was raised—Charles Miller's circle of friends—would regard them as a traitorous rabble and welcome them with a hail of lead rather than with a hail of friendship.

Donald Mackay marched with the rifle company next to Joshua. He had sobered up, but his face was haggard and his step seemed to drag a bit. Several times the soldiers in ranks behind him complained and not too kindly advised him to quicken his pace.

"This is a great day for Canada," Mackay called out. "We should savor this moment."

"How would you savor my rifle butt up your ass, Mackay?" said the rifleman behind him.

"Patience, Williams, you bloody Welsh bastard. You spent so much of your life underground in a mine that darkness means nothing to you. But if you'd been raised on the highlands of dear Scotland and knew about sun, you would be able to tell night from day. You would get used to seeing where you're going rather than moving by instinct. Which is the long way of saying I can't see three bloody inches in front of my face. Who the hell thought of attacking in the dark?"

"Mackenzie," said Williams.

"Did he, the dear boy? Then he must have had his reasons, so stop complaining," answered Mackay.

"You're the one who is complaining."

"I was not. It was you who said I didn't move fast enough."

Joshua started to laugh at both of the men. But Lount turned on his mount and ordered quiet in the ranks.

They had moved about one-half mile south of the Bloor tollgate. Joshua could make out the outline of William Sharp's farmhouse coming up directly in front of them. Suddenly, light flashed before his eyes; his ears felt the concussion of the mass of lead flying over his head.

"We're under fire," Mackay shouted. "May the Lord of Battle, the God of Hosts give victory to his chosen people."

"Spread out. Hit the ground," Lount ordered.

The men obeyed his order. Joshua found himself spread-eagled and facedown in the dirt of the road.

Lount raised his sword. "Fire," he shouted.

The rifles fired a volley blindly ahead. Joshua busily reloaded. He turned to get a cartridge from his cartridge box at his side. Behind him he saw the pike men scattering. They were not filling out the front, however; rather, they were moving in confusion off the road toward the footloose army behind them.

"Where are they going?" Joshua asked in astonishment of no one in particular.

Lount ordered another volley, and the muskets of the

company blasted down Yonge Street toward Sharp's farm.

Michael Brant came running up from the rear, calling Mackenzie's name.

The rebel leader swerved on his pony to meet Brant.

"What's happened?" Brant called out. "The army is panicking behind us, Will. Word has spread that the Tories are lined up along Yonge Street right into the heart of town and that the whole rifle company was shot down with the first blast."

"My God, man, get the officers to hold them on the road. We can't be chasing after our own men."

"How many are wounded?" Brant asked, worried about Joshua.

Lount polled his men.

"Two" he responded. "One dead."

"But that can't be!" said Michael. "I myself saw the whole front rank cut down."

"That's how I trained them," Lount replied. "If they were fired on, they were to hit the dirt and return the fire."

"Well, we've got a bloody panic on our hands. Some are so frightened they are running back to the tollgate."

Mackenzie kicked the sides of his pony and raced toward the rear to try to stem the retreat.

Sam Lount grabbed Joshua, Williams, and Mackay and ordered them to scout ahead. Joshua crawled on his belly in the snow-dusted dirt of Yonge Street, with Williams ahead and Mackay coming up from behind.

Williams waited for Joshua to come alongside and then signaled him to cross the road to their left and reconnoiter that side toward the Sharp farm. Mackay was sent in the other direction.

The darkness in front of Joshua seemed totally impenetrable. Behind him he could hear the fading commotion of hundreds of men in full retreat. He hoped that Mackenzie and Uncle Brant could restore order, but mostly he hoped he would not be so frightened of what lay ahead of him that he would betray his fear to the other men of the rifle company.

The ground was cold and Joshua shivered as he moved

ahead. He came to a rail fence. It was dark and he could not see beyond it. At any moment he expected to be blinded by the flash of gunfire. He stopped moving forward. Suddenly he heard Mackay call out.

"There are no goddamned Tories in sight. The bastards have fled."

Then there was silence.

Joshua screwed up his courage and moved toward the railing.

He heard something scurry away off to his left. But from the sound of it it had to be a small animal. He rose to a crouched position and stepped around the fence post. Now, even in the dark, he saw signs that men had spent time crouched behind the fence. They were all gone now.

"All clear on this side," he called out.

"The road's clear, Captain Lount," Williams called out.

Lount ordered his men back on their feet and joined Joshua at the fence. He examined the ground on both sides of the road.

"Damn it, they didn't have more than thirty men posted here," he cursed. "And they stopped our whole goddamned army."

"I am sure Mr. Mackenzie will get them back on the road."

"Boy, something you ought to know about Willie Mackenzie. He can talk his way from here to the land of Goshen and back and there ain't no better man in this world with words. If I needed someone to write for me or speak for me I'd want William Lyon Mackenzie. But he couldn't organize a family picnic, much less an army. Right now our bloody army is scattered all over the countryside. I'll be surprised if he can get it back together by next week. The bloody march on Toronto is over. There's just us—you, Mackay, Williams, me, and what's left of the rifle company, which I think will be about a third gone by the time we get back to taking roll call. There ain't nobody between us and Toronto now that this picket's dispersed, but there ain't enough of us to do the job. I've got a bad feeling, boy. I think we're going to regret this night real bad. I think Will Mackenzie's war of liberation just came to an end. And if it wasn't so tragic, it would be kind of funny."

On the next day Charles received word aboard his steamer in Toronto Bay that the attack on the city had failed to materialize and that in all probability the Mackenzie rabble were in great disarray. He ordered the steamer to place itself in a condition of readiness but not to sail without his orders. The regular run to Kingston was canceled.

He regretted his decision almost immediately when he heard the bell in the cupola of Upper Canada College began to toll. That had been the signal that attack was imminent. But once ashore, he found Colonel Fitzgibbons on the dock. By the grin on his face Charles knew that the word was good.

"Charles," the colonel called to him, "word has come from Lower Canada. Another battle outside Montreal and the frog rebels are beaten. Papineau has fled and all his forces are in retreat or worse. Now Lord Gosford can send his regulars to us."

Charles grabbed the adjutant general by his shoulders. "That is good news," he laughed.

"But we'll not await them. We're going out after the bastards ourselves. We've got the loyal militia, men like you and me. Even the archdeacon plans to ride with us. We're going to hang that bastard Mackenzie, by God we will."

Charles went pale as Fitzgibbons spoke. Perhaps it had not been wise to return to shore so quickly.

"By the way, where have you been since I last saw you?"

"I was placing the steamer in shape to pick up troops to reinforce us."

"Good. Is she ready to sail?" Fitzgibbons asked.

"Not quite yet."

"Why wait? We need more men."

"Then I'll order her to sail immediately," Charles said after some hesitation. He wanted to object but he could not without arousing suspicion.

"You'll join our march out to Montgomery's Tavern, of course," Fitzgibbons continued.

"Of course," Charles confirmed, "but I'm surprised Sir Francis would allow it."

"I can't pay too much attention to Sir Francis. I woke him up three times last night with reports on Mackenzie's drive on the city and he did nothing. He forbade me to place troops outside the city limits. I disobeyed. I put Sheriff Jarvis on Yonge Street, south of the Bloor tollgate, and he stopped Mackenzie's advance. Thirty men against thousands. It reminds me of Thermopylae."

Charles looked at Fitzgibbons in amazement. "You mean Jarvis's men were wiped out?"

"Of course not. Not one was hurt. I meant the few against the many."

"Well, I can think of better examples, James. Let's not get carried away."

"There's no denying our boys were brave."

Charles shook his head. "What remains to be done?" he asked.

"We await reinforcements from the town militias. But not too long. We've almost a thousand men under arms and two fieldpieces. I propose to ride out and drive the rats out of their nest."

Charles was instantly sure that what Fitzgibbons had suggested was the worst thing that could possibly be done. He knew he had to get to the governor and prevent Fitzgibbons from endangering all their lives.

"Don't be too hasty, James. We must have a council of war to effect all of this. Sir Francis must call it. And since my steamer is the sole means of escape for the lieutenant governor's family, I suggest that it remain in the bay until His Excellency's family is aboard. We can sacrifice our lives and risk life and limb for Her Majesty, but the women and children of Her Majesty's servants must be safe."

"Of course, you're right about that, Charles. I hadn't thought about it. But we are no longer in danger in the town. We need not think of defeat."

Charles received an audience with Sir Francis Bond Head as soon as his presence was made known to the lieutenant governor. Head was still wearing his dressing gown and he had not been shaved. His desk was cluttered with military maps of the town, the surrounding forts, and York County to the north of the city.

"Miller," he greeted Charles, rising from his chair. "It's good to see you. I need all the calm heads about me I can find." He grabbed Charles's hand and shook it vigorously. "I'm sorry about your boy. Perhaps after all this is over we can squelch it. Evans was a good man but he was rather forward with the ladies. Perhaps there was something to what the boy's grandmother claims. I mean about Joshua's protecting the Winslow girl from Evans."

Charles looked the governor directly in the eye. "I'll ask no favors for Joshua Miller, sir. He will be responsible for his own actions and I'll not have the girl's reputation harmed in any way. She is innocent and virginal. Jessica Brant's story is a slur on Allison's reputation and I shall not tolerate it. As you said, Evans was a good man."

Head looked at Miller quizzically. "Have it your way," he said after a brief silence. "Right now I have more pressing problems."

"Yes, I know. I think your biggest one is Fitzgibbons."

"The man's close to lunacy," Head said vehemently. "He wakes me up in the middle of the night with wild stories that the red-wigged midget is on the move. Wanted to rouse the whole town. I had all I could do to keep him from ringing the church and school bells all over the city. Could you imagine the panic if we had done that?"

"Worse than that," Charles spoke with some vigor. "I just heard him say he's sending an army out to Montgomery's Tavern. He tried to order my steamer out of the bay to pick up reinforcements along the lake towns."

"You object?"

"Most vigorously, sir."

"Why?"

"For one, we should barricade and defend this town

68

until Lord Gosford is able to send regular troops. The French rebellion is crushed. Mackenzie's rabble will not stand up to Her Majesty's finest."

"You're right about that. You advise caution, then?"

"Most certainly!"

"Now what about the steamer?"

"Well, Your Excellency, I held it in the harbor as a means of escape for your party, Lady Head in particular. I do not think the rebels stand any hope of taking the town from us, but we should never take the chance of allowing the families of Her Majesty's servants to be held hostage."

Head looked genuinely gratified. "I shall not forget what you have just said. It is good to know that during trying times men of intelligence will rise to the fore, and men of generous heart as well. Thank you, Charles."

"I'd appreciate it, sir, if Judge and Mrs. Winslow and their daughter could be invited to transfer to the steamer as well."

"I'm sure the ladies will accept, Charles, but you'll be hard pressed to get the judge to go. The last time I saw him he had his beaver hat on his head and his musket on his shoulder preparing to join the muster."

"My God, a man of his age has no business acting like that. I'm fifty-eight. He must be sixty-five at least."

"The good judge is a vigorous man. He may be sixty-five but he has a sixteen-year-old daughter."

Charles shrugged. He didn't care about Judge Winslow, so long as mother and daughter were safe and sound. He was determined to make the daughter his bride. All he would need was the consent of a living parent, be it father or mother.

There was a soft rap on the door.

"Enter," Head called out.

A civilian aide entered the room.

"There's a delegation from the town to see you, sir."

"Oh, Christ, that's all I need now."

"On the contrary, Christ is precisely all you need now," boomed the voice of the archdeacon, the Reverend John Strachan, as he entered the study.

69

The line of march stretched out of the town and up Gallows Hill, one thousand men strong. There were middle-aged men like Judge Winslow in their finest suits of clothes, weapons of war slung across their shoulders. Most had not fired a gun in anger since 1815, twenty-two years earlier. They were followed by the younger men, eager and yet nervous about going to war for the first time. Bringing up the rear was the military artillery, two horse-drawn fieldpieces, and a brass band.

The archdeacon, accompanied by a priest, rode in the middle of the column. He was in a jubilant mood. It reminded him, he said, of the Yankee attack on muddy York back in '13 when he alone had kept his head and saved the town. Now he had joined forces with Fitzgibbons and bullied the governor into offensive action. That monstrous atheist Mackenzie would die today, or at least he would take his first step toward the gallows.

Sir Francis Bond Head rode in the middle of the column not far from the archdeacon. Beside him rode Charles Miller. Miller was annoyed at having been trapped ashore instead of remaining aboard his steamer. Yet there was no turning back without raising eyebrows all over Toronto. These people were fools to attack a desperate enemy instead of waiting for the regulars. The whole town had gone mad, lining the streets and cheering their ragtag army on its way to destruction. Charles had noted several pro-Mackenzie reformers in the cheering crowd. Well, they had good reason to cheer. The governor had allowed himself to be forced into fighting a fight he couldn't win.

Fitzgibbons led the van. He rode his horse and issued instructions from its back. Once they passed the tollgate he sent flanking parties to the right and left on either side of Yonge Street.

The sun was warm at midday for December and the dusting of snow had totally disappeared. The column moved in a straight line over the hill toward Montgomery's Tavern.

Charles was wondering where the enemy had gone to when suddenly musket fire came from the brush and tree stumps on either side of the road, causing men to drop to the ground for cover. Fitzgibbons stood in his stirrups and waved his sword. He ordered his men to spread out and continued to advance on the woods. The Tory flanking column came up quickly and opened fire. The horses pulling the artillery were turned around and the muzzles of the fieldpieces brought to bear on the enemy line. The first cannonball tore through the treetops. The aim was far too high. But falling branches from the trees, combined with ever-increasing musketry on the flanks, unnerved Mackenzie's men. Charles could see many of them begin to run for cover, back toward the inn. Again the artillery fired and the cannonballs landed in the midst of the retreating rebels, bouncing on the frozen soil and skimming along the ground to the terror of those who ran from them.

Even from his vantage, Charles could see several unmoving bodies in the midst of the enemy retreat. The muskets of the Toronto loyal militia were beginning to find targets. Now the whole rebel force was in full flight. The fieldpieces were rehitched to the horses and the column again moved north. Once in range, the artillery commander began a bombardment of the tavern building itself. The cannonballs went through windows and crashed through the roof, panicking the unarmed recruits, who began to scatter in every direction. The spirit of Mackenzie's army collapsed when the tiny man in the red wig was seen scurrying toward the north atop his pony. The Upper Canada rebellion was over.

Joshua had been sent with Captain Lount's rifle company to feint against the Don River Bridge and hold the militia in Toronto. The feint had not worked, primarily because no one in Toronto realized that Lount's men threatened them. Joshua missed the "battle" at Montgomery's Tavern, but he and his company could hear it. The captain force-marched them back in the direction of the fighting too late—the battle was over.

Once he realized that the army had broken up, Sam Lount addressed his company.

"Boys, I am afraid it is every man for himself," he called out.

The men hesitated at first but then broke ranks and headed toward the north, where most of them lived.

Joshua was confused. He knew he should flee, too, but first he wanted to find his Uncle Michael. The last time he had seen Brant he was sitting as part of Mackenzie's staff in the taproom of the tavern.

Following his companions, Joshua slipped into the woods that covered the countryside to the north on either side of the roadway. But unlike the others, he turned toward the east and then to the south to double back on Montgomery's Tavern. He had to hide several times to avoid the search parties that scoured the woods looking for rebels. Finally from a small knoll he caught sight of the tavern. A wisp of smoke rose from its windows, followed by tongues of flame. It had been torched. There was no sign of his uncle.

Joshua continued to watch the scene from the hillside throughout the afternoon. The tavern burned briskly. The winds changed direction and blew the heavy smoke toward Joshua's hiding place. He crawled back down the hillside to avoid the smoke.

Toward evening the wind shifted again and Joshua could resume his observation post. He saw prisoners marched into the tavern courtyard. Their hands were tied behind their backs and halters were placed around their necks, linking them all together. Joshua recognized Sam Lount as one of them, but he did not see his uncle.

He was hungry and cold. His spirits were lagging. He had no idea where to look for Uncle Brant, and without his uncle he had no idea about what to do next or where to go. He sat in the darkness of the hillside with only the flickering light of the burning tavern making it possible to see.

"Well, I can't just sit here," he said aloud. He rose to his feet and began to walk down the hill toward the flames.

Militiamen strolled around casually. There seemed to be no more discipline on the Tory side than there had been on the rebel side. All he had to do was walk among them and hope he was not recognized. He went from cluster to cluster of militiamen. He saw no more prisoners. Just when he was about to give up, he recognized a brown homespun-clad figure with a felt hat on her head carrying a bundle. He knew it was Willie Mackay. She dodged from the light of the campfire near the edge of a clump of trees.

Joshua looked about him. No one was watching. He, too, entered the underbrush and set a course that he hoped would intercept hers. He moved as silently as he could. But in the darkness it was difficult to avoid branches, bare of leaves, that snapped back at him like whips when pushed aside.

He had gone too far, he was sure. He should have found her by now. The pain that shot through his head nearly paralyzed him. He twisted to see what had come from behind but he was unconscious before he hit the ground.

The cannons roared again and again. Joshua tried to stuff his fingers into his ears but it did no good. Each thunderbolt crashed into his consciousness, pulling him away from the black void in which he found himself toward the red glare from two identical caves. Just before he awakened he realized the caves were the lids of his own eyes. The thunder subsided and gave way to a throbbing in the back of his skull. He focused his eyes with difficulty. The brown dirty face of Willie Mackay stared down at him.

"Josh, I'm glad you came back. I nearly messed my breeches when I saw it was you I clobbered. But you came on like such a bear, such a city boy lost in the woods, I couldn't take any chances."

He tried to sit up, but he got no further than raising himself on his elbows.

"Willie Mackay, I do think someday you will really succeed in killing me."

He saw the pained look on her face and regretted his comment.

"I'm sorry," he offered. But the tears began to roll down her cheeks.

"I'm sorry," he said again. "Damn it, what I said wasn't so bad," he complained.

"It ain't you at all." She sniffed as she spoke. "It's my dad. You sort of set me remembering."

Joshua looked at her in silence. It dawned on him that Mackay had not been with them at the Don Bridge. In fact, Joshua had not seen him since Sharp's farm.

"I made him stay behind this morning. Josh, he got sickly drunk last night. I think it was the disappointment. He knew we had lost our chance. When morning came he could barely stand. I stole his pants until you and Lount's boys marched off. He took a stick to me and rapped me good across the rump. I can still feel it. Josh, it is the last thing he ever did give me. They put a ball in his head in the woods this afternoon. The goddamned Tories orphaned me, and all I've got left from him is a bruise. I hope it don't never go away."

She was sobbing now. Joshua reached up and pulled her head toward his chest. He held onto her while she wept. His dirty jacket was soon soaked with tears.

When her tears had stopped, she sighed and rested against him. Finally he pulled away from her and looked at her from arm's length.

"Where is your father?"

"They buried him. There was only a couple dead on our side. The Tories didn't lose anyone."

"Have you seen my Uncle Michael?"

She looked beyond her shoulder and turned around. There on the ground behind where he himself had fallen was the pale, blanket-covered form of Michael Brant.

Joshua twisted around and stared into Michael's face. Its pasty grayness convinced him that Michael Brant was another victim of Mackenzie's folly, or, worse, of Joshua Miller's folly. He bent his head down to Brant's chest. He could hear a beat. His uncle was alive.

Joshua pulled back the blanket. Brant's shoulder had been struck by a musket ball. The wound had been washed and dressed. It was clear that he needed a surgeon so that the deadly lead could be removed.

74

"I did the best I could for him. He was awake earlier. He told me he was hit while he was in the tavern. He crawled out before they set fire to it. He made it to the underbrush and collapsed. That is where I found him. I was looking for my dad."

"Willie, I think you saved my uncle from those bastards. My grandmother isn't going to forget that. Neither am I. You won't be alone. We'll take care of you."

"I can take care of myself," she responded defensively. "My dad was mostly not around, and when he was, he was mostly drunk. *I* took care of *him*. Now I ain't got no one to take care of anymore."

"I think we both have Uncle Michael to take care of. That is, if you are willing to help me."

She looked at him contemptuously. "Do you think I dropped him in these woods and stole a blanket to cover him so that I could walk away now? Sometimes, Joshua—shit, why only sometimes? why, all the times—Joshua Miller, you are dumb. You don't know your soup bowl from your chamber pot."

Joshua ignored her insults.

"Uncle Brant has to get to a doctor. I suspect we could find a friendly one in the northern towns. I think we ought to set out there."

"That's a chamber pot thought," she said. "Mackenzie lit out for the north. Every officer of the queen and every self-styled rebel-hater is going to be scouring the northern towns. I say we do the opposite—we head right back into Toronto. We take him right to your grandmother's house."

Joshua started to laugh at her. "That's like taking him back to be hanged."

"They're not going to hang Michael Brant. He's rich. He's important and he's got many friends who side with him. It's people like my dad who get killed. It's farmers who get hanged, not lawyers with rich families. Besides, everyone in the northern towns is going to be running for cover, surgeons and lawyers. Most people would enjoy hanging a sawbones."

"Most would enjoy hanging a lawyer, too," Michael

Brant said in a feeble voice, shocking both Joshua and Willie. "Josh, the girl is right. Get me back to the city. If you can help me, I'll walk."

Joshua looked dismayed. "What makes you think she's right?"

"Because if you can get the lead out of my shoulder, then both of us can make it across the lake to the United States. We might even get your father to help us. After all, he has all kinds of boats."

"He hates you."

"But he's your father. But one step at a time. First let's get back to town."

Joshua was sure they would be stopped at the Bloor tollgate. But Toronto was celebrating a victory, and no one expected fugitives to try to sneak back into the town. The tollgate itself was unmanned. Joshua and Willie, supporting the weakened older man, walked straight down Yonge Street to King Street, into the heart of Toronto. As they approached Bay Street, Michael sighed and started to collapse at the knees. The boy and the girl caught him before he fell to the ground.

"Just a bit further, Uncle Brant," Joshua urged.

Michael smiled. "Don't bring me directly inside. Find out where Phinias and Lillie are before you take me in. They are clearly the source of our troubles. Jessica must have figured that out, but for all of her huff and puff she's too forgiving a woman."

They half dragged, half carried Brant around to the mews in back of his Bay Street mansion. Joshua tried the back door to the house. It was unlocked. He stepped through into the kitchen. The room was dark. Even the stove showed no glowing embers. No dinner had been cooked in the Brant household that night.

Joshua entered the hallway. There was a light coming from the parlor. He walked cautiously down the hallway and stepped back into the shadows. He peered into the room. The old lady sat by herself. Her shawl was pulled over her head and her lips seemed to tremble. The house was deadly silent except for the ticking of the clock above the mantel in the parlor. Joshua realized that her lips were not really trembling. She was speaking, almost in a whisper. It was a language Joshua had never heard before, but he knew she prayed.

"Grandmother," he called out softly.

Jessica was startled by the sound of his voice. She rose and peered into the darkness of the hallway.

Joshua stepped into the dim light. Jessica's shawl slipped down from her head to her shoulders and she moved toward him. She threw her arms about the boy and squeezed him. She was no longer strong. Not like the girl who could work twelve hours a day in a seamstress shop as she had once done. But still her emotions were so great that Joshua had to squeal and tell her that she was hurting him.

"Michael?" she questioned.

"Here, but he's been hurt."

Fear replaced the joy in her face.

"Where are the servants?" Joshua asked.

"In hell for all I care," she responded with anger. "Where is my son?"

"Come with me." Joshua took her hand and led her into the kitchen. He opened the outside door. Both Michael and Willie entered.

Jessica led Michael to a kitchen chair. She pulled the army blanket off his shoulders and tore open his shirt. She handed the blanket to Willie.

"Who are you?"

"Willie Mackay," Joshua responded. "She saved Uncle's life."

"I can speak for myself," Willie said belligerently.

"Is what the boy said true?" Jessica asked.

Willie nodded.

"Consider yourself a friend, child. Now take that blanket and drop it in the stables behind the house. It probably has lice in it. Don't put it near yourself."

"Damn," Willie said, "I've had lice before, ma'am. They ain't nothing to be afraid of." She went out the back door.

"Real little lady, isn't she?" Jessica commented with a smile.

"She's a good girl," Michael interjected.

"Well, my son, you've had to wait until you're fifty to get yourself shot."

"I'm not fifty and you've got to get that lead ball out of me."

"I know that, boy, but we've not had a built-in doctor in this family since Eli Stoddard died. I'm going to have to get that ball out myself. Joshua, go up to the old sitting room. In the cupboard you'll find a carpetbag with Eli's instruments in it. Bring it to me."

"Why not get a real doctor?"

"Because, you silly ass, everyone in Toronto knows you were with Mackenzie and that Michael took you there. Every doctor in this town will take one look at either one of you and summon the constable. I don't want Michael patched up for the hangman. Now get me the bag," she insisted.

Willie came back into the kitchen.

"Girl," said Jessica, "can you start a fire?"

Willie said nothing but stepped out into the back where she had seen logs and kindling.

"Mother." Michael looked up into her face. "Do you really know what you are doing?"

"I watched Doc do it many times. I helped him. After Elizabeth left and your father died, he asked me to assist him. I know what I am doing."

She went to the pantry and pulled down a large bottle of West Indian rum. She pulled the cork.

"Start drinking," she ordered, handing the bottle to her son. "But don't drink all of it. I'll need some to pour over the instruments."

"Why?"

"I don't know why. All I know is that Eli used to do it. Now shut up and drink."

Joshua returned to the kitchen with Eli Stoddard's bag.

Willie, her arms loaded with wood, stumbled through the door from the yard. She dropped her load with a loud crash on the floor.

"Boy," Jessica yelled at Joshua, "don't just stand there.

Give the girl a hand and get the fire going. I want hot water too."

Michael had downed half the bottle of rum already.

"Good digging, Mother," he joked as she pulled a scalpel and a pair of narrow steel tongs from the bag.

Finally she found what looked like a sharp steel rod.

"Here it is," she said to herself.

"It's wicked-looking," said Michael, his speech already slurred.

"Can you climb up on the table?" she asked him. He could barely get to his feet.

"Joshua," Jessica called.

The boy came to her side.

"Help me get your uncle up on the table before he gets too drunk and can't help us himself."

Michael, despite the pain of the wound, started to get giggly.

"Mother dear, you used to tell me to keep my elbows off the table. Now you want me to put my ass on it!"

Joshua lifted his uncle at the waist and boosted his rear onto the table. Michael lay back himself.

Jessica lifted his head and gave him another large mouthful of rum. The fire was already roaring in the stove and the room became pleasantly warm.

"Put some water on to boil," Jessica ordered the girl.

Willie went to the pump to fill the kettle and placed it on the stove.

Jessica poured some of the rum into Michael's open wound. He gasped and started to sit up.

"Joshua," she called to her grandson, "hold him down."

Joshua grabbed his uncle's shoulders and pinned him down to the table. Michael groaned in pain.

"Hurry up with that water," she called out.

Willie brought the steaming kettle.

"Get some cloths from the drawer below the sink," Jessica ordered. She soaked a small towel in hot water in a basin and added some of her homemade soap. She washed Michael's wound carefully and cleaned his chest and shoulders.

79

He was almost delirious from pain and rum. She took the steel rod, poured some of the liquor over it, and gently inserted it into the wound. Again Michael's whole body stiffened. Joshua pressed down on his shoulders and Willie tried to control his legs.

"What are you doing?" the boy asked.

"Shut up," Jessica said gruffly. "This is what Eli did. He followed the path of the bullet until he felt it with the sounding rod."

Michael tried to escape the ever-pressing pain in his shoulder by twisting away from it. But Joshua held him firmly. Jessica kept the pressure on the sound. Deeper and deeper it probed.

"There it is, I have it, I feel it," Jessica called out.

She took the scissorlike instrument from the table and again poured rum on it. She inserted the tongs to follow the path of the sound.

Michael fainted.

"Thank God," she said as she peered down at his shoulder almost as if she could see deeper into it. "There, the tongs are touching the ball. Now to get a grip."

She maneuvered the instrument first to one side and then to the other.

"Careful now," she said, "I think I've got it. Slowly now." A look of triumph crossed her face as the tongs, grasping a flattened piece of lead, came out of the bloody hole in her son's shoulder. She quickly removed the other instrument and washed the whole wound with liquor and hot water. Then she bound it with clean cloth.

"I think we've done it," she said to the two youngsters. "Now let's get him to bed and get some sleep ourselves. In the morning we'll decide what to do about all of us."

Joshua did not wait for the morning to come. Somehow or other he had to get to Allison. She had to clear his name in the death of Captain Evans. When he was cleared, then his uncle would have a chance to explain why he had fled from Toronto.

As soon as the house quieted, Joshua opened the door

80

and tiptoed down the hallway and down the stairs to the front door.

The night air was bitter. Winter had now truly descended on the city. Down along the waterfront it was possible to see swirling columns of steam rising into the black night as the lake gave up its heat to winter. By morning a heavy coat of ice would have formed on Toronto Bay. Joshua shivered. He wished he had the fur coat he had left hanging in the hall closet just a few houses down Bay Street. He retraced the last carriage ride he had shared with his father. He turned left on Newgate Street. The houses and shops were quiet and the street was dark. He cut diagonally across the street and reached the corner of York. The mud puddles in York Street had frozen, giving the avenue the appearance of a frozen canal.

Joshua was walking briskly but he could feel the pinch of the cold on his face. The tips of his fingers had gone numb. He blew his warm breath onto his hands and then shoved them inside the waistband of his pants.

He crossed over Hospital Street and came to Queen Street. He could see her house now. Up to this point he had not even considered how he would find Allison. It was at least two in the morning. She would be in bed. If he knew which was her bedroom, he could try climbing up on the porch and rapping on the window. But he would get only one chance to pick the right bedroom with that method.

There was one dim light shining in the front window on the York Street side. Perhaps that was hers. He picked up a handful of gravel from the house walkway and hid behind a cedar bush that grew alone in the front yard. He hurled a gravel pebble at the window. The stone struck the windowsill with a clatter that Joshua was sure could have been heard all the way down at the college in the square over by John Street. Nothing happened. He threw another pebble. This one struck the windowpane, bounced backward, and rolled down the sloping porch roof into the yard. A shadow appeared in the window, and the lamp was raised and then drawn away, as if someone was trying to get a better look outside and realized that the light would interfere with the view of the dark lawn. The sash was thrown open and Allison's beautiful head and shoulders, wrapped in a satin-covered comforter, appeared framed in the open window.

"Who is it? Who do you want?" she called. Her voice sounded worried, almost frightened.

"It's me!" he called and stepped from behind the cedar.

She stared at him. Her eyes widened. Now he was sure she was frightened.

"Go away, Joshua Miller. You've been nothing but trouble for me."

"Allison, listen to me."

"No, you go away. Do you hear me? I never want to see you again. People talk about me because of you."

"Allison, you've got to tell them the truth. If they catch me I could hang."

"You won't hang. Not if you go away someplace where they can't find you."

"I've got to talk to you," Joshua pleaded.

"No," she said finally and slammed the sash down.

Joshua was growing angry. Her selfishness was costing him too much. He moved quickly to the porch post and climbed up it. When he was high enough, he threw his leg over the porch roof and grabbed a fingerhold on the wooden shingles with his right hand. He pulled himself up and onto the roof with the strength of his arms. He knelt on the sloping roof for a second and then crawled up to Allison's window. He knocked on it. She was not going to be allowed to ignore him. Maybe she would run to her parents, but then they would have to confront him too. He was determined to force her to tell the truth. He rapped a second time. He thought he heard voices behind the closed window. He didn't care. Finally the window was thrown open. Joshua did not wait to be invited. He climbed through and stood in the dimly lit bedroom of Allison Winslow.

He stood as if struck dumb. Standing naked in front of him was his own father.

Joshua did not know what to do or say. He had never

seen his father naked before, and he certainly had never found him in these kinds of surroundings.

Allison moved nervously from the window to her bed. It was clear that she had nothing on under the satin quilt.

"Well, if it ain't the Miller rebel," Charles said glibly to his son.

Joshua felt as if he had been punched in the stomach. He did not know where his voice had gone. He tried to speak but only a croaking sound came from his throat. He felt as if he were going to be sick.

"I see the fair Allison and I have taken you by surprise. It is true that I have compromised the lady's virtue, my boy. But I intend to make it up to her. You see, Joshua, Allison has consented to become my bride. I am sure she intends to be a good mother to you."

"You're a bloody hypocrite," Joshua yelled.

"You're right," said Charles. "I do not practice what I preach, but you know the old adage, son, don't do as I do, do as I say. You are a mere child. I had hoped by doing my duty I might spare you from the sins of all flesh."

"But she's the same age as me."

"True, but dear Allison is no child. In fact, I suspect that Allison never was a child. She seems to know instinctively what I like, and I know exactly what she likes."

He smiled lasciviously at her as he spoke. Joshua followed his glance and watched as Allison relaxed as if mesmerized by his words. She leaned back into her pillow, and the comforter fell away from her breasts and she smiled back at her naked lover.

Joshua felt as if he were being choked.

"I've got to get out of here," he said.

"Smart move, my boy. In fact, as much as I love to amuse myself with the thought of Allison as your mother, I think her maternal duties will be short-lived if you don't leave Toronto. Indeed, if you don't leave, we may have to. I don't believe, as much as I loathe my gross brother's even grosser offspring, that it would be proper for Mrs. Miller and myself to be present for the hanging."

He smirked, and Allison started to laugh along with him.

"Allison," Joshua called out to her. She shocked him. The beauty of her face was marred by the sneer on her lips.

He broke for the door and flung it open. The doorknob banged against the wall with a thud. He no longer cared whom he awakened. He raced down the stairs to the front door. It was bolted. He drew back the bolt and ran out the front door into the night.

Charles watched the boy flee. He knew that Judge Winslow was parading like a fool around the countryside looking for rebels. Dear Mrs. Winslow was icebound on the steamer in the harbor along with Lady Head. After receiving the judge's blessing, Allison and Charles had intended to return to the ship. But the ice made it all impossible. He had returned the girl to her empty home and "chaperoned" his own beloved for the night. No matter, the wedding would be very soon.

He turned to look at the girl. She had thrown off the comforter and lay exposed to his view. By God, she did affect him. He went to her side and bent down and kissed her stomach, tracing his tongue on the fine golden fleece he discovered there.

"Allison, I have so much to teach you. And never before was there such a pupil."

"Teach me about love, Charles."

"About love, yes, and about pain." He could feel the yearning for her growing within him again. All his life he had waited for such a woman. Now he had her—he would never let her go.

Joshua did not know where he ran when he first left the Winslow house. Somehow or other he had crossed Yonge Street and Church Street. He had been running along King Street until he found himself at the junction of Market and King. This was the Toronto outdoor market. But at this hour of the early morning the whole area was deserted.

He sat down finally on an empty barrel. He put his head in his hands and began to weep. Everything had gone wrong. He had been prepared to leave an unkind, even cruel, father behind him. Now he could never ignore Charles Miller. The feeling that he had for him was pure hate. And never would he be able to forget the sight of Allison lying on the bed.

He had been afraid even to think about what her body might look like. In fact, he had not even been able to think such thoughts without feeling he would debase her. He was horror-struck that he had seen her, and had come to realize that she was capable of lust.

He shivered. He was chilled to the bone. If he continued to sit in the empty market he would be frozen to death by morning. He heard a rat scurrying from under another crate. He rose from the barrel and began to walk along Market Street toward Bay Street and the Brant residence.

As he turned the corner of Yonge he saw a group of men walking down the middle of the street. It was dark, but he was sure they had seen him. If he turned and ran the alarm would be raised. He walked directly toward them.

The leader of the patrol called to him. "You there, halt in the queen's name."

Joshua stopped. He knew that voice.

"Well, I'll be damned, boys. It's the little snot, Miller, who is wanted for killing a queen's officer and for going over to the rebels. I'll see the little fucker hang."

It was Master Buckam, the choirmaster. Joshua no longer feared the alarm being given. He turned and bolted back down Market Street. One of the patrol fired a pistol. A ball went whizzing over Joshua's head. The boy ducked and zigzagged down the center of the street, then turned to his left and raced up Church Street into the churchyard of St. James. He knew that several of the patrol were older men and would not be able to keep up with him. He ran past the apple orchard where Willie had ambushed him only last summer, then entered the cemetery. He ducked down behind one of the larger headstones. He had to catch his breath. He heard several voices at the entrance of the yard. Two men entered. He recognized

85

Buckam even in the dark. The oak tree behind him creaked in the chilling wind and its branches seemed to protest the cold that penetrated to its core.

The night was cloudless but there was no moon. The two searchers were heading into the graveyard. Joshua tried to bring his heavy breathing under control before it gave him away. He took a deep breath and sighed. He could hear the breathing of his two pursuers now. He did not know what to do. Should he bolt again and risk another gunshot or should he wait it out? The men were among the stones now. They said nothing to each other but merely kept moving forward, crouching low and peering behind each stone as they passed.

From behind him Joshua heard the low hoot of the owl that lived in the orchard and the whooshing of its wings as it took off from its perch. It flew directly at Buckam. The boy jumped in fright but he went unseen. Buckam screamed as the dark form came looming from the black night at him. His companion's musket fired harmlessly into the air. Both men started to laugh nervously when they realized they had been frightened by the churchyard owl.

"Let's get the hell out of here," Buckam said. "The little shit has probably already hightailed it home. I think the Miller place is on Bay Street below King. Let's keep a watch on it."

Joshua waited until they left the yard. He crept from behind the stone and ran as fast as he could across the yard. He hopped over the stone fence and raced down New Gate Street and across Yonge to Bay Stret. They would be looking for him farther down the street. But he was in no mood for another chase. He opened the front door of the Brant house and closed it quickly behind him. He leaned against the door, trying to catch his breath. He looked up the staircase and saw his Grandmother Jessica standing with a candle at the top of the landing.

"What is it, Joshua?" she asked. "Where have you been?"

"It's no good, Grandmother. They know I'm in Toronto and it won't be long before they connect me with you. I've got to get out, and Uncle Michael must flee too."

86

Willie came out of the guest room rubbing her eyes. She stood next to Jessica and listened as Joshua told his story.

When Jessica had heard the full story she turned and entered her son's bedroom. Michael Brant was slightly feverish but he was soon alert when his mother relayed Joshua's story.

"I'm afraid coming to the city was a mistake," he said, climbing out of his bed. He staggered and almost fell when he made it to his feet.

"You're not well enough yet, Michael," Jessica pleaded.

"If they take me, Mother, I'll be a lot less well."

"Where will you go?" she asked.

Willie stuck her head sheepishly into the room. "Mr. Brant, sir, I know where there is a boat, sir. It's got a sail."

"Not on a night like this." Michael rejected the idea.

"Don't say no so fast," Willie protested.

"My dear child, ice is forming on the lake. What good will a sailboat do? Besides I know nothing about sailing boats."

"I do," said Willie. "And the ice is forming only in the harbor. This boat is beached on the peninsula out near the light. The ice ain't formed out there yet. It'll take some more days of this kind of cold and no wind to do that. But there's a wind tonight."

Michael looked at his mother. "What do you think?"

"It's frightfully dangerous," Jessica protested. "You'd be on the lake with two children. You could freeze to death. Besides, where could you go?"

"To the state of New York on the other side of Lake Ontario. We'd all be safe there. I could send for you in spring."

"You'll be pardoned before that, Michael. You're no rebel. You never have been. Get your warmest clothing. I'll get a basket of food."

Within the hour, Michael, Willie, and Joshua were out on the street working their way cautiously down Bay Street toward Front Street and the harbor.

Jessica watched them leave. The tingle of her son's parting kiss still lingered on her cheek. Now she was truly

87

alone. She stood at the back door and shuddered. She could not have known that she was really not alone, that the self-righteous eyes of Phinias, the carriage man, were watching her. Jessica closed the back door and locked it. Cautiously Phinias stepped from the stable and followed the fugitives out into the streets. He would find Buckam and the patrol and inform them of the traitors' attempted escape.

Michael seemed to get stronger after they crossed Front Street and made their way to the docks along the waterfront. Nevertheless, he still needed to lean on Joshua's shoulder for support. Willie ran ahead, making sure the path to the peninsula that formed Toronto Bay was clear of constables and citizen militia.

The older man was still in pain and had not totally recovered from the large quantities of rum he had consumed when Jessica operated on him. He was more talkative than Joshua would have wished. Voices carry in the quiet of the night, and he did not want to attract any curious dockside denizens.

"It's really very ironic, you know, Joshua."

"Yes, sir," Joshua said, hoping to shut him up.

"What's ironic?" Michael questioned him.

"I don't know. You're the one who said it."

"Well, don't agree with something unless you know what it is."

"Yes, sir," Joshua agreed. They were silent for some moments. Only the sound of breathing interrupted the silence.

"You're not going to ask me the source of the irony are you, boy? I'll tell you anyway. It wasn't so long ago that my father and his family fled from the United States to a haven in Canada. Now here am I reversing the process, a fugitive in my home seeking refuge from whence we came."

"Let's just hope we get the boat and get across the lake."

Michael reached under his greatcoat and pulled a pistol from out of his waistband.

"Can you handle one of these?" he asked. "I think you should carry it. I'll be little use in a fight. I can't fire left-handed and I'm slightly tipsy."

Joshua took the pistol from his uncle. He had never fired one before, but he had fired the old brown bess and he was not afraid of firearms.

Willie came running back toward them.

"The path to the lighthouse is clear," she said breathlessly.

The three of them bent low as the wind off the lake thrust its icy fingers into them.

"My jeezus, it's going to be some sail," offered Willie. There actually was a note of glee in her voice.

They were out of the town now. The rocky shoreline to the bay opened to their view, and despite the wind there were almost no waves close to shore.

"It's really cold," Michael said breathlessly.

"It's not that much further now," said Willie. She scurried ahead and then turned sharply.

"It's here," she said, jumping up and down with excitement.

Joshua and Michael rushed to join her. She pointed at the wooden tublike craft that lay at an odd angle on its side on the beach.

"That's going to sail us across Lake Ontario?" Joshua asked. The disbelief in his tone was equally shared by Michael Brant, but he felt compelled to counter it to keep up their spirits.

"With this wind we'll be across the midpoint border to safety in no time. Willie, check the rigging and the sail. Joshua, she looks a bit heavy. Can we get her down to the water with your two arms and my one?"

Joshua walked around the boat to the far side. There were several smooth round logs that had been used to roll it onto the beach.

"I'll get her launched," he said. He placed a roller beneath the stern. He pushed his shoulder into the bow and shoved with all of his strength. The craft did not budge an inch. Joshua grunted heavily and fell to his knees.

"Damn, Willie," he said, looking up at the girl, who was sitting in the boat and fixing the mast in place. "I'm trying to budge this thing and you're sitting in it. Let's try to work together."

"Josh, let's not get nasty. We need each other if we're to succeed," said Michael.

Willie pouted a bit and then leapt over the side of the boat to the hard sand.

"The bottom has frozen to the wet sand," Joshua said. "Give me some help."

Willie placed her small body on the opposite side of the bow. On signal from Joshua, both of them shoved. Still there was no movement.

"Once again," Joshua called out. This time Michael stepped up to the boat and placed his shoulder against the center point of the bow.

"No, Uncle," Joshua said.

Michael ignored him. "All together now, shove."

The three strained with all their might. There was a cracking sound as if ice were breaking up, and slowly the boat started to move on the roller. Michael and Willie stood up and continued to push more easily now. Joshua ran to the stern and shoved a second roller under it to keep up the momentum. Soon the stern of the boat jutted into the lake and only the very tip of the bow held the craft to the shore. Willie worked feverishly on the sails while Michael collapsed exhausted in the stern.

Joshua sat next to him. He felt his uncle's forehead, but in the cold it was impossible to tell if he was feverish.

"We had better set sail as soon as possible," Michael said in a voice just loud enough to be heard over the wind and the flapping of the sails. "I think my wound has begun to bleed again."

"Josh," Willie called out, standing in the bow.

Flickering lights, torches carried by a body of men, could be seen in the trees, moving toward the beach.

"Damn," Joshua cursed. "Can we shove off, Willie?"

"I haven't got the rigging ready. I wouldn't be able to navigate. Not in this breeze."

"Then we'll have to hold them off to give you time."

He leapt down from the boat onto the beach and went out boldly to meet the search party. He recognized Buckam and Phinias immediately. He raised the pistol and pointed it directly at Buckam's heart.

"Hold it right there," he shouted. "One more step and the choirmaster is a dead man."

"We've caught up with the traitors," Phinias yelled.

"I call on you to surrender in the queen's name," Buckam called out pompously.

"Not likely," Joshua responded. "Willie, you give a yell when you're ready. Now, Master Buckam, you remain right where you are. If any one of your deputies even moves a muscle..." He did not have to finish the sentence.

"You could only get one of us, Miller. There are twenty of us here."

"True, but you'd be the one I'd get, choirmaster."

Buckam was clearly frightened by the tone of Joshua's voice. The boy meant what he said.

"Now take it easy, boys. We've got time." Out of the side of his mouth, he whispered to Phinias: "Once they're bobbing out there on the waves his aim won't be true, but ours will."

The wind seemed even stronger now and blew into Joshua's face, pushing his pants and jacket against his skin and chilling him. Phinias shifted his weight from one foot to the other.

"Tell your man not to move again, Buckam. I might just misunderstand his intentions," Joshua warned.

"For God's sake, you fool. Stand still," Buckam ordered.

"Joshua, we're ready!" Willie called out. "Hurry, I've got the mainsheet. Hop in, we're launched. Hurry, the bow has caught the wind."

Joshua steeled himself. Every instinct in his body was drawn to the bouncing tub of a boat, but he knew he hadn't enough time to make it without giving Buckam time to pick them off.

"You sail, Willie. Take him across the lake."

"Not without you," she called in desperation.

"No choice, it's too late. This way at least two escape. Take good care of him."

Willie called back to him in anguish. The bow of the boat had turned to port and the wind had caught the sail.

The boat leapt forward, its bow plowing into the choppy waves. It seemed almost to fly across the waters of the lake.

Joshua wanted to turn around to see them disappear but he dared not take his eyes off Buckam, not until he was absolutely sure that Willie and his uncle were beyond the range of the patrol's muskets.

Buckam was satisfied. He would have loved to bring in Brant, but it was more than enough glory to arrest young Miller and start him on the path to the gallows.

"All right, Miller," Buckam said. "Your friends have escaped. Put down your weapon and come with us to town. You'll get a fair hearing."

"Not by a long shot," Joshua responded. "I want all of you to drop your muskets."

"Let's cut out the charade, Miller. Give up."

The tension on Joshua's trigger finger grew tighter. Buckam sensed it from the look of Joshua's torchlit face. Buckam ordered the muskets dropped.

"Now put out the torches. Put them out."

Again the men of the patrol obeyed when Buckam ordered them to comply.

Suddenly the beach was drenched in blackness. Joshua moved instantly. He raced down the beach away from the patrol. He heard shouting and curses as several constables crashed into each other searching for muskets and torches. He knew that at least three or four of them would be hot on his trail. He turned to his right and raced up the beach for the woods. He could hear the footfalls behind him. He could not stop and get his bearings. He raced through the underbrush, tripping once on a fallen log and flying face-first into the frozen ground. He pulled himself back onto his feet. He could still hear shouting on the beach. He saw shadows in the bushes behind him. He ran forward again and soon broke through the trees and bushes on the bay side of the peninsula. Once again he was on a beach. The darkened shadows of the buildings of Toronto could be made out dimly across the bay.

He knew that his pursuers were directly behind him but he was not going to surrender. The moment for gambling had arrived. He ran down the short sandy slope to the water's edge. He placed his foot onto the firm white ice of the shoreline. No time for second-guessing. He moved out onto the ice. He moved quickly. If he took time to look for the right place to put his foot he'd be captured. He ran across the ice's surface. He could hear deep moaning sounds coming from under him. Occasionally a sharp crack like a rifle shot penetrated the night and overwhelmed even the rushing sound of the wind. He only hoped that the wind would not cause the ice in the bay to break up too soon.

When he had first ventured out onto the ice, he had thought he heard a musket fire, but he had heard nothing since. Toronto seemed closer now. He could actually distinguish one building from another along the shore. He struck out toward the west end of the town. He wanted to avoid the docks. And he did not want to enter Toronto and have to attempt an escape from within the town. He would have to take the overland route to the United States via Niagara.

"I might as well begin that journey right now," he thought aloud. He had only a hundred yards or so of ice to cross. He looked behind him. He could make out the figure of a small man moving quickly toward him. He recognized Phinias, the carriage man. Joshua stopped, raised his pistol, and fired. He knew he had missed, but the noise and flash had frightened the carriage man. Phinias's feet slipped from under him and he landed with a crash on his behind. Instantly a loud splintering crack cut through the ice toward Joshua. The boy leapt aside. Water gushed upward and poured over the flat surface of the ice. He heard Phinias's scream for help as the frigid water closed about him. Joshua tuned out the sounds and ran as fast as he could move toward the shore. The ice was breaking up behind him but he had a clear path toward the old garrison house and fort west of the city. Normally that would have been the worst spot to try to escape from, but he remembered that days before Sir Francis Bond Head had emptied Toronto of its garrison—an action that in itself spurred rebellion. Now it was an action that was going to help one very cold and frightened rebel to escape.

Joshua thought he would freeze that night in the woods north of Toronto. He dared not light a fire and the night was cold. He was wrapped in the warmest clothing that Jessica Brant could find for him, but no clothing, not even the warmest fur, could keep a man warm on such a night.

With morning the sun brought a bit of warmth to the air. Joshua set out west through the woods. He kept the lakeshore to his left at all times. He knew eventually it would bend around to the south and lead him to Niagara and the American border. He was hurrying now. Willie and Michael had escaped with all the food. He was proud of their escape and slightly amazed by his own. But the pangs of hunger were working on his morale. Whenever he smelled smoke or saw a cabin in a clearing, he avoided it. But that became more and more difficult as his hunger built. He could not afford to confront any settlers without knowing where their sympathies lay. But he would have to steal from the next cabin.

For a long time he saw no more clearings and began to wonder if he had missed his chance. But in the early afternoon he found a hut with a small barn. He could hear hens clucking in the yard; where there were hens there were eggs. He had eaten raw eggs before.

He slipped around the edge of the clearing so that he could come up behind the barn while keeping the cabin itself in sight at all times. He could not face the thought of being caught by some farmer trying to protect his chicken coop. He waited for some sight of the inhabitants of the cabin. He could hear laughter coming from inside. Just as he rounded the corner of the barn, he came face to face with a large mongrel dog. When it caught sight of Joshua, the dog started a loud baying, as if it had treed a raccoon.

Joshua started to move backward toward the woods, but the dog grabbed his pants leg in its ancient teeth and pulled back, digging its hind legs into the ground.

The cabin door swung open and a farmer carrying a

musket raced toward the barn. He got Joshua in his sights and ordered him to halt. The boy knew that his luck had finally run out. He turned to face the farmer, but his eyes drifted beyond and fell on the small man with the disheveled red wig who came up behind him.

"Well, I'll be damned," Mackenzie said. "Call off your dog, Sean. He's one of mine."

Joshua was still in a daze when he finished a breakfast of hot corn bread covered with fresh butter and honey, and three boiled eggs. He was on his second mug of coffee when Mackenzie sat down across the rough board table of the farmhouse and began to question him.

"They got Lount and VanEgmond, I hear."

"I don't know about Colonel VanEgmond, sir," Joshua responded after swallowing another mouthful of coffee. "But I did see Captain Lount all tied up."

"They'll probably hang both of them. They are a revengeful lot, those Tories." He pronounced the impending deaths of his two associates without emotion. "How about your uncle?"

Joshua told him the story of Michael Brant's escape in the boat with Willie Mackay.

"I'm glad," said Mackenzie. "I'll have to get in touch with Brant just as soon as I make it across the border."

"Will you be leaving tonight?"

"Tonight?" Mackenzie laughed. "I don't have that kind of time to waste. I'll be leaving immediately. I assume you'll want to come with me."

"Yes, sir, but won't it be dangerous traveling by daylight? They must be looking for you."

"Oh, yes, they are looking. I'm told they're distributing posters all over the province and that they have organized a troop of three hundred Orange Lodgers just itching to lift my scalp." He raised the wig a few inches off his bald head and then brought it back down in place.

Joshua started to laugh.

"But I've got my friends here in the countryside. The common folks side with me. We'll be safe. All the way to the border."

95

Joshua finished his coffee.

"Let's go, young man. You and I are walking to the United States."

They continued to follow Joshua's original path along the lake. They stopped at cabins for food. Sometimes it was clear that the inhabitants knew exactly who it was that they entertained and at other times they neither knew nor cared.

Mackenzie had a way with the poor, with struggling farmers. He spoke their language. They fed him; they put him up for the night; they gave him rations to continue his journey. Some farmers gave them rides in hay wagons. Joshua stayed at his side, in awe of the man's power with the people.

A few miles below the falls of Niagara they crossed over into the United States. Joshua had expected some sort of guard to be at the border, but there was nothing so dramatic. At one point they came down the shore of the fast-moving river. Mackenzie hailed a boatman, agreed to pay him three pence to take both him and Joshua to the other side. Once they put a foot down on the far shore they were safe. Mackenzie paid his fare but asked the boatman to wait.

He sat down on a large rock that jutted into the river. He removed his shoes and started to wipe the riverbank's mud from them.

"A man should always have clean shoes when he goes to town," he lectured Joshua. "And I have a mind to go into Lewistown or on to Buffalo and set up my headquarters in exile. Are you sure you want to come with me?"

By this time Joshua was totally under the spell of the man who seemed to be able to wave his wand and drive away all the forces of danger that had surrounded and terrified him before.

"I'll follow you anywhere," Joshua responded.

"Now, young fellow," Mackenzie interrupted him, "I want you to think long and hard before you respond to a question like that. When you set foot on this side of the river you become an exile, a man without a country. Right across that river is home, Canada. I'd like to be there, not here, but if I go back they'll hang me and my work will be for naught. If you go back . . ."

"They'll hang me too," Joshua said.

"Oh, if you go back to Toronto perhaps they will, but it's an awfully big country, our Canada. I could use a good young man like you to continue my war, but that country over there needs you too. If all the good people, the people who love freedom, leave, then there's no hope for Canada."

"You want me to go back?"

"I think you ought to go back. Back to somewhere where you're not known and where you can start again. Someday I'm going to go back, and when I do I am going to need young men like you who care about our country. Someday the republic of Canada is going to be formed and I'm going to be its president. So while I clean off my shoes, you get your tail back into that boat and go home. Go west, Joshua. You've got family there. At least that's what your uncle told me. Technically the West might belong to the Hudson's Bay Company, but it is still part of our land. If you have the chance to live in Canada rather than in exile, boy, grab it. I'm sure Michael Brant would agree with every word I am saying. Go on, now."

Joshua was unsure of himself. He wanted to stay with Mackenzie but it was clear to him that the little man did not want him. He hesitated, but Mackenzie insisted.

"That's it, boy. Here's the fare." He flipped a coin, which Joshua caught in the air. The boatman looked at Joshua strangely as the boy reboarded. Soon he found himself in midriver. He watched Mackenzie put his shoes back on his feet and disappear into the American woods.

Part Two

THE RED RIVER COUNTRY

IV

Fort Garry, Spring and Summer 1841

In an endless procession the horse- and ox-drawn two-wheel carts came rolling through the gates of Fort Garry. In the heat of the late afternoon the stench of the offal and reeking buffalo skins with which the carts were loaded was overwhelming. Cart drivers, smelling almost as bad as their cargo, yelled at horses and oxen and each other. The hunt was over, but this time the mostly Métis-led caravan had had to wander more deeply into the prairies to find the buffalo herds. The skins, the fresh meat, and the pemmican that the buffalo provided guaranteed another comfortable year for the Red River Settlements.

Dark-skinned women and children dressed in European clothes jumped off the backs of the carts and joined in the mass confusion in the center of the trading post. Rifles were fired into the air. The sutler's store was opened and men disappeared into it to return a few minutes later carrying small kegs of brandy or rum.

Indian women, whose lodges lined the outside walls of the fort, poured through the gates. They stopped the young men and made unmistakable gestures toward themselves with their hands. A group of young hunters approached an Indian girl of no more than sixteen. The most forward of the men, a broad-shouldered hulk of a man dressed in buffalo leather pants and woolen shirt, walked up to the girl. His features betrayed his mixed blood. His hair was dark brown and his skin a pale brown.

"*Combien?*" he called to her.

101

She look at him, then at the five or six young men behind him.

"*Combien?*" she responded.

"*Tous.*" He laughed and grins broke out on the faces of his companions. She held up five fingers and the grins disappeared. The broad-shouldered leader turned his back on the girl and the men held a small parlay.

Finally the leader turned around and held up three fingers. The girl, without much hesitation, held up four.

"*Bien,*" said the leader. Almost immediately he started to undo the string laces on his pants as he approached the girl.

The girl shook her head and walked away into the alley. The man hurried after her, his pants almost down to his knees. His companions followed him eagerly into the alley.

Joshua Miller had just arrived at Fort Garry the day before the buffalo hunters. It had taken him over three years to reach his destination—not that he had been single-minded of purpose.

The day he left William Lyon Mackenzie on the Niagara, he had made up his mind to come to the Red River Settlements to find the man his father, Charles, had suggested was his real sire—Stephen Miller. He had risked taking a job as a deckhand on the Miller line steamer from Fort Erie to Detroit. It made only one voyage before entering drydock at Amherstberg. The cold descended on the lake, and with the ice all navigation was ended.

He crossed over the border to Detroit and joined a group of fur trappers who ventured into the wilderness of the Upper Peninsula and over into Wisconsin looking for what few beaver might be left in those territories. He was totally inexperienced in the woods, and the trappers used him as a beast of burden to carry equipment, heavy metal traps, and eventually the skinned beavers when they returned in the spring.

During that first winter Joshua learned much. The trappers taught him how to survive in the woods, and in the spring, as they returned to Fort William on Lake Superior, they taught him to handle a canoe.

At Detroit he had written to his grandmother, telling

her of his whereabouts. There was a letter from her waiting for him at Fort William. Michael had made it safely to New York state. He had moved on to Boston and lived with Joshua's aunt, Margaret Nowell Conrad. Her husband, the congressman, had died in the spring, and she was indeed glad to have her cousin with her. Michael had brought Willie with him, and Margaret set out to make a lady of her. His uncle, his grandmother informed him, had taken no part in Mackenzie's effort to continue the rebellion with raids across the border. Joshua steeled his emotions when he came to the part about Allison. She had married his father in a grand ceremony at St. James. The town was scandalized by the difference in their ages, but Jessica tried to soften the worst part: Allison was now pregnant, and his father had publicly denounced him as a rebel and a traitor and cut him out of his will.

He received no more news for the next three years. He spent three winters trapping on the Lake of the Woods. The furs were meager; the area was overworked, the trappers complained. This spring he had the opportunity to ride out onto the prairies to the source of the Red River. Once he reached it he made up his mind. He traded his horse for a canoe from a Sioux family that lived on the banks of the river, and he paddled northward. The flooded spring waters allowed him to travel without too many portages. At some point, without his knowledge, he crossed the line back into British territory and into Rupert's Land, the private preserve of the Hudson's Bay Company. Still he followed the river to the point it was met by the Assiniboine at Fort Garry.

Joshua had filled out with the hard work. His shoulders and chest were broadened and he had lost his boy's physique. In this period his body grew into a man's body. He had watched the little charade between the buffalo skinners and the Indian girl. He felt stirrings of similar desires in his own body, but he had not taken part in quick couplings under the bushes that constituted the love life of the trapper, and he did not wish to begin now.

Joshua picked up his gear and headed for the company store. The one room was jammed with buffalo hunters. In

103

the confinement of the indoors, they reeked all the more of dead animals, sweat, and stale tobacco juice. Most spoke rapidly in French and most were Métis, with their strange mixture of white and Indian ways.

Joshua overheard a small group of men, including the storekeeper, speaking English.

"Excuse me, gents, for butting in, but I'm looking for someone," he said.

The men stopped speaking and stared at him with clear hostility. Strangers asking questions about people would always be so greeted by this close-knit community.

"I'm looking for a fellow by the name of Stephen Miller."

"What do you want him for?" an old man with enormous sideburns questioned.

"He's my uncle, my father's twin brother."

"So, what you want him for?"

"I've been living in the back country down in the States for some time. I heard he lived up here so I came to say hello."

"Seems like a helluva distance to travel just to say hello," said another man, whose accent marked him as a Scot but whose black Indian braids would have caused quite an uproar back on the Clyde.

Joshua was becoming frustrated. He turned to walk away from the group when finally the storekeeper himself relented.

"There be no one in these parts by that name, lad. Although I do recall a fellow some decades back who had a place downriver from the fort. His name was Miller. I don't recall his first name, but he headed out west after a flood wiped out his crops."

"Do you have any idea where he might have gone?" Joshua asked.

"West is all I recall. Not much farming west of here. I guess he was planning to trap."

"Would anyone here have received any word from him?"

"I suspect McAlistair knew him best. They were

neighbors. Shared each other's farms for a while. I suspect he'd be the best person to talk to."

"Where would I find McAlistair?"

The men looked at each other.

"I'm not sure I'd want to find that one," the man with the sideburns said. "He's one best left alone."

Joshua smiled. "First you tell me to go see him, then you tell me not to. What's the matter with him?"

The storekeeper just shook his head. "It's not for me to say. Follow this bank of the river downstream for two miles. You'll see three farms. Two of them abandoned. The third one belongs to James McAlistair and his squaw."

"Thank you," Joshua said as he started to the door.

Before he could leave, he heard several Métis speaking to each other. He saw one man make the sign of the cross quickly as if to ward off the evil eye.

Joshua had no trouble finding the farms. He beached his canoe and hailed the farmhouse. He could tell from the reaction of the buffalo hunters and the Scottish farmers that James McAlistair was a man they feared. If he was that sinister, Joshua did not wish to take him by surprise.

He pulled his canoe up onto the landing beach. He turned to walk up to the farmhouse and looked straight into the muzzle of a rifle.

"I suggest you get back in your tub and get the hell out of here," said the voice from behind the muzzle.

Joshua looked past the gun to the man. He looked to be about thirty, with long black hair that he tied in the back. He had a droopy black moustache. His eyes were hazel and they seemed to look right through Joshua.

"Are you McAlistair?" Joshua asked.

The man remained silent.

"My name is Joshua Miller and I'm looking for my uncle, Stephen Miller."

The man's eyes searched his face and Joshua thought he detected a softening in his facial expression.

"I guess you really are. That doodad about your neck— Stevie used to wear it." He lowered the gun and turned

105

around swiftly and started up the incline from the river toward the farmhouse. "Come," was all he said.

Joshua followed him into the house. It was a simply furnished one-room cabin. The open fireplace had a stove jammed into it that served for both heating and cooking. An Indian woman dressed in buffalo hide with a band of colored beads around her head was roasting two prairie hens over the fire.

"We got a guest," McAlistair said to her. She turned around to look at Joshua and her eyes registered surprise.

"This is the boy, isn't it? Elizabeth and Stevie's boy."

Joshua studied her carefully. "You know me?"

The woman's face broke into a great smile. "I lifted you from your mother's body. I cut your cord with my own knife." She walked to him and threw her arms about him. "I am Cree Woman. It is good that you returned to the land of your birth, Joshua Miller."

Jamie McAlistair sat at his table watching the two of them. Joshua looked over at him. There was no warm greeting, no friendliness coming from him. He sat sullenly staring into the fire.

"Mr. McAlistair?" Joshua addressed him.

"He's dead. He was my father. My name is Jamie."

"Jamie, I've come looking for Stephen Miller. I was told you might know where he is."

"He is long gone. I think he went loony after the floods wiped us out. Started drinking. Said he was going out looking for his Elizabeth, but we all knew she had drowned in the lake."

Cree Woman stared at Jamie and then went back to her fire. The men would eat the hens. She would find something else for herself—perhaps some pemmican.

"You've heard nothing from him since? How long ago was that?"

"At least ten years ago. But the way he was drinking, I doubt if he would still be alive."

Joshua's disappointment was obvious.

"You can stay with us. I'll tell you as much as I can about those times. They were bad times for both Cree

Woman and myself. We both lost our families to the Indians."

"To the Métis," Cree Woman corrected him.

"Same thing," said Jamie bitterly.

The Indian woman brought the roasted birds to the table. She placed a bottle of whiskey with them.

Jamie pulled the cork from the bottle with his teeth.

"Taste some of this." He offered the bottle to Joshua.

Joshua looked around for a cup.

"We don't stand on niceties here. Take a swig."

Joshua let the liquid fill his mouth. Then he swallowed. It burned all the way down to the pit of his stomach.

"Good, eh?" Jamie said, smiling for the first time since they both met. He took the bottle from Joshua and took an enormous gulp. Then he turned his attention to the small hen. He took hold of the leg and stuffed the whole thing into his mouth. He pulled an almost clean bone out of it and dropped it onto the plate.

"Have another drink." He nodded toward the bottle. "Cree woman makes it."

Joshua was still having trouble talking after the first swig. He was not ready to try another. He started to pick at his hen. He was hungry, and soon he was devouring it as completely if not as vigorously as Jamie.

The older man consumed about half the bottle of whiskey. Joshua took another swig finally, and Cree Woman took a cup to her place by the fire where she ate the warmed-over dried meat.

"You can stay with us," Jamie said as he sat back in his chair. "You're practically like family. You was the first person I ever did see get birthed. Tomorrow I am riding out onto the prairies looking for game. I haven't gone on the buffalo hunt in recent years," he said. A strange look came into his eyes. The hazel-brown-green almost seemed to turn glassy. He remained silent for a long minute.

Cree Woman came to his side and touched his shoulder. He reached over and brought her hand to his cheek. Joshua was puzzled by the two of them. The woman looked old enough to be Jamie's mother, but it was clear that they were lovers. Suddenly Jamie came back to life.

"As I said, I'm going hunting tomorrow. I go out for a few days before I plant, and then after planting, at least once a week before harvest. Mostly I get antelope, but sometimes some prairie hens, and every once in a while a stray buffalo. But that's not too often anymore. The hunt has driven them farther and farther away from the Red River and the Assiniboine. Do you know anything about the life on the prairies?"

"I spent only a few weeks in Crow and Sioux country south of the border."

"Can you ride a horse?"

"A bit."

"You'll have to do better than that to live out here. Partial to a canoe, ain't you?" Jamie chuckled. "That would be Stevie's boy. Come tomorrow, you and me will ride out there and I'll show you a thing or two."

That night Cree Woman made up a sleeping mat for Joshua in the loft. Away in the corner of the loft, Joshua, even in the dark, could make out the outline of a doll. Children used to live here. But there was no sign of them now. He took off his clothes and lay down on the soft buffalo robe. He pulled the edge of it up to cover his naked body.

The night air even in the late spring was chilly, and the fur felt soft and warmed his body. Down below he heard Jamie and Cree Woman speaking low to each other. They whispered at one point, as if they did not wish Joshua to overhear them. Then there was silence for some moments. That was followed by sounds that Joshua did not recognize at first. In fact, the sounds frightened him—a low moan, a cry of pain. Then it dawned on him what was happening in the bed beneath his perch. He covered his head with the buffalo robes to try to cut out the noises that embarrassed him so.

The next morning Joshua and Jamie McAlistair rode out from the farm into the open prairie. The vistas opened for miles about them, rolling grassy knolls giving way to a few miles of flat plains of grass and then some low hills. The sun was at their backs as they rode west. Their pace was quick, or so Joshua thought until Jamie caught sight of motion by a small creek in the bushes.

"Antelope," he called out and spurred his brown mare into action. He went galloping off in the direction of the creek.

Joshua kicked the sides of his gelding with his heels. The horse quickened its pace but still he was left far behind. He lost sight of Jamie over on the far side of a hillock. He continued to ride forward. He heard a rifle shot. He kicked his horse again and came to the top of the hill. Below him Jamie had dismounted. He hoisted the carcass of a dead antelope over the back of his mare. By the time Joshua arrived at his side, he had tied the animal's feet together beneath the horse's belly.

"You don't take after your mum, Josh. She was a natural on a horse. Better than any white man I ever seen. Only an Indian could have kept up with her."

Jamie remounted and rode beside Joshua. His eyes seemed to dart in all directions, watching for signs, searching the sky, squinting in the glare of the sun that rose high above them, exploring the horizon.

"You said yesterday that Stephen Miller went searching for my mother. Why would he do that when he knew she was dead?"

"We never did find her body. But no one could have lived through that storm on Winnipeg. I was there. But later, when he came back, we kept hearing stories about a white woman living with the Cree, and then it was with the Assiniboine and later the Bloods. The story was always the same . . . a white woman, a white squaw who could always outride the men. That's what got him looking. He set out west and never did come back."

"Jamie," Joshua asked, "I'm still a bit puzzled."

"Why should you be any different?" McAlistair quipped. "What about?"

"Back at Fort Garry when I first mentioned your name, people seemed to back away from me—like they were afraid."

"Were they white folk or Métis?" Jamie asked, searching Joshua's face.

Joshua thought a moment. "I don't rightly recall," he said finally.

"Probably Métis," Jamie said. "You know, your Uncle Stevie and I had one hell of a serious run-in with those folks. People out here have long memories."

They rode on in silence without sighting any more game. About noon they halted at the side of a creek that ran south into the Assiniboine River. Jamie took a roll of pemmican from his saddlebag and offered it to Joshua.

"I could go me a nice cup of hot tea, right now," Jamie said, "but I don't think I should make a fire out here on the prairie."

"Why not? We've got wood," Joshua offered. There were several dried logs from long-dead trees along the creek bank.

"You don't need wood to make a fire out here. All you need is dried buffalo chips." Jamie's eyes continuously searched the horizon.

Joshua followed his gaze. He saw the white column behind the hill just as Jamie turned from it.

"Is that smoke?"

Jamie didn't bother to look back. "No, it's dust. I suspect there's a small band of buffalo strays behind there."

"Should we ride over after them?"

Jamie looked at him in annoyance. "I'm not equipped to be hauling buffalo back to the Red and I ain't like those wasters. They kill the damn beasts for the tongue and leave the rest to rot. Let's mount up."

They rode farther, but Joshua noted that the dust on the horizon never really disappeared. It always seemed to parallel them. Jamie seemed not to notice it, and the one time Joshua drew his attention again to the dust the older man ignored him.

Joshua decided to overlook his companion's moodiness. He was enjoying himself; riding on the open prairie gave him an overwhelming sense of freedom—freedom from restraint and confinement. He relished the idea of standing in the stirrups and seeing for miles in all directions. He barely noticed that the sun was now shining directly in his eyes. When he did call it to Jamie's attention the man continued his silence.

"I assume we're not going back tonight," Joshua finally said.

"Correct," Jamie said. "A night out in the open prairie is part of your education. Let's find us a good spot for a camp."

"Maybe near some buffalo chips. If tonight is anything like last night, a fire will be real welcome," Joshua said.

"No fires. That's a sure way to signal hostiles that you're waiting to have your scalp lifted."

"There are hostiles around here?"

"Indians are always hostiles. Even the friendly ones. There are plenty of Indians about. So from my point of view, there are always hostiles about. Over there." He pointed to a flat piece of open ground. "That's as good a place as any. That way you can see anyone who comes at you just as soon as they can see you."

They dismounted when they reached the campsite. Jamie hobbled both horses while Joshua stared at the sun as it fell lower in the sky, turning the whole world in that direction rose, pink, and gold.

"I've never seen anything quite like that," Joshua said.

"Some sight, eh?" said Jamie without even bothering to look up.

He had cut the bonds on the antelope's feet and the animal landed on the ground with a thud. Quickly Jamie dragged it clear of the mare, and with his enormous hunting knife he slit open the animal's belly, reached his arm into the gore, and pulled out the antelope's liver.

"Tonight's dinner," he announced with a broad smile across his face.

He cut the organ in half and offered one of the pieces to Joshua. The young man took it gingerly in his hands. Jamie bit into the raw liver and pulled a huge chunk of it away with his teeth.

Joshua thought he was going to be sick. Jamie meant it when he said they would have no fire. He would have to eat the raw liver if he was going to eat at all. He couldn't do it. He could not even watch Jamie eat it, with the blood dripping down his chin and from the end of his moustache.

111

McAlistair looked up at him. "You going to stand there holding that thing or are you going to eat it?"

Joshua held out his hands to him. Jamie grabbed the liver and was soon devouring it. He finished and wiped his hands on his pants. He cleaned his chin and moustache on his shirtsleeve.

"There's some pemmican in my bag, if you're up to eating," he said finally to Joshua. "There's also a bottle of Cree Woman's brew. Get that for me too."

He finished cleaning out the cavity of the antelope, then buried the intestines. He tied the carcass to the back of Joshua's gelding.

"No sense making critters with keen smell curious about what we're eating."

The sun had set, and with a suddenness that surprised Joshua it was dark. He sat next to Jamie munching on the strange-tasting dry buffalo meat that was the staple diet of people of these settlements.

Jamie had set up his saddle as a headrest and was already stretched out on the ground, his saddle blanket pulled over him to keep him warm. He offered Joshua some whiskey. The younger man accepted it gratefully. He needed something to wash down the dry meat. Joshua placed himself against his saddlebag, emulating McAlistair.

"Jamie," he asked, "what kind of a man was Stephen Miller?" Guiltily, he realized that he had used the past tense. It was as if the expression "going west" was equated with disappearing from the earth. He had picked it up from Jamie's tone. Jamie thought Miller was dead.

"I'd have been proud to have had him as my pap," Jamie said finally after some silence.

"I'm pretty sure I know what he looked like. His twin brother raised me. But can you tell me anything more about him?"

"I'll tell you one thing about him. He knew how to keep his mouth shut when his companion wanted to sleep."

Joshua said no more. He lay looking up at the myriad of stars that popped out suddenly in the black sky. Before long he drifted off to sleep.

He awoke suddenly. He had been asleep for hours. He

was sure of it. Something was moving between the horses. Joshua rose on his elbows and turned over to awaken Jamie. His hand touched air. His companion was gone. Joshua reached for the knife that Cree Woman had given to him. He crawled into a crouched position ready to spring forward.

The black form moved forward. Joshua breathed a sigh of relief. It was Jamie.

"Where you been?" he asked.

"Christ, can't a man take a piss without a formal inquiry? You're worse than my wife."

Joshua leaned back against the saddle pillow.

"Are you sure we didn't have visitors?" Joshua asked him. But either McAlistair was already asleep or he was not speaking. Joshua was sure it was the latter.

In the morning Joshua went to unhobble the horses. He called out to Jamie.

"McAlistair, someone was here last night weren't they? Someone tried to steal the horses. Your mare's hobbles have been cut. And they didn't loosen. This cord was cut with a knife."

Jamie smiled. "On the prairies you have got to stay alert or else you end up walking. Every Indian, or Métis for that matter, even those that consider themselves your best friend, thinks that he has a fumdamental obligation to relieve you of your horse."

"How the hell can you sleep out here, then?"

"If you're alone, you don't. If you're with someone else, you take turns."

"Why didn't we do that?"

Jamie looked harshly at Joshua. "If you think I am going to trust my hair to the likes of you, you've got another thought coming. You'll know you ain't no tenderfoot, boy, when I ask you to take a watch."

Joshua shut his mouth again. McAlistair was not gentle with another man's feelings. But what he said was so obviously true that the younger man had to accept it and try to learn from his harsh teacher.

They mounted their horses and headed first to the south and then off to the east. They had traveled about five or six miles when Joshua saw them. There were birds circling in the sky—large birds. He looked over at Jamie quizzically.

"Buzzards. There's something dead over there."

Joshua's curiosity was great. He took the lead and spurred the gelding in the direction of the birds.

"Miller," Jamie called out, "we've got no time to go investigating every dead creature on the prairies."

But Joshua had already reached the top of the knoll to the south of them and disappeared on the other side. Jamie cursed and kicked his mare into action.

The birds scattered when Joshua rode into their midst. He got off his horse and immediately became ill.

There were eight of them, Indians and Métis. Four men, two women, and two children, all dead. But they were worse than dead. The eyes of the children had been picked out. That could have been the work of the birds. But the birds could not have done to the men and women what had been done to them. All were naked. The men had been emasculated, and their severed organs had been shoved obscenely into their bodies. The women's breasts had been severed from their bodies. Yet none of their faces registered pain. All seemed almost to be sleeping.

Joshua leaned against his horse, horrified by the sight. Jamie rode up next to him in silence.

Joshua looked up at him.

"What in God's name has happened here?"

Jamie looked down coldly at the bodies. "They look to be Cree and some Métis. I suspect they ran into some group that came out after their horses. Blackfoot, I suspect. Blackfoot hate Cree enough to do these things to them. You don't have to be a tenderfoot to die out here on the prairies. Come on."

"Aren't you going to bury them?"

"I'm not burying no Indians," Jamie said. "Besides, we ain't got nothing to dig with." .

He pulled on his horse's reins and moved away from Joshua. Joshua remounted and joined him. They rode home in silence.

V

Fall 1841

Throughout the summer Joshua rode out with Jamie on his shorter hunting trips, but he feared the night on the prairies and rejected Jamie's offers if he knew they would be gone longer than one day. Still, even on the short trips, he learned skills from McAlistair. He also helped Cree Woman with the chores on the farm. At night he listened to them make love. He got over his initial embarrassment. Now when the sounds began he actually listened, although their love sounds were peculiarly mingled with sounds of pain. But the listening turned to frustration. He was nineteen years old and he had never made love with a woman. He would turn over on his side and allow his hand to slip down his belly to his crotch. He would find himself hard and take what little consolation he could from his palm.

All three of them worked from dawn to sunset during the wheat harvest season. There were no more trips out onto the prairies. Joshua swung the scythe again and again until his shoulders ached. But he knew his job was easier than Cree Woman's. She bent over to pick up the cut sheaves of wheat and loaded them into the cart Jamie drove. Joshua offered to switch with the Indian woman, but she rejected his offer. Jamie never offered. When he came to relieve Joshua with the scythe, Joshua again offered to switch with Cree Woman.

"She don't drive the team, boy. You're embarrassing her. She's a squaw. She expects to work. You take it away from her and you take her self-esteem away with it."

Joshua said nothing, but he was convinced that Cree Woman would really not have minded a few turns driving the wagon. He was convinced that McAlistair's arguments were no more than rationalizations for putting most of the hard work on his wife.

Before the cold set in, they completed the harvest. Jamie took the thrashed wheat in his cart to the wind-powered mill upriver near the fort. There he would stay while the wheat was ground into flour and bagged. Some of it he would sell to the company and the rest of it he would bring home for their winter's bread.

Joshua sat helping Cree Woman peel some potatoes. He was feeling good about his life on the McAlistair farm. He knew, because Jamie told him, that one-third of the acres that they worked had belonged to Stephen Miller. Miller had deeded the farm to Jamie when he left, but it was clear that McAlistair was not reluctant to share the land with the boy he thought was Stephen and Elizabeth's son. Joshua even considered asking Jamie's help to rebuild the burned-out homestead where his mother and uncle had once lived so happily. His own home was an idea that appealed to him. There were some girls, single girls, at Fort Garry. Some were of mixed blood and some were Scottish or Irish girls, daughters of farm families. None of them were Allison Winslows, of course. The memory of her beauty filled his mind and he stopped dreaming. He laughed aloud. She was his stepmother now and had probably produced a little brother or sister for him. He threw down the potato he had peeled to almost nothing.

"May I borrow the gelding?" he asked Cree Woman. "I think I would like to ride out on the prairies a little way," he said.

She could tell he suffered some inner anguish and she nodded assent. He went to the barn and a few moments later appeared before the front door astride the large gray horse.

"I'll return for supper," he called to her.

"Be careful," she warned him. "Jamie has taught you much but even he does not know all."

116

He smiled at her and turned the horse's head to the west. He rode carefully through the recently harvested fields, but once he was beyond them he kicked the horse and gave him his head as he raced across the rolling sea of high grass.

Cree Woman watched him disappear. She saw his musket leaning against the wall behind the door. It was foolish of him to take off onto the prairies without it. Jamie had not taught him nearly enough.

He let the horse run past the point where he should have turned back for dinner. He had to get over the fluctuations in his moods like this—one moment thinking of settling down to family life and the next thinking of Allison and allowing her memory to drive him to silly distractions like riding off into the prairies. He looked about him. He was not far from the spot where Jamie had killed the antelope. He turned his horse toward a stream. Both of them could use a drink. He came to the bushes that grew beside the creek and allowed the gelding to trample through them until he came to the water's edge. The horse seemed nervous.

"Steady," Joshua said to him.

He searched the ground for snakes or something else that might have spooked the animal, but he saw nothing. He let the bridle fall loose, and the horse bent his neck to reach the trickle of fresh water. Joshua slipped from the saddle to the ground. The gelding shied from the movement and pulled to the left away from him. Joshua kept the reins in his hands and knelt down to drink. The water tasted brackish but it was cool.

As he raised his eyes to look across the stream, he saw three pairs of brown, bare legs. He lifted his gaze slowly and took in the loincloths and the muzzle of a musket aimed directly at him. The three Indians said nothing. Joshua stood and raised his right hand palm outward to signify that he was friendly. The three, still without a word, stepped across the stream. The gelding reared up in fright. But one of the Indians grabbed the reins from Joshua's hands and quickly quieted the animal. Joshua remembered what Jamie had said about horses and even the friendliest of Indians. He feared he would be walking a long trail back to the farm. He would be lucky if he returned for tomorrow's lunch, much less tonight's dinner. And then he would have to explain the loss of the horse to McAlistair.

The Indian who grabbed the gelding's bridle unhitched the saddle and allowed it to fall to the ground. He was the oldest of the three, and Joshua could only assume that he was their leader. He leapt onto the gelding's back. Again the horse reared, but the Indian was a superb horseman and soon had the animal under control.

A second warrior bent down and searched through the saddlebags. He pulled out a bottle of Cree Woman's brew that Jamie always insisted be kept there. He pulled the cork and sniffed it. He let loose with a whoop of joy. The last warrior walked directly up to Joshua, looking him over as one would evaluate horse flesh.

He said something in a language Joshua did not understand, then grabbed at the young man's homespun shirt and pointed to his own bare chest. Joshua removed his shirt and gave it to the Indian. As the warrior examined it carefully, a smile broke across his face. He raised the shirt to his nose and sniffed. He held his nose in disgust and threw the shirt on the ground. Next he pulled at Joshua's pants.

"Well," Joshua said aloud, "if all I lose is my horse, my whiskey, and my pants, I guess I've gotten off lightly."

He stepped out of his pants. The Indian took them and slipped his legs into them and pulled them up about his waist. The loincloth bunched up about his middle. His two companions started to laugh. The third allowed the pants to fall about his feet. He stepped out of them. He pulled off his loincloth and pointed to Joshua's undershorts. Joshua stepped out of his shorts. The Indian put them on and then pulled the trousers back on. He pranced about for a few moments, swinging a war club about his head and singing in a high-pitched falsetto.

Then the leader atop the gelding spoke harshly to the

118

dancer, who stopped and gave the leader a resentful glare. The two of them spoke in guttural tones to each other. To Joshua it sounded like an angry exchange. The elder man pointed to the sun, which was clearly in its waning stages. Finally he made a sound that to Joshua sounded like resignation.

The man wearing Joshua's clothes approached him. Joshua was sure the leader had given permission for his death, but the Indian merely stared at the locket of gold that Joshua wore around his neck. He grabbed it and broke the chain and shoved the locket into his pocket. Then he grabbed Joshua's arms and twisted them behind his back. In seconds they were bound together with rawhide. Another rawhide noose was thrown over his head. His captor jerked the line and dragged him forward. Joshua had only one choice—to move forward in the direction of his captor.

They crossed the creek and climbed the hill on the other side. On the far side of that hill the Indians had left three ponies. Joshua's horse had sensed their presence even if he had not. The two Indians on foot hopped on the backs of their ponies. Joshua stumbled and fell on his chest and stomach. His captor let out a yell and started to urge his pony forward. If he were dragged along the prairie floor Joshua knew he would be killed. He jumped to his feet and started to run behind the pony. The Indian had not bothered to take his shoes and he was able to run. His captor slowed down. It was no fun unless he dragged his victim. The Indian's companions caught up with him. The leader on the gelding led his pony behind. At first Joshua hoped they would let him get on the pony, but no such offer was made. They seemed in no great hurry and allowed their ponies to move at a slow gait. It was not hard for Joshua to keep up. But as the sun fell lower and lower into the western sky, the fall air became chillier. He was cold, and without his clothes he felt very vulnerable and very defenseless.

After they had traveled about five miles, the three Indians dismounted. Joshua's captor started collecting buffalo chips for a fire but the leader again spoke to him harshly. The younger man dropped the chips and looked at his leader with contempt. The older man kept shaking his head and repeating an expression, "mu-dra."

Each of the men spread a blanket on the ground and each cut a slice of pemmican to eat. No one offered Joshua any food. The man who had found the whiskey bottle kept it clutched to his chest. Finally the others persuaded him to share it. But when he felt they had had enough, he withheld it, and the three of them began to argue. Joshua sat down gingerly on the prairie grass, his hands still tied behind him and his neck thethered to the foot hobbles of his captor's pony. The leader finally, after much argument, struck a deal. He received another mouthful.

The younger Indian sat disconsolate. He went to his pony and got Joshua's shirt. He handed it to the holder of the bottle. The whiskey man, as Joshua came to think of him, sniffed as the captor had done. He seemed not quite so offended. He handed the bottle over. Joshua's captor took a long swig. Too long, in the opinion of the whiskey man, who became enraged and grabbed the bottle. The captor's eyes flashed with anger and he grabbed for the homespun shirt. The leader had to step between them. Again he yelled at them. Again he used the same expression, "mu-dra." It seemed to sober the other two a bit.

As night set in on the prairies, the three Indians became more and more subdued. As the dark settled down on them, Joshua had the feeling that they were afraid. The slightest noise, from the sound of animals scurrying across the grass to the distant howl of a larger animal, startled them, and they would search the darkness about them with fear. They argued about who would stand watch and who would sleep. It was the leader who sat out the first shift. He ignored Joshua, even when he grew so cold that his teeth started to chatter.

Joshua finally worked his body around so that he could lie down without strangling himself. His mind was a jumble of images, of anger with himself for allowing himself to fall into the hands of these immature but clearly dangerous men. He had no idea what they intended to do to him. But at least he was alive.

He fell into a fitful sleep. He heard the changes of the watch and on each occasion he heard the new guard mumble "mu-dra" almost as if it were an incantation to ward off the evil spirits of the night.

In the morning with the first light the raiding party was up. No longer were they frightened children. With the sun's rising they became the bold warriors who had captured him yesterday.

Joshua had trouble getting to his feet. His muscles ached and his body was bruised and insect-bitten. He was also growing desperate. Cree Woman would probably have ridden out looking for him. She would then ride for Jamie. The fact that Jamie had not found him already disappointed him. At any moment he expected his friend to rescue him. But no one came.

Instead, his captor walked over to him. He pointed to the spot on the gelding where his testicles should have been. Then he laughed and pointed to Joshua's crotch. The white man froze. Did these men mean to do to him what Jamie had done to the horse? The captor went over to his pony's side and pulled his loincloth from the bedroll he had just strapped to the pony's back. He approached Joshua with it, but instead of running it between his legs and over the rawhide belt, he tied it like a towel around Joshua's waist. He looked admiringly at Joshua. The two companions joined him and started to laugh. The captor called out to him, "Wu-mun, wu-mun." He started speaking in a high-pitched voice and wiggled his hips. Joshua realized that he was imitating a woman and that the Indian had been speaking English and calling him a woman.

"Wu-mun," he said again, "no ball."

But the leader soon tired of the game. He leapt onto the gelding's back and led the extra pony to where Joshua stood. The other two Indians hoisted him onto its back and tied his feet together beneath the animal's belly.

At last, Joshua thought, he was going to ride.

The other two mounted and the four horses set out at a

121

fast clip across the prairies. It was only as they moved farther and farther west that Joshua realized that by riding and moving at a fast pace, they were diminishing his chances of rescue. Would Jamie ever be able to follow the trail of four ponies on the dry plains? Whereas earlier in that day riding had been a relief to him, as the day wore on it became more and more a source of despair.

The Assiniboine encampment was in a sprucewood forest along the banks of the river that bore their tribal name, although Joshua was totally unaware of which tribe had captured him when he entered the village behind his captor, his hands tied in front of him as he sat astride the pony. They had traveled for two days, always following the same ritual. No fire at night. The nights seemed to terrify them. But come the sun, they became bold and brave warriors.

They arrived at the encampment at sunset but this time they showed no fear. Each of the warriors donned his finest. Joshua's captor, who had not removed his pants from the very first day, also draped the white man's shirt about his shoulders like a cape. They rode through the spruce trees, following a clearly marked horse trail. As they entered a clearing of about twenty-five tipis, the women of the camp let loose a shrill high-pitched yell, a curious sound made by flapping their tongues up and down. The other warriors stepped from their lodges to see what success their compatriots had had.

Clearly the greatest prize, now that the whiskey was gone, was the gelding horse. The leader rode him proudly through the encampment amid the admiration of both men and women. His squaw began to sing his praises in a high-pitched monotone. Joshua's captor paraded Joshua about the village as well.

"Look what I found out on the open prairies."

"What is it, Swift Bear? I do not recognize what you have captured," yelled an old wrinkled man whose blanket was drawn completely about him to keep out the cold. Only his enormous nose and a high feather protruded from it.

"I myself am confused," said the young man. "When we stumbled upon him he appeared to be a white man; he certainly smells like one."

The crowd of admirers laughed in appreciation. They had all heard about the strange odor of the whites.

"But he did not fight to save himself. It's true that if he had I would have killed him. But he would have died like a man. Instead, he let me count coup. Since he did not resist, I did not take him seriously any longer. Instead, I exercised my rights. I took his clothes from him. And lo and behold, he possesses the body of a man but he is not a stallion. He is big like a stallion but docile like a gelding. So we decided to dress him not like a man but not like a woman either. More like a man with no balls or a woman who can't bear young. No, I'm not sure what he is either. But he is my slave. Of that much I am sure."

A teen-aged boy, still not graduated to warrior status, voiced the fear that his elders dared not express.

"Such a strange creature," the boy said. "How are you sure he is not mu-dra?"

The crowd fell into a shocked silence. Suddenly all the fun was disappearing. Swift Bear turned to his prisoner. He rode up next to Joshua's pony and slapped Joshua in the face. The blow was a stinging one, leaving the imprint of the Indian's hand on Joshua's cheek. The white man gritted his teeth. He would take whatever they dished out. If that helped him survive, so much the better. He was determined to meet his fate without giving them the benefit of a reaction.

Swift Bear pulled away the knotted loincloth, exposing his captive's manhood to the gaze of every woman and child in the encampment, and still he would not respond.

"So much for mu-dra. The spirit of the night that kills is not man enough to protect himself from shame—not likely."

Again the crowd laughed. This time their laugh was one of relief.

Joshua's face had gone red from the slap he had received. The inflammation hid the flushed embarrassment he felt from being naked among these strangers. He was afraid that they still intended to kill him. And if they did, his only hope was that it would be swift.

Suddenly the crowd in the village square parted and a whisper ran through it. The Medicine Cow Lady walked from her lodge and approached the war party.

"My sons have been successful," she said as she eyed the gelding. "It is a fine horse. Is it yours, Swift Bear?"

The young man looked in annoyance at Crooked Bow, the war party leader.

"No," he acknowledged. "It is his," he said, pointing to Crooked Bow.

But the attention of Medicine Cow Lady was already distracted. She stared at the white man.

"He is my prize," Swift Bear bragged.

"Not much of a prize is he, sitting there on a horse naked as the day he was born. Has he no shame?"

"None," answered Swift Bear.

"Then maybe you should kill him before he breeds and his race spreads."

"No," argued Swift Bear, "first I want to use him as my slave. I am told that the whites have slaves, that the white men who are black are made to work for the white men who are white. I want a white man's slave. No Indian would be a slave. But I would be an Indian who owned one."

The old man with the nose spoke up. "It's not so! I have seen Indian slaves. A tribe far to the south, south of the Crow and the Sioux, the people I have heard called the Pawnee, they will be slaves."

Medicine Cow Lady walked over to examine Joshua. There was something attractive about him, something familiar. She shook her head. She would not think of such things. Those were days past, days never to be recalled.

"Let us cook a feast to honor our returning warriors," she called out.

Again the women let loose with their strange yell. Swift Bear reached over and yanked Joshua by his blond hair and pulled him from the pony's back. He leapt from his own horse and grabbed the halter from about Joshua's neck and led him to his mother's lodge. She would appreciate having him, he thought. He could help her with the heavy work. He pushed back the lodge entry skins and placed his foot on Joshua's buttocks and shoved him through. His mother sat wrapped in her blanket before the fire. She looked up at the yellow-haired white man in amazement, then ignored him.

"You did not come to greet me," Swift Bear complained.

"I am in mourning. You know that. I could not attend celebrations."

"Mother, my father has been gone for five years. No one has found any sign of him."

"I will stay in mourning until his spirit is at rest. Mu-dra has his soul, I know it."

It was a source of constant battle between them. Swift Bear wished his mother, who was still strong, to take a new husband. That way he would be freed of the responsibility of feeding her and could take a wife and move to her lodge and begin his duties of feeding her and giving her babies. He had the girl all picked out, if only his mother would stop her endless mourning.

He grabbed Joshua's hair again and forced him to his knees.

"This is my slave."

"I heard you bragging outside. Why do you insist on bringing a man with no shame into my lodge?"

"It pleases me to abuse him," Swift Bear responded.

"Dress him," his mother commanded him.

A smile crossed Swift Bear's face. He went rummaging among his mother's things. He found her old antelope-skin shift. The rawhide frills were almost totally gone and all the painted decorations had worn off. Swift Bear handed the shift to Joshua.

The white man looked at it and then let it fall to the ground.

Swift Bear picked it up in anger and tried to force it over Joshua's head. The prisoner's hands were still bound but he used them to ward off his captor's attempts.

The Indian was now in a rage. He picked up a piece of kindling wood that rested near the fire. He struck Joshua a fierce blow across the shoulders. The stick broke into pieces. Joshua sprawled on the ground. The Indian jumped on top of him with the dress and tried to force it over his head again.

Joshua crashed his knee into the man's groin. Swift Bear screamed in anguish. He rose slowly to his feet holding his crotch. He was breathing heavily. He picked up another piece of wood, this time a stronger piece, and he slashed Joshua across the buttocks with it.

Joshua cried out in anguish. Swift Bear struck him again. This time an ugly black-and-blue welt appeared on his arm and shoulder. Something snapped in Joshua's mind. Suddenly he was back in his bedroom in Bay Street and the Indian who beat him so thoroughly was no longer Swift Bear; it was his father, the sneering tormentor of his boyhood.

The third blow struck his back, but Joshua rose to his feet. He lowered his head and charged into the Indian's belly. Swift Bear let out a lungful of air and fell to his knees. His mother, now alarmed, stood and screamed that mu-dra had entered her lodge.

Others came running into the lodge to see the white man standing over the fallen warrior. Several warriors subdued Joshua while Swift Bear's mother helped her son to his feet. Medicine Cow Lady entered the lodge. Her eyes took it all in in one rapid glance.

"The slave without shame has wakened from his trance. Clearly there are some things that shame him. What did you try to do, force yourself on him and unman him?"

Swift Bear's face went red. "That humiliation is reserved for defeated warriors, not geldings."

"And yet this gelding is standing with his head high while this lodge smells with the farts he kicked out of you."

Several of the warriors started to snicker at her words. Swift Bear was again in a rage.

"I decree his death by the fire," he shouted.

"Then you will be as empty-handed from this war party as Big Elk, who even now clutches his empty whiskey bottle and cries in his lodge."

"I will not be empty-handed." He reached into the

pocket of his pants and held up the gold locket. It caught the reflection of the lodge fire and glittered gold to their eyes.

Several of the Indians gasped in awe. It was made of the metal that the whites killed each other for.

Medicine Cow Lady looked at Swift Bear and his medallion.

Then she spoke. "The white man does not die. I claim him as my share of the loot of the war party."

"You can't, he's mine," Swift Bear shouted.

The woman exuded haughtiness. Her dignity had been offended by this pup. She hissed at him.

"You challenge the authority of Medicine Cow Lady? I, who have kept mu-dra from the village since the day I came here, who escaped from mu-dra's vengeance on the Cree? I am shamed. I will withdrew my protection. I will still my medicine."

The warriors who held Joshua in check now pulled back from him and Swift Bear. Her words terrified them. Swift Bear's mother started to wail the death song, and Swift Bear himself seemed shocked by his boldness, then terrified by it. He fell to his knees and bowed his head.

"Forgive me, Assiniboine Mother," he begged. "The prisoner belongs to you."

Medicine Cow Lady said no more then. She turned on the prisoner and spoke to him in English.

"Joshua, come with me!"

Stunned, Joshua followed the Indian woman out of the tipi. One minute he was sure they were about to kill him, and the next he was called by his name in his own language and told to follow.

Medicine Cow Lady entered a large tipi made from the skins of buffalo bleached white by the sun. It was filled with rich furs and decorated with the finest beadwork and drawings. She handed the boy a beautifully woven Indian blanket.

"Cover yourself with this. Sit down by the fire and get warm. I'll get you some venison. It's cold, but you must be hungry anyway."

Joshua merely stared.

127

She handed him a bowl of meat and sat down next to him by the fire.

"It's a long story, Joshua, and there's no beating around the bush. You are Joshua Miller, son of that snake Charles Miller of York!"

Joshua nodded yes.

"I am Elizabeth Stoddard Miller, your mother."

"She's dead," was all Joshua could say in his amazement.

"Perhaps you're right," said the woman. "I'm really Medicine Cow Lady, the Assiniboine shaman woman. I have taken over the spirit of Elizabeth Miller."

Joshua shook his head to clear it. "My Uncle Stephen told everyone in York that my mother drowned when their canoe capsized on Lafe Winnipeg during a storm. He saved me but could not find her."

"Where is your uncle?" she asked, her heart beating wildly, hoping not to hear the answer she feared.

"I don't know," said Joshua. "He left me in Toronto years ago and then went west. No one has seen him since."

"Did he kill your father as he promised he would?"

Joshua was confused now.

"No, he didn't. He left me with Grandmother Brant, but my father took me from her."

Elizabeth brightened when she heard the name Brant. "My mother, she still lives? And my brother?"

"Yes, both of them. I have a letter from her. Uncle Michael lives in Boston. He sided with Mackenzie in the rebellion. So did I. We had to flee. Are you really my mother?"

Elizabeth smiled. "I should have recognized you. Imagine not knowing my own baby. I nurtured you within me. I nursed you at my breast. I knew every fold of baby fat on your body, and I failed to recognize you."

Joshua smiled. "It was the locket, wasn't it?"

She nodded. "A charmed piece of jewelry in our family. We've had a sorry history—more tragedy and suffering than any family deserves. But all who have worn that Nowell locket since the first one have been saved in one

128

way or another by it. I believe it is blessed. Blessed by the spirit of your great-great-grandmother."

"When they took me I thought it was the unluckiest day of my life. Now I discover it led me to the best good fortune I have ever had."

He reached over and touched her face. She drew him to her and ran her hands through his blond hair and down onto his face. Tears ran down her cheeks.

"Oh, my Joshua, don't leave me ever again. Don't ever let me be alone. I have been so alone."

In the morning they talked. He told her of her husband's remarriage to Allison Winslow. He said nothing about his relationship with Allison, but to his surprise she guessed. He told her of his adventures in the rebellion, the escape of her brother to the United States, and his own escape with Mackenzie. It was clear to him that she had little use for Mackenzie's radicalism. She was too much the daughter of Eli Stoddard and Aaron Brant to approve of the rebellion in Upper Canada. But most of all she wanted news of her mother and Eli Stoddard. When Joshua told her that Eli had died and that Jessica thought Elizabeth was dead, Elizabeth wept bitterly.

Finally he told her of coming to the Red River country looking for Stephen and finding Jamie and Cree Woman.

"They still live on the farm, then, and together?" She laughed. "Oh, I'm delighted to hear that. He was a strange and troubled boy, forced by violence to do things way beyond his years—in fact, way beyond anyone's years. I am happy for both of them."

She looked at him seriously. "In case you are still puzzled by it, if it means anything to you, Joshua, your real father is Charles Miller, although I wish it wasn't true. I would so love you to be Stephen's son. But you mustn't think he did not love you. He was a big, lovable wild man. He felt deeply even if he didn't always think deeply."

"You think him dead, then," Joshua said.

"I think he died with me back on Lake Winnipeg. That might sound self-flattering but I think not. I think it is true. But as you can see, I did not die. I became an Assiniboine goddess."

"How?" Joshua questioned.

"I got back in the canoe and it floated to the far shore. I was found by Indians, Cree first. They took me to their fishing camp on the shore of the lake. I tried to ask them to go looking for you and for Stephen. But nobody spoke English. I think I cried for three weeks. I was so weepy that Steals a Horse, the warrior who found me in the canoe, decided I was bewitched and left me alone. They all did. Thank God for that. I don't think I could have handled their advances—not then—not just after losing your uncle.

"We left the lake and went out onto the plains again. I tried to make signs that I wanted to go east. They refused. At first, I believe, they were just trying to thwart me. But later—later they had reasons. Trouble came from the east. Then one day, Steals a Horse did not return from a war party. None of them did. All five were missing."

"What happened?"

Elizabeth avoided Joshua's question. "His squaw chopped off two fingers as a gesture of mourning. I suppose I was his woman slave. Something was expected of me, too. Instead, I waited until no one would miss me. I took a horse and left the camp. After about three days' travel without food or water, I collapsed. The Assiniboine found me, and here I am."

"Twenty years later?" Joshua exclaimed. "Why didn't you come east to the settlements or send word?"

"Why should I? I believed that you and Stephen were dead. I never doubted it until I saw that locket today. I had nothing to go back for and so I stayed."

"How did you become boss?"

She avoided looking at him. "Force of personality, no doubt." She laughed, but it was clear to him she was keeping something from him. He did not push her for answers.

"Now you can leave, though. We can both go back to Fort Garry."

She shook her head. "The Assiniboine will follow my orders, Joshua, but they will never let me leave. They regard me as magic. They feel safe as long as I am with them. As a result, they will never let me go. I probably could escape. I am a magnificent horsewoman, even if I do say so myself. And these years on the prairie have done nothing to harm that gift. But they would track me down and bring me back before I was gone a day. No, I am destined to remain here."

"Well," said Joshua, looking at the luxury of her tipi, "I've been in worse places."

"I could make them let you go," she said with the terror of loneliness gripping her heart.

He smiled at his mother. "As long as you stay, I'll stay. But I sure would like to get word back to Jamie McAlistair and tell him where I am."

"I'll try to arrange it," she said. "My people are terrified of leaving these woods. They have moved from the open prairies to the spruce forest for protection. The next war party may not be for some time. But when it does go, I will instruct them to deliver a letter to Jamie. I think they will do that for me."

"What are they afraid of?"

"They have many enemies," Elizabeth said as a blank look came over her face. "Now, what can we do about you?" she said, as if putting evil thoughts behind her. "You will remain in my lodge. I will officially adopt you as a son. Some old ladies will gossip and talk about us, but they will not dare say it in front of their men. The warriors would beat any squaw or child who gave offense to me. Can you ride and hunt, Joshua, or did my husband turn you into a city boy?"

"I will hold my own," he said proudly if not truthfully.

She beamed at him. "I am sure you will," she responded. "But first, the warriors wear loincloths, leggings, and a shirt. I can't have you walking about with a blanket around your middle."

She looked at him fondly and spoke in a soft low voice that he could barely hear.

131

"I prayed to old Father Thomas's gods, I prayed to my mother's Hebrew Avenger. I even tried direct prayer to dear old Eli. I think I knew the very moment that he left this world. My dear old Eli. I don't know which of them heard my prayers, but your coming has answered them."

Then she stuck her head out of the lodge and asked in Assiniboine for clothes for her newfound son.

VI

Assiniboine Encampment, Fall 1841

Within thirty-six hours Joshua decreed himself lazy and
fat. He had done nothing but feast on fresh venison and
luxuries that his mother's people showered on him as her
adopted son. He slept late in the day and then lounged
amid the furs while his mother cooked him meals. Finally
he became disgusted with himself. He rose from his
wolfskin mat, adjusted his loincloth, and announced his
intention to investigate the encampment.

The lodges of the Assiniboine seemed strangely out of
place among the evergreens. The lodge skins were sun-
bleached like his mother's, which they never would have
become here in this forest. The tribe had clearly spent
time out on the open prairies before coming here.

The air was cool on this sunny autumn afternoon, and
most of the lodges had smoke rising from them. The
horses of the village, including Jamie's gelding, were
corralled on an island formed by the slow-running creek
that split the camp. Medicine Cow Lady had ordered the
camp built at the ford of the creek so that horses could be
kept secure at night. During the day, boys took them to
several open meadows in the forest to pasture.

There were women washing clothes in a stream, and
despite the coolness of the day, several children ran naked
under the watchful eye of the women. One little boy
wandered upstream a short way. He looked about himself
surreptitiously and, seeing no one watching him, he let fly
with a stream of urine. Several of the women caught sight
of him and started to yell and pick up their clothes from

the water and rocks. A broad-hipped woman with a young child strapped to her back rose swiftly and grabbed the boy by the hair just as he was about to dart away. She smacked his bare behind and sent him downstream with a good scolding. The boy, his face an angry red, moved where his mother pointed and squatted down to complete his business in the river.

Joshua decided that upstream was preferable to downstream, and he walked along the creek's edge. He saw Big Elk and Swift Bear conversing with each other. He nodded to them but they ignored him.

He was soon beyond the encampment and out of sight of the mothers and their children. He sat on the boulder beside the creek and removed his shoes. His ankles were black from the dust and sweat. He wished he had some soap. There was fine-grained sand by the river's edge. He picked some up in his hands and scrubbed his skin with it. He took off his shirt and his loincloth. He smelled as bad as the Indians claimed he did. The river was barely two feet deep here. He sat in the chilly waters and splashed his skin, raising gooseflesh all over his body.

He heard giggling from the underbrush of small spruces across the stream.

"Stop spying," he called out.

There was silence. He stood up and again there were giggles. He was tired of these people making fun of him. He ran across the stream and parted the bushes. Three or four young girls ran away in terror. One tripped and fell. She bruised her knee on the ground and she grabbed it in pain. Joshua walked over to her. Now he was sorry he had not just ignored them and dressed. He offered to help the girl regain her feet. She looked away from him.

"Clothes, put on," she said.

Joshua started to laugh. "You speak English."

"Yes," she said, still looking away from him.

She was fair-skinned, with jet-black hair. Her eyes were almond-shaped. Her nose was straight and her chin pointy. She was young and with a figure that was just beginning to show in the one-piece dress of antelope that she wore.

134

"Wait here, please. Don't go away. I would like to speak with you. I want to get my clothes."

He hurried back to the stream and waded across it. He fumbled with his loincloth, checking it several times to make sure nothing showed. Then he laughed aloud. He had just stood before the girl totally naked. Why should he now suddenly worry about a small exposure? He picked up his shirt and shoes and retraced his steps across the stream. She was gone. He felt suddenly cheated. He had wanted to speak with someone who spoke English. He needed to communicate. His mother spoke English but he wanted to speak with someone his own age. He did not admit to himself that it was the companionship of a young girl that he sought.

That evening Elizabeth announced that they would have visitors. She roasted slices of antelope meat over her fire and baked a corn bread on hot stones. She pulled a clay jug from under the buffalo robes.

"This is the secret of Medicine Cow Lady's power with the tribe, Joshua."

She pulled the stopper out with her teeth and offered it to Joshua. He sniffed it. It smelled sweet. He tasted it. It was wine—no, stronger—a brandy made from berries. He was not exactly sure what kind of berry it was, but he knew the liquor was strong.

"Medicine Cow Lady has many visitors to taste her medicine," Elizabeth joked, "and the medicine affects the knees. All who partake become weak in the knees and wobble from side to side when they go back to their lodges. My mother would not recognize the recipe, but she surely would have recognized the method and the effect."

Joshua took another sip from the jug. He sat down on his wolfskin. Elizabeth looked at the flush on his face.

"How are your knees?" she asked.

"Wobbly," he responded, with a silly smile on his face.

Just as Elizabeth finished her roasting and her baking, the flap of the lodge was pulled away and the old man with the large nose and the feather came into the tipi, followed by a fat squaw wrapped in the blanket that had enveloped

135

the old man on the day Joshua had entered the village. Following both of them was the girl Joshua had met that afternoon by the river.

Elizabeth greeted the two adults warmly. She wrapped her arms around the woman and touched both her cheeks with her own. She did the same to the girl. The old man she patted on his protruding belly.

"May your bowels loosen and give off with more than just wind," she said to him. "My medicine pours from me into your belly."

The man grinned at her. "Cow Lady," he laughed, "I have another problem down lower. Would that you could straighten it out."

"Oh, would that you could," teased his wife. "The Great One knows I can't and He knows I tried."

Elizabeth feigned embarrassment. Perhaps some medicine from the jug. The old man's eyes lit up at the mention of the brandy, and he looked over at Joshua, who still held it.

"Medicine Cow's calf has been sampling, I would say by the look of peace that is on his face." He laughed a wild, high-pitched, gleeful howl.

The old man took the jug from Joshua and patted his blond head. He wanted to see if the hair was real. He had long heard of white men with false hair. He had known a Blackfoot who had counted coup on a French trapper. When he went to scalp the trapper, he came away with a handful of hair without ever using his scalping knife.

"Joshua," Elizabeth addressed him in English, "these are my best friends among the Assiniboine of this band. This is my brother, Eagle Face, and his wife—I don't know her name. Before I came here she made some medicine that she would have no name. So no one calls her anything other than Eagle Face's Wife. This is their daughter, Rainbow. Her real name is Girl Asleep in the Meadow Awakened by the Light of the Rainbow After the Storm. You can see why she is called Rainbow."

"Rainbow and I have met," Joshua interjected, nodding to the girl.

"Medicine Cow Lady's calf is very pretty man everywhere," Rainbow said, smiling and blushing at the same time. "You like Rainbow English?"

"Yes, I like it," Joshua replied. "How did you learn it?"

"It's not been easy," Elizabeth laughed, "but I knew I would forget my own language if I couldn't speak it to someone. But the girl does awful things to the language. Sometimes I find myself doing the same strange things. It's been good to have someone around who speaks English, not Rainbow English." She reached down and squeezed Joshua's shoulder.

Eagle Face and his wife took turns sipping Elizabeth's brandy and carrying on an animated conversation with her in Assiniboine.

Joshua stared at the girl. The light of the fire reflected on her fair skin. Her narrow, beautifully shaped eyes moved from person to person as they spoke, and seemed to come alive with interest as the conversation continued. But she did not speak. Finally Joshua reached over and touched her arm to gain her attention.

"Why did you run away this afternoon?" he asked.

The girl blushed and looked away from him. "It was my girl friends' idea to spy on you when we saw you go by yourself to the river."

"Why should they want to do that? Didn't they see enough on the day I was brought into the village?"

This time she turned crimson. "That was the reason. They had seen too much."

"When do I get to view them?" he asked boldly.

Elizabeth interrupted her conversation with her friends. "Never mind, boy, unless you want to take one of them as your wife."

She stood up and began to serve the meal. Joshua ate in silence and listened to the strange sounds of the Indian language. He continued to stare at Rainbow. She was very beautiful. It had been a long time since he had had the opportunity to stare at a beautiful girl—not since Allison. The memory of the wife of Charles Miller shattered his peaceful mood. Suddenly it was clear that the conversation between the Indians and Elizabeth had also changed in tone. Eagle Face's Wife was terrified and Eagle Face himself seemed angry.

Rainbow looked at Joshua. "My father complains of our neighbors the Peigans. They come to the spruce trees from the setting sun. They warn Medicine Cow Lady and our band to leave. They say we are antelopers."

Joshua started to laugh but checked himself. Eagle Face glared at him. He saw nothing funny in their enemy's challenge to their right to be in the spruce forest, especially after so long a time.

"I'm sorry," he apologized to Elizabeth, "it's just something that Rainbow said."

"I know the feeling," she responded with a smile. But Elizabeth was not in a cheerful mood. She grew more serious as the conversation continued. Several times he heard the expression "mu-dra" used.

"What does *mu-dra* mean?" he blurted out.

There was a deadly silence in the tipi. Only the swishing of the wind in the spruces above them broke the silence.

"It is of no concern to you," Elizabeth remarked.

"If I am to live among you, I must know what you know."

Again there was silence. Joshua glared at his mother. He resented their secrecy. Finally Rainbow spoke.

"Mu-dra is an evil spirit. It comes at night to those caught alone or in small groups on the prairies. Its teeth are like knives sharpened on flint. It turns men into women and women into men. But it cannot find us here among the trees. Medicine Cow Lady brought the trees to us. Mu-dra has not found these trees with the Assiniboine in them. Not since we have been here, five winters now. The Peigans know this too, and now they flee mu-dra into the spruce trees."

Joshua watched Elizabeth as Rainbow spoke. She never smiled. Did she too believe in mu-dra? he wondered.

The talk of the Peigans and then of mu-dra had put a damper on the party that even the berry brandy could not lighten. Eagle Face lifted his buttocks slightly off the floor of the lodge and farted. He grimaced.

138

"Your medicine has not done the trick yet, Cow Lady," he complained.

His wife smiled, revealing several gaps in her teeth.

"We will try again tonight," she said.

"I do not need your help to move my bowels, woman," he complained to her.

"Oh." She looked crestfallen. "I thought you referred to the other problem."

"She patted my belly only," he said in annoyance. "No doubt if *she* had worked on the other part of me I'd have no trouble."

Eagle Face's Wife glared at him. Elizabeth decided the party was over. She stood.

Eagle Face struggled to his feet. Rainbow rose and helped her mother to her feet.

Joshua stood next to Rainbow.

"May I see you tomorrow?" he whispered to her.

"Your eyes are there," she said, touching his face and smiling.

"No, I mean may I talk to you?" He started to laugh. "I know, my mouth is there," he repeated her joke. "Mother," he called to Elizabeth.

She looked at him with pure love. They both realized it was the first time he had addressed her by that name.

"Mother," he repeated softly, "I want this girl to stop teasing me and to promise to see me and talk to me tomorrow."

Elizabeth turned to Eagle Face's Wife and spoke rapidly to her. The old woman's face brightened immediately, and Eagle Face threw back his shoulders. He smiled and placed his hand on Joshua's shoulder. Joshua smiled back and returned the gesture. The old Indian started to grin and bow and pat Joshua's shoulder. His obvious joy was contagious and Joshua soon found himself repeating the old man's antics until he and the family left the lodge.

"What was that all about?" Joshua asked.

"You just agreed to marry Rainbow."

"I what?" Joshua shouted.

"No harm done, she is a lovely girl."

"I know, but at least I should have known what I was doing."

"You certainly seemed attracted to her, and I know how she already feels about you. No matter, the wedding will never take place."

Now Joshua became defensive. "Why not?"

"Because you agreed to meet the most outrageous bride price this band has ever heard of. You promised Eagle Face four ponies. He said you could have Rainbow as soon as he got his horses. You, however, don't have any horses, and neither do I. The one gift I don't get from the Assiniboine is a horse."

"Why didn't you stop me?"

"I'm not sure I wanted to," she admitted. "You are with us now. A few ties—a wife, little ones—they will tie you to me and this life more securely."

"Mother, be at peace, I am not going to leave you ever again."

"Thank you, Joshua. Maybe we can get you some horses."

Word that Medicine Cow's calf had promised four ponies for Rainbow spread rapidly through the camp the next day. But in the telling the story became more elaborate. Eagle Face bragged that his new son-in-law-to-be had agreed to take these ponies from their enemies the Peigans. When Elizabeth tried to downplay his exaggeration, Swift Bear began to mumble once again about a woman in man's clothing. Elizabeth began to regret that she had allowed the need she had to tie her son to her place him in danger. She vowed to keep the story from him.

Joshua and Rainbow agreed to meet each other by the stream. He found her sitting on a rock with her feet dangling in the water. He sat down next to her.

"My mother does not know where she is," she said, pointing to herself.

Joshua chuckled.

"That is funny to you?" Rainbow asked.

"No, it's just that I still am not used to some of your expressions."

"I sound foolish." She looked hurt.

"No, Rainbow." Joshua made her look at him. "You speak my language very well. I could not begin to speak Assiniboine. My expressions would make you weep rather than laugh."

She smiled and started to laugh.

He realized he had touched her for the first time. The skin of her face was delicate. He leaned over and pressed his cheek against hers.

She pulled away from him and scowled.

"You have prickers," she said, running her hand against the grain of the beard on his face.

"I have no razor," he explained. "Soon it will grow longer and become soft like the hair on my head."

"And other places," she giggled. "White men are strange."

"Oh, we're not that different. Not in the essentials," he said boldly.

He lay back on the rock and stretched out his body. He was very excited by her nearness and by the suggestive nature of her words. She lay back also but leaned on her elbow to look at him. She was aware of the swelling beneath his loincloth. He ached for her to touch him, but he could not bring himself even to look at her.

"Joshua," she said after some minutes of embarrassed silence, "I have not known man before. I want you to know."

"I believe you," he said. His voice broke from the dryness in his throat.

She looked hurt for a second. "I want you to know," she repeated.

He looked at her strangely.

"I am sorry. Again I make a mistake. I mean to say, I want to know you."

He turned his head to look at her and his face broke into a wide grin.

"I want to know you too, Rainbow, and I have never known a woman before either."

Now it was her turn to grin at him.

"But is it required," she said, "that we must know each other on top of the rock? It is a bed of little comfort."

He jumped down from the rock; his loincloth barely

covered his excitement. He held her hand and she slid off the rock to the ground.

"I know a place where the spruces make a shelter," she said and took him by the hand.

He walked awkwardly by her side. He blushed. She did not notice it. She had searched the narrow path that they walked in the forest until they came to a small brook that gurgled its way down to the creek.

"Here," she said, pushing aside some bushes. The ground was covered with dried spruce needles. It was not a soft bed but far more comfortable than the rock by the stream.

Joshua lay down first. He watched as the girl loosened the ties on the front of her dress and pulled it up over her head. She stood before him naked. Her breasts were small but they stood out from her body gracefully. Her belly was flat but without muscle and gave the impression of softness bordering on chubbiness. Her hips flared gently from her sides and descended gracefully into long sensuous legs.

Joshua stared at her beauty.

"Do I please you?" she asked softly.

"You are very beautiful. Come lie by my side."

She spread out her dress next to him and then sat down by his side. She peeked over at him and took the cloth he wore about his middle into her hands and slowly and gently removed it. She smiled when she saw him. She touched him and he moaned. He gently pulled her head down onto his chest. He kissed her hair and her eyelids and the lobes of her ears and finally lowered his mouth to the nape of her neck. Now it was her turn to voice her ecstasy.

She rolled onto her back and he knelt between her legs. She gazed up at him, the paleness of him, the strange golden hair with which he was covered, the strength of his muscles. She wanted him inside of her. He lowered himself and she felt him touching her. She reached her hand down to guide him to her. Then she lay back and waited. She knew it would hurt. Her mother had warned her of that. The pain began and then she felt a tearing. He lowered himself and wrapped his arms about her, relishing the feel of her gripping him. They would be slow this first time. She wanted this to last forever. She wanted it burned into her memory. This first joining with her lover. And she wanted his seed to bear fruit within her and to make her big with child.

Joshua used every bit of willpower and self-discipline to force himself to go slowly, to make it last. The spasm of pleasure that ran from his groin throughout his body blotted out all other awareness. They relaxed in each other's arms, still joined together. When he became hard again, they "knew" each other a second time. But this time it was fast and bordering on the violent.

They lay exhausted and sweat ran down Joshua's back. The fresh September air soon cooled them both. Rainbow was embarrassed by the blood that covered him when they separated. He grew frightened, terrified that he had harmed her with the strength of his passion. She assured him that her mother had warned her of the bleeding and told her it was normal.

"Come with me," she said, rising from their spruce-needle bed and leading him by the hand toward the creek where they first met.

They walked together hand in hand into the creek. She cupped some water in her hands and modestly turning her back on him, washed herself. Then she turned around to face him, and again taking water into her cupped hands, she poured it gently over his groin. She took him into her hands and rubbed him to make sure all the blood was washed from him. The effect of her hand on him was electric. Once again he grew hard. He drew her to his body, wrapped his arms about her frailness, and lowered his mouth and kissed hers for the first time. She opened her mouth to gasp for air and he filled it with his tongue, searching her, probing everywhere. He knelt down and entered her there in the water. This time also it was very quick.

They went back to their bed of spruce needles and sat down just to stare at each other. Joshua played with the spruce needles and dropped little handfuls of them in lines on her belly, over her stomach, up between her

143

breasts. He feasted on the sight of her, and he knew he loved her as he could never love anyone else.

"When you become my husband," she said after a long silence, "I will place my lodge pole here," she said.

"Is there any symbolism in that?" he asked.

"Do not brag. You are no lodge pole."

He looked a bit distressed but then shrugged it off. "I seemed to have promised much to buy you from your father."

"Too much. You look before my father the fool."

This time Joshua broke out laughing.

"I have done it another time, have I not?" she said.

He nodded, still laughing.

"But you should not have bragged about taking horses from the Peigan."

Joshua stopped laughing immediately. "What have I done?"

"You said you would buy me with four Peigan ponies. Does that mean we must wait until spring before we can be married?"

Joshua had no desire to tell her he had promised no such thing. It was clear to him that although she told him he had been foolish to propose so much, nevertheless she could not help feeling cherished by so foolish a promise. But after a day like today, a day in which she gave him pleasure such as he had never known in his life, he was glad he had honored her with such a foolish promise.

The wind cut through the spruce trees with a wailing rush, and the gray, rain-laden clouds came rushing off the prairies toward the three young men as they lay prone on their bellies. Darkness fell upon them with even greater suddenness than normal, thanks to the approaching storm. Before them, nestled in the clearing at a bend in the river, lay the Peigan encampment. Beyond it, protected by the river bend, lay a herd of enemy horses.

Joshua waited impatiently as Swift Bear crawled slowly forward to get a better view of the encampment and to see how many warriors would be guarding the herd as night fell. It had disturbed the white man that only Swift Bear

144

and Big Elk had agreed to go on the raid with him. He knew nothing about stealing horses. He could not go alone. Several young men spoke noisily about going out on the raid in the spring, but Joshua was impatient. He wanted his bride's gift now.

He wished his companions were men with whom he had better relations, but he needed knowledgeable companions. Elizabeth, fearing for the safety of a newly discovered son, had argued against their going, but he had ignored her and she had not used her influence to discourage his companions. She wanted Rainbow as a daughter as well. Eagle Face held a banquet for the young men the night before they left, and Medicine Cow Lady had blessed them to protect them from mu-dra.

Both Swift Bear and Big Elk were clearly relieved when they found the Peigan band living in a forest rather than out on the open prairie. They said nothing, but Joshua could see their relief on their normally impassive faces.

They had stalked the camp for two days and a night thus far. Last night the moon's light in a cloudless sky bathed a clearing and the horse herd in its reflective light. Swift Bear, who was in command of the party, had vetoed a raid in such conditions. But tonight the clouds would blot out the moon. The storm had already made the horses restless. Even on the slope above the village, the three raiders could hear them snort and stamp their feet at each roll of thunder and each howl of the wind. Tonight they would get their chance.

Darkness descended on them, broken only by streaks of lightning. Swift Bear crawled forward from the rim of the hill. He motioned with his hand for Big Elk and Joshua to follow him. The three men crawled forward together. They swung about on the left side of the hill, staying as long as possible in the fringe of the forest.

Elizabeth had told him his task was to steal four horses. The other men would be more interested in counting coup. But she insisted that Joshua was not to take part in the fighting. The rest would be easy. Just follow the other two men.

Joshua wished he could speak some Assiniboine so that

he could converse with Swift Bear about his plans. He had four rawhide bridles with him. He had no experience driving a herd and therefore would have to control each horse. He could tell by the way they moved that Swift Bear, who for the first time led his own raiding party, was planning to approach the encampment from the northwest, from the prairie side. Big Elk perceived the plan at just the same moment. He grunted something at Swift Bear and the two men exchanged harsh words in a whisper. Once again Joshua caught the ever-recurring "mu-dra." It was clear that Big Elk's love of whiskey had made him go on raiding parties, and that his need for it was greater than his fear even of the night spirit.

The rain slashed down at them with an icy chill. Particles of sleet were mixed with the cold raindrops and stung their faces and bare arms. It pushed them on. The sooner the raid, the sooner they would be able to return to the warmth and comfort of their lodges in their own encampment.

They made a wide circle out into the grassland. The night was pitch-dark and the wind bent the grass flat against the prairie floor. It made an eerie, frightening sound as it whipped through the stalks. Swift Bear had wanted to wait until all were asleep in the Peigan encampment before he struck. But he was cold. And attacking it while all were in their lodges and not expecting the attack was deemed good enough. Every time the lightning zigzagged through the black night, Big Elk would start in fright.

Joshua could not recall when they had changed direction. That had occurred gradually when they had completed their arclike swing to the north. But suddenly he realized that the river was now on their left and the dark outline of the spruce trees again appeared in the lightning, but this time in front of them.

Swift Bear directed them to the river's edge and they reentered the forest, following its course. The herd would be directly ahead of them now. Swift Bear and Big Elk suddenly split company, one going right and the other to

146

the left. Joshua knew that two men normally watched the herd. They would be dead if they watched tonight.

He stayed put, waiting for his companions to return. Both did within minutes. They were empty-handed and disappointed. Joshua felt relief that no youth had been forced to give up his life for the sake of his bride's gift.

The three men were now totally drenched with rain and sleet. Swift Bear signaled toward the horses. Joshua followed his lead and Big Elk disappeared in the other direction again.

The leader of the party was soon in the midst of the horse herd. Joshua looked about for horses. They all looked alike to him—small, scrawny, and unshod. He looped a lasso of rawhide over the head of one pony. Swift Bear looked at him with contempt. He knew he was being evaluated by a man prone to be contemptuous. He did not have much time to select. Yet he did not wish to bring home inferior stock and humiliate Eagle Face and Rainbow.

Then he saw him—black and large—standing away from the herd. It was a stallion, a superb horse. Swift Bear saw the horse at the same time as Joshua. But the Indian was swifter than the white man. He moved rapidly toward the stallion and attempted to leap onto his back. The horse reared high in the air just as lightning brightened the sky, outlining the blackness of stallion and the warrior frantically attempting to retain his seat.

The horse screamed, almost sounding human, and then bucked, kicking his rear legs out and twisting violently from one side to the other. Swift Bear went flying backward over the horse's tail and landed in a heap on the water-soaked ground.

Joshua ran to the Indian's side. Swift Bear moaned in pain and held his limp shoulder. The horse shied away from both of the men, stamping his feet in anger. He was a white man's horse originally. Joshua could see the remnants of iron shoes still clinging to his feet. He could see recently administered whip marks on the horse's body. It was clear to Joshua that the black stallion was frightened, probably terrified of his recent Indian owner.

Joshua called out to him in English and the horse seemed instantly soothed. The boy walked carefully over to him. The horse looked away and snorted. Joshua reached out and stroked the velvet nose. The horse did not back away. He decided to take his chances and tossed the rawhide halter over the stallion's head. Then he lay on his belly across the stallion's back. He balanced there precariously for a moment. If ths horse bucked now he was finished. But the stallion barely moved. Joshua swung his leg over and sat upright.

Behind him he heard a war whoop. Big Elk had arrived at the rear of the herd and would now stampede it into the Peigan village.

Joshua had to act quickly. He reached for the halter of the pony he had already selected and handed it to the still dazed Swift Bear. He quickly selected two more animals from among the herd ponies, which were now beginning to crash into each other in panic. Joshua moved the stallion into the middle of the herd and looped his rawhide over the head of the two selected horses. Now he had them. He turned and saw that Swift Bear had remounted, still favoring his shoulder.

Big Elk came from behind the herd and leapt on the back of one of Joshua's ponies. The white man kept a grip on the neck of the stallion. It was a big and powerful horse, accustomed to a bit and reins, and Joshua was not sure he could manage the beast. At the same time, he would not let go his extra pony, who crowded next to the stallion and who received a nip on the back of its neck as payment for its boldness.

Swift Bear and Big Elk were now screaming at the top of their lungs. There was shouting coming now from the Peigan village. A musket shot rang out. The horses began to race toward the lodges.

The plan was working perfectly. All they had to do was ride through the camp up the hill and into the spruce forest—following the river back to the Assiniboine lodges.

The great stallion raced ahead of the ponies. Joshua bent low along the horse's neck and held on with all of his strength. He sped past lodges and excited people. Someone fired at him and missed. He was moving up the slope of the hillock. Many of the riderless horses resisted the steep upgrade and ran to the right and to the left. Joshua, astride the stallion and leading the pony, soon found himself alone at the top of the hill. He pulled back on the horse's mane with his arms in an effort to slow him up. The stallion twisted sideways and finally, complaining loudly, came to a halt. Joshua turned around to see what was happening behind. He caught no sight of his two companions.

"Damn it," he cursed. "Where the hell did they go?"

As if hearing his question, Big Elk, astride his pony, came racing away from the confusion of horses, people, and overturned lodges. He rode straight-backed on the horse, holding his loot high above his head with both hands. It was a keg of brandy.

Of Swift Bear there was still no sign. Big Elk reached Joshua's side. His smile was enormous. He smacked his lips together, almost tasting the contents of the barrel. He turned his pony and looked for his friend. He made a sound of disgust with his mouth when he could see no sign of their leader. He waved his hand as if to dismiss Swift Bear and started to ride off into the woods.

He signaled for Joshua to join him. Joshua could see several Peigans chasing ponies. It was important to get a head start, to be off into the woods, into the dark and the rain before the Peigans could get mounted. Suddenly Swift Bear, astride his pony, dashed from behind a burnimg lodge. Several Peigans tried to intercept him on foot. He struck at one with his war club. The blow landed lightly on the man's shoulder and Swift Bear screamed a cry of triumph. The Peigan seemed to sink in shame and no longer tried to pursue him.

Swift Bear emulated Big Elk's solo ride except instead of a keg he held a more grisly trophy in his hand—a human scalp dripping blood. Big Elk was already in the woods when Swift Bear came up to Joshua. Both of them kneed their horses and rode into the dark after their companion.

Behind them the confusion subsided. The fires were put out, lodges were righted. One family set to wailing death songs of a scalped twelve-year-old boy not yet even initiated into the rites of a warrior. Four horses were counted as missing. The Peigans would add this night to a list of grievances to settle with the Assiniboine.

The three riders rode through the spruce forest for many miles. When they were sure no one pursued them, they dismounted in a small clearing surrounded by large spruce trees. Swift Bear did a small dance, waving his trophy in his hand and calling out the number of times he had counted coup on the Peigans.

Joshua felt sick about the scalp, although he knew there was no stopping Swift Bear from living fully the ways of his people. There was nothing he could do now anyway. Joshua was more concerned about Big Elk. He had smashed open the wooden keg and discovered that it was filled with whiskey. He was downing it in huge gulps, spilling some down his chest. He sat down under a spruce and clearly intended to spend the night drinking. Swift Bear sat next to him, trying to coax some whiskey from him. Big Elk provided him with one swallow and then another. Soon the two of them were tipsy and shortly thereafter they were both totally drunk, with no thought whatever about making the rest of the journey to the Assiniboine encampment.

Joshua climbed back up onto his stallion and pointed to the ponies.

Swift Bear and Big Elk merely laughed at him, spilling whiskey over themselves as they gestured drunkenly.

"Well, if you don't care, why should I give a damn?" Joshua said to them. He took all three extra bridles in his hand and started to move away with the ponies. He estimated a ten-mile journey ahead of him. Despite his elation over the raid, he was wet and cold. He wanted to get back to the warmth of his mother's lodge. His companions could walk back once they had sobered up. He guided his horse out of the clearing into the woods and back to the riverbank. He led the rest of his bride's price behind him.

Joshua arrived back at the camp in the middle of the night. A true Indian warrior returning from a successful raid would have spent the night outside camp so that he might return in triumph in full daylight to the admiration of the entire village. Instead, Joshua tied his horses to a tree behind Elizabeth's lodge and quietly entered the tipi. He longed for the warmth of his wolfskin bed. He stripped off his loincloth, his leggings, and the sopping-wet shirt. He did not awaken Elizabeth. All he wanted was his bed. He slipped his legs down into the soft fur and drew it up over his shoulders. His face sank into the silklike texture of the fur. His eyes focused briefly on the hot coals that were the sole remains of the evening's fire. He was asleep in seconds.

In the morning the whole village was astir. Joshua still slept, but everyone could see the horses tied behind Medicine Cow Lady's lodge and all knew that he had returned in triumph. Swift Bear's mother poked her head nervously out of her lodge. Her son had not returned and she worried. Big Elk had no mother to worry about him, and his wife had left him for a man in another Assiniboine band two summers before because she could not stand his drinking. He was, however, a cousin of Eagle Face's Wife.

Eagle Face sat before his lodge wrapped in his blanket, accepting the congratulations of all the men and women of the band. He would soon come into possession of great wealth, thanks to his daughter's beauty. The ponies were modest horseflesh, but the stallion was the finest horse in the band. Far better even than Crooked Bow's gelding—the horse he had taken from Joshua—if only because he was capable of breeding with the band's mares and improving the quality of the mounts for the entire encampment.

As soon as the white calf of Medicine Cow Lady awoke from his sleep, he would make the presentation. Within Eagle Face's lodge his wife fussed over Rainbow's hair and clothes. She would be sitting in all of her finery when her future husband came to call.

Elizabeth finally grew tired of waiting. She knelt beside her son and shook his shoulder. Joshua's eyes flashed open. He saw his mother staring down at him with a great smile across her face.

"My son is a warrior, an incomparable warrior. You did

precisely what you said you would do—a real horse and three ponies."

"I had some help from Swift Bear and Big Elk."

"Word is that they have not returned yet."

"They are probably sleeping it off. Big Elk had a whole keg of whiskey. He intended to get powerfully drunk, and Swift Bear looked like he was willing to help him."

Joshua slipped out of bed and quickly dressed as his mother prepared some corn bread for his breakfast. He wished he could look in a mirror. Today was an important day. As he had promised Rainbow, his beard had grown longer and the hair was softer to the touch. He found some salt in one of Elizabeth's clay jugs and took a stick of it to brush his teeth with. He walked out of the lodge. The day after the rainstorm had dawned icy cold. But today Joshua was determined to take a wife, and he intended to be clean. He walked to the river's edge and followed it down to their rock. Off among the spruces he saw a new lodge with fresh, beautifully decorated buffalo skins covering it. He knew it was Rainbow's work and it was their honeymoon lodge.

He removed his loincloth and leggings and soft leather moccasins. The water in the creek was numbing. He could not wade into water like this. He screwed up his courage and dived headfirst into the cold. He was determined to stay under for ten seconds. He started to count slowly. At seven he screamed and ran out of the water toward the embankment. He grabbed himself with both arms to try to keep warm, but with no success. His body had a rosy tint all over, almost as if he had stayed out in the sun too long. He looked down at himself, all shriveled and almost disappeared. He chuckled.

"Poor Rainbow," he said. She was expecting a lot more.

He was still cold. He cursed his failure to bring something to wrap himself in. He dressed and raced shivering back to the lodge of Medicine Cow Lady.

Two hours later he led his stallion and ponies from his mother's lodge to the lodge of Eagle Face. Elizabeth followed the procession, keeping her distance. A crowd had already assembled at the old man's tent. He sat, still wrapped in his blanket, which protected all of him but his giant beak from the biting cold. The crowd cleared a path for Joshua and his magnificent gift.

Eagle Face sat impassively as the white youth approached him. Joshua stood before the man he wished to make his father-in-law and suddenly realized they could not communicate. He turned in desperation and saw his mother step forward to speak for him.

"O great nose," she said, "my bull calf made rash promises to fill your old age with wealth if he could have your only child as his bride. As you can see, he has fulfilled his promise."

Eagle Face did not stir. Everyone knew what his answer would be—had to be—but it would not be proper to ignore the forms.

"She is my only daughter. She is the joy of my wife. My wife has taught her all she knows. What sorrow will come to her. It will not be compensated for by ponies—mediocre ponies at that."

"Mediocre ponies and one magnificent stallion. Eagle Face will go to his next war party mounted better than any Assiniboine on the prairies or in the forests. No Cree may touch him. No Blackfoot, no Blood, no Peigan, no Sioux."

Eagle Face could not keep his eyes off the horse as Elizabeth described him. Nor could he keep his composure any longer.

"Yes, I want that horse," he cried out.

Several women whispered to each other. They were scandalized. Eagle Face had given over Rainbow in indecent haste. Perhaps the men understood. If pressed, all would have given three daughters and even their wives to own such a steed.

"Wife," the old man called out in his croaking voice. "Bring out our daughter. She is bought by the calf of Medicine Cow Lady."

Then he threw off his blanket. He was bare-chested, clothed only in leggings and loincloth. His belly protruded and hung down over the top of the cloth, yet he was surprisingly nimble. He sprang to the back of the stallion. The horse, again under the control of an Indian, reared in

153

panic, but Eagle Face kept his seat. The crowd scattered from the path of the kicking, twisting animal. Eagle Face kneed the horse. It charged across the village square and out across the meadow. The old man reined the stallion in. Again the horse reared on its hind legs. Eagle Face turned the stallion's head and once again charged, this time back into the encampment. He jumped from the back of the horse when he reached his lodge and yelled into the sky with the sheer joy of the experience.

"That was better than the last time with my woman," he exclaimed.

"I doubt that, friend," Elizabeth said solemnly. "The problem is that the last time with your woman was too dim a memory."

He howled with laughter at her joke, as did all the bystanders.

"Do you intend, however, that my son be as old as you are before he sees *his* woman?" she jested. "I have not yet seen your side of the bargain upheld."

The old man was chagrined. "Woman, bring out our daughter before I take a stick to you."

The flap of the tent opened and Rainbow stepped out. She was dressed in an almost-white antelope-skin shift decorated with beads and quills. Her hair was braided, with a vermilion ribbon entwined in the braiding.

A murmur ran through the women bystanders. Most complimented the wife of Eagle Face on the appearance of her child, but several whispered condolences that so important a moment should be blighted by her husband's rudeness.

It was clear from the expression on the countenance of Eagle Face's Wife that she too felt the insult. But Rainbow was oblivious to all but Joshua. She did not look at him directly. She kept her eyes shyly downcast, as was appropriate for the occasion. But she missed not one motion he made. She caught the smile he had given her when she appeared. Despite her downward glance, she could see that his beard had lengthened. It was strange how these whites grew hair all over their bodies. She would make him scrape this yellow fuzz from his pretty face when the appropriate time came.

Eagle Face, still holding his stallion, took his daughter's hand and placed it in Joshua's.

The crowd cheered, and Joshua gently drew Rainbow to his side. Protocol required Eagle Face to give his blessing, but he mumbled a few unintelligible words and leapt back on his horse. He had lost all sense of decorum out of the joy of owning such a beast. Again he raced through the village.

Eagle Face's Wife entered her lodge and then returned to the entryway with a bundle of essential items that her daughter would need in her own lodge. Rainbow took them and touched cheeks with her mother. Joshua took her by the hand and they left the crowd gathered around Eagle Face's Wife consoling her, both for the loss of a daughter and for the poor behavior of her man at such an important moment in the family's life.

Elizabeth followed Joshua and Rainbow until they came before her lodge. She entered alone and then returned with Joshua's sleeping mat and a musket. She handed them to Rainbow to take to her new lodge.

Joshua tried to carry them for her, but his mother waved him away.

"As an Assiniboine warrior it is your responsibility to protect your wife's lodge and to keep it filled with meat. It is Rainbow's task to take care of your needs."

Rainbow blushed, and Joshua started to laugh.

"We both have needs," he said.

Elizabeth chuckled. "Tend to them, boy," she said, patting him on the cheek and then kissing the girl on the forehead.

Joshua and Rainbow walked together to the river and then along its bank until they came to the place where Rainbow had built her lodge. They came to the entryway and Rainbow started to lift the flap so that she might precede her new husband into her lodge. Suddenly, however, she found herself swept up into his arms.

"All we've had so far, my bride," he said, "has been Assiniboine customs. Among my people a man carries his bride to their wedding bed."

She leaned her face against the nape of his neck. She

could feel the strong pulse of his blood course through the veins, and she could feel the pent-up power of the muscles in his arms and chest. He was a strong man, a provider and a protector.

She had taken some of the best furs her mother could spare and she had lined the floor and sides of her marriage lodge with them. He took her across the lodge and gently set her down among the beaver pelts that covered their bed. He spread out his own wolfskin and sat down next to her. Someone had preceded them to the lodge and set out bowls of pemmican stew and fresh antelope meat, and there was also a jug of berry brandy. Joshua easily recognized the handiwork of his mother.

"Rainbow," he asked, "are you sorry that this will not be the first time for us?"

"The first time was not as good as the second and the third time was best of all. I look forward to the fourth." She blushed as she spoke, shocked by her own boldness.

"Let's not waste any time, then." Joshua laughed.

He helped her out of her dress and she lay back, nestling her body into the furs. He removed his clothing and lay down beside her, pulling the wolfskin over both of them to keep them warm. The lodge was chilly. In their desire for each other they had forgotten to start a fire.

Rainbow placed her face against his chest. She examined it and noted the fine blond hair that sprouted from it. She grew alarmed.

"This hair on your chest, will it grow long like the hair on your face?"

He started to laugh. "You don't like my beard, do you?"

She smiled shyly and shook her head.

"I'll shave just as soon as I can find a knife as sharp as a good razor," he offered. "Now what else don't you like? My mother tells me that Indians think white men smell very foul. I washed myself in the coldest water in North America this morning just so I wouldn't give offense to you."

She moved her face closer to his arms and sniffed. "You should have stayed in the water longer."

"If I had," he said, drawing her hand down to his groin, "this would have shriveled up into nothing."

"Then I am glad you still stink."

"You little witch," he said as he grabbed a tiny bit of the flesh of her bottom with his thumb and finger.

She squealed more in anticipation of pain than from the actual hurt. She grabbed his arm and tried to hold him off. She knew he was too strong and so she attacked with her fingers, running them lightly across his ribs and down onto his stomach. He was violently ticklish and almost instantly constricted into a ball, knees drawn up, neck pulled down, howling with laughter. She continued to attack him. He roared and begged her not to touch him anymore.

"Promise you'll not pinch me again," she demanded.

"I promise," he said, gasping for breath.

"Good," she said. "Now get back to behind pinch."

"May I?"

She looked at him warily. He had a devil's gleam in his eye and she realized she had made a mistake. "I mean before pinch. Now, what before pinch?"

"You had just told me that I stink," he volunteered.

"I'm sorry," she said.

"So am I," he responded.

"Not as much as I am. I have to smell."

Now he became sensitive. "Do I really smell that bad?"

She realized that she had teased too much. She nuzzled his armpits and kissed both of them.

"Rainbow has teased you. You are a beautiful man."

He leaned down and kissed her mouth. She remembered from the last time and opened it for him to probe. They kissed passionately, stopping their deep kissing only to place their lips on eyes and nose and chest and throat and breasts.

She reached down and touched his erection. "I am glad you are warm under the furs," she said. "I would be disappointed if it was shriveled and not ripe like a squash."

Suddenly he started laughing again.

"What has Rainbow done? Is touching you like this the same as making you tickle?"

157

"No, that doesn't tickle," he said, stretching sensuously under the furs. He was glorying in the feeling she sent through him.

Finally he was afraid he would not be able to check himself. He pulled away from her and raised himself on one elbow. He looked into her face as she lay beneath him.

"Girl Asleep in the Meadow Awakened by the Light of the Rainbow After the Storm," he called her by her name in Assiniboine, "consented to join with Medicine Cow Lady's bull calf. I love you very much and now I would like to prove it to you with my body."

She closed her eyes. "I have longed for you since the last time," she responded.

He lowered his body gently on top of hers.

The snow came two days after Joshua and Rainbow were married. The storm came from the northwest, roaring out of the flatland between the two branches of the Saskatchewan River. The clouds swept in, black and heavy-laden with snow, which they dumped in the basin of the Assiniboine River. Within an hour the spruce trees surrounding the young couple's lodge were groaning under their white burden. Five hours later the storm had passed on, heading for the Dakota territories to the south.

After the storm the sky cleared and the cold settled down. Joshua loaded log after log on the fire to keep the inside of the tipi warm. The snow piled about the lower third and helped to insulate the lodge. And the hot smoke rising through the smoke-opening at the top prevented the cold air from circulating down to them. Still they lay wrapped in the furs, rising only to eat and feed the fire. Then they fell back into each other's arms and lost themselves in pleasure.

Elizabeth trudged through the heavy snows toward her son's lodge. She was wrapped in furs. She had kept the old women away to give the young lovers the feast they deserved, but when Eagle Face's Wife joined in the outcry she had no choice but to fetch her son.

She could tell from the lack of footprints in the snow that

Joshua and Rainbow had not even ventured out of the lodge, and it grieved her to have to disturb them. But disturb them she must.

"Joshua," she called out. She heard a stirring inside the tent. After a few moments her son appeared, wrapped in his wolfskin bedding. He looked at her in surprise.

"I would not disturb you except there is great concern in the village. Swift Bear and Big Elk have still not returned from the raid. It is more than three days now—three days of snow and bitter cold. Swift Bear's mother and Rainbow's mother, who is cousin to Big Elk, are making a great commotion in the village."

Joshua frowned. He did not wish to leave Rainbow but he knew what his mother asked of him. He was the last to see the two warriors. He alone knew where he had seen them last. He was gripped by fear that the Peigans had tracked them down and fallen upon them as they lay drunk.

"I'll join the search party," he offered.

She nodded her thanks to him and departed.

Joshua returned to his bride, who had already begun to tidy up the lodge and prepare a breakfast and a bundle of food for traveling.

He knew she was disappointed and that he would have to disappoint her further.

"You will have to leave the lodge and go back to your mother," he told her.

She looked at him as if he had slapped her. "That would disgrace me," she said, her eyes flashing defensively. "People would say that next you would take back the man horse."

He put his arms around her and could feel the resistance to him building in her. "I don't want you to be alone while I am gone."

"I have a fix for that," she responded. "I go with you. You cannot speak the language of the Assiniboine yet you need to tell them where Swift Bear and my cousin of the whiskey are. You will need me to speak for you."

Joshua did not want to be separated from her, but he knew it could be dangerous for her to accompany him.

"All right," he agreed. "Now may I put my arms about you?" he asked, smiling.

"Always when you give to me what I want."

He swept her into his arms.

When he got to his mother's lodge, Joshua found that the idea of a massive search party had already been abandoned. The snows were too deep for the Indian ponies. Yet Medicine Cow Lady had to do something to soothe the fears of most and the terror of Swift Bear's mother. She would have gone out herself, but no one in the village could face the greater terror that the lack of her medicine in the encampment would generate.

Finally Eagle Face offered to ride his stallion along with Joshua, who would borrow Crooked Bow's gelding. They were the only two horses large enough and strong enough to make the journey.

Joshua was tempted to break his promise to Rainbow and leave her with his mother. But he knew that Eagle Face and he could never understand each other without her. He helped her up onto the gelding, then seated himself behind her.

They set out, following the course of the river that wound its way through the spruce forest. They had only ten miles to cover to arrive at the spot where Joshua had left his companions. Although the horses were strong, they had a difficult time plowing a path through the deep snow.

Eagle Face led the way. He knew the spruce forest well and had explored it for Medicine Cow Lady before they moved the encampment there from the prairies. He said little, primarily because he could only have spoken to his daughter and he did not believe that girls should be involved in men's work such as this. He disapproved of his son-in-law's decision to bring his wife along. He would not bless her participation with words. He rode wrapped in his favorite blanket. The cold was seeping into his old bones and he wished he had wrapped himself in furs like the young one. But this was a potential war party. One had to look the part. He would not face the Peigan wrapped in furs like one prepared to be raised onto the burial platform.

160

He thought about death much more often now. Until the mu-dra had struck the prairies, he had never worried about death. As a young man he had charged into the lances of the Sioux and raided horses as far away as the lands of the Blackfoot without once thinking that he might not survive. He could face Sioux lances without flinching. He was an Assiniboine warrior. It was expected of him. But how did anyone face the knives of mu-dra?

He urged his stallion on through the snow. He was sure he knew the spot Rainbow had described after speaking with Joshua. Swift Bear and Big Elk were fools. He too enjoyed the white man's drink, but they could have enjoyed a good drink even more if they had taken the keg back to the village with them. They had grown too impatient and too selfish. If they had brought it back, Big Elk would have had to share it with relatives—even cousins by marriage. He paid no attention to the two lovers who shared the gelding. They had eyes only for each other and were of no help to him. He searched the snows for signs of Peigan. There were none.

They were close now to the spot. Eagle Face turned the stallion left, away from the river. The snows deepened. He urged the stallion forward. The black horse snorted and twisted its head. It was a magnificent beast, he thought, and more than compensated him for having a white man mate with his daughter.

There, up ahead, was the clearing. He could feel the gelding press closer to the stallion. The white boy had recognized the place as well and his interest was finally aroused.

There under one spruce tree the snow had piled into drifts. It had done it under no other spruce tree. Something was wrong.

Eagle Face rode directly to the mounds of snow. He knew now what he would find. He slid down from the back of his stallion. He began to dig in the snow. Joshua joined him. They uncovered a foot and then a whole leg, frozen stiff and looking almost as fresh as if the owner were still able to move it.

Joshua was heartsick. He recognized the arm holding

the empty keg. He really recognized the keg. It was Big Elk's arm. He told Rainbow to go back a distance and hold the horses.

Eagle Face uncovered the middle of what had been Swift Bear's torso and gasped.

"Mu-dra!" he cried out in terror.

Rainbow stiffened in fear. The old man stepped back in horror. Joshua stepped around him to see what had frightened him so. He saw that Swift Bear's abdomen had been sliced open and his still pink entrails had oozed onto the ground and stained the snow red. Yet there was not much blood in the snow. The ground under the snow was drenched in it.

Joshua felt sick to his stomach. He dug away some more snow and saw that Swift Bear had been castrated and that his penis was missing. Almost mechanically he worked to uncover the bodies. He knew what he would find when he uncovered Big Elk. Eagle Face stepped even farther away and kept repeating "mu-dra" over and over again.

Joshua could not hold it back any longer. He turned from his wife and father-in-law and spewed his vomit into the snow.

When he felt he could regain control of himself he rejoined them, but the horror of what struck his eyes triggered a memory. A memory of last summer. He had seen this slaughter before out on the prairies. A party of Cree had been slaughtered and maimed in exactly this fashion. He remembered Jamie's explanation.

"Ask your father," he said to Rainbow. "Could this be the work of the Blackfoot or the Peigan?"

Eagle Face shook his head after he listened to Rainbow translate. He stepped warily toward the corpses and pointed to their untouched scalps. He turned to his daughter. "Only the evil one kills like this. He takes no trophy, except on occasion he will take the manhood of a warrior and the breast of a mother. But the evil spirit has no interest in what a true warrior will regard as a trophy of battle. He has for the first time struck in the spruce forest. We are no longer safe. Medicine Cow Lady has lost her power to protect us."

Joshua was disturbed by the old man's last remark. It implied a threat to his mother. But Joshua underestimated the shrewdness of his father-in-law. He was terrified that the evil spirit had struck at last in the forest. But still he could not bring himself to believe that the protective magic was gone. Nor could he bring himself to tell the village. Maybe it would not happen again—especially if no one spoke of it. The old man knew that if he returned with the two bodies, and he must return them for proper burial, there would be no hiding how they had died. The village would know they were the victims of the evil spirit. It would terrify them. But did they have to know *where* Swift Bear and Big Elk died? He would tell the village for its own good that they had followed the trail of two drunken men out into the prairies. There, they had discovered the work of mu-dra. The three of them, therefore, must sit by these corpses for most of the day before they rode back with them. The ride into the snow-battered plain would have taken much time. He felt better after he worked out this deceit. The Assiniboine needed to believe that Medicine Cow Lady could protect them. He needed to believe it, too, even with the gory truth staring him in the face.

VII

Assiniboine Encampment, Winter 1842

There were times during the white endless winter that Joshua lost all track of time. Day was followed by night, sunrise by sunset. He recalled how in Toronto he would easily recall which day of the week it was. Was it a schoolday? Or a weekend? These had been significant and highly meaningful questions to him then. Now he was not sure of the month, save that it was a winter month. All seemed the same. The winds drove the clouds down upon their forest home; the snow swirled in small cyclones among the spruce trees and piled against Rainbow's lodge. And when the flakes ceased falling, the wind swept the new-fallen snow into white swirls that sometimes left portions of the forest floor bare and piled drifts several feet high in other parts.

Joshua rarely bothered to dress any longer. He only ventured out to get wood from the pile Rainbow had collected before their marriage, and then more often than not, he merely threw his wolfskin about him and jammed his feet into his moccasins.

They made love to each other every night, except for that first one when they returned with the bodies of his companions. Swift Bear's mother had slashed her arms with a knife and then had cut off a finger of her right hand to allow her body's suffering to mirror the anguish within her. Eagle Face's Wife sang Big Elk's death song, as was proper, but made no further display of sorrow.

But neither the screaming of the one woman nor the dignified wailing of the other told the true story of the anguish of the Assiniboine band. Mu-dra, the dreaded one, had struck down sons and cousins before, but this was the first time since Medicine Cow Lady had led them into the forest. A burden that all thought had been lifted from them had returned. Those not directly affected consoled themselves that the young men had foolishly, in their drunken stupor, wandered out into the prairies. But they had done that before, when they captured the white man who lived among them, and they had returned safely. A pall fell upon the whole village.

That first night Joshua and Rainbow merely held onto each other. He questioned her about mu-dra, although it was clear she did not know very much. She calculated her own age at about seventeen summers. It had all begun before she was born. At first it had hit only the Cree, the gruesome slaughter that terrified them. The Assiniboine had taken little notice of it until stories came from Cree captives about the killing. The Cree at first thought it was their enemies. But the evil one did not try to count coup or take scalps. The Indians of the plains would rather wound and let their enemy live so that he would bear the scar and remember his defeat at his enemy's hands. His continued life was a memorial to the superiority of his foe. But not the evil one. He killed at night while all slept. He killed man, woman, child indiscriminately. He reveled in denying to the warrior his sex so that he could have no joy in the next world. He took the breasts from mothers so that they might bear no babies.

The mu-dra spread west eventually. It struck the Assiniboine next, and they were told by Peigan women they had captured that even the western Blood and Blackfoot had fallen victim. No one was safe.

But then Medicine Cow Lady came to them from the Cree. She said she had dreamed of a safe place where the sky was blotted out by black trees at night and the evil one could not descend from the sky and find them.

Rainbow then stopped her narrative and shivered despite the fact that Joshua's body warmed hers. She began to weep.

165

"He has found us, even under the cover of our trees. He will visit again."

Joshua stroked her hair and pulled her even closer to himself. "I'll protect you," he whispered in her ear. "No one can touch you with me beside you."

She wrapped her arms about his chest and fell asleep with her head resting against his arm.

Joshua drifted off to sleep after his wife, but his dream was disturbed by the flash of a hideous knife slicing and twisting into his flesh. From the wounds came the screams of hundreds of sufferers.

With the passing of days and then weeks, the sense of doom seemed to fade. The winter dragged on and indolence took control of the two lovers. They ate the winter stores of pemmican and cornmeal washed down with the beer made from spruce. It tasted to Joshua the way turpentine smelled, but even his mother insisted he drink it to ward off the scurvy.

One morning in late winter, Joshua looked down at his naked body on awakening in the morning and recognized a bulge where once a flat belly had been. He elbowed Rainbow, who slept at his side. She raised her head sleepily to look at him. She was suddenly aware that he had pulled the furs from both of their bodies and was staring at them.

"What bothers you?" she asked.

"Look," he said, pointing to the incipient belly. "I'm going soft."

"Rainbow will take care of that," she said, taking hold of him in her hands.

"Not there," he laughed at her and gasped at the same time as bolts of pleasure passed upward from his groin.

"You have some other place that grows hard? You have kept the secret from me well, husband."

"No," he said and grabbed his belly with his hands. "This grows fleshy."

She turned onto her back and assumed the same position that he was in. She looked at the protruding roundness of her own belly. Joshua looked at her as well. His face

166

went blank for a second, then he turned to her in shock.

"I was trying to remember when you had the flow last. You're pregnant, aren't you?"

"I think so. My mother claims it must be so. Your mother already picks names."

He reached over and touched her belly with an awe-inspired reverence. Then he leaned down and kissed her belly.

"You will be a happy father?" she asked him.

"I will be happy to be a father and a happy father both."

She looked away in mock anger. "You make my English seem funny."

"It requires no effort on my part at all." He laughed. "I am sorry," he said to her finally. "You have made me very happy. In fact, I grow impatient. I want to meet this new person." He bent forward and put his ear to her naked stomach.

"Hello in there," he said, "this is your father speaking. I have just found out about you. How are you doing?" He listened. "No answer," he said, looking up at his wife. "The child probably only speaks Assiniboine."

She laughed. "That is better than letting him speak Rainbow English."

He kissed her on the mouth and then lay back down next to her. A frown crossed his face. He looked at her, trying to frame his question but not entirely sure how to say it. Finally he blurted it out.

"Does this mean we have to stop doing it?"

"I asked my mother that too. She said there are ways and things a woman can do to amuse her husband."

Joshua placed his arms behind his head and sighed. "Well," he smiled, "I am waiting to be amused."

Rainbow ignored him and continued speaking, "And she said that there are things that a man may do to please his wife."

"Really, what?"

Rainbow giggled. "I can't say it out loud."

"No one can hear you but me."

"I don't care."

"I tell you what: Whisper it in my ear," he said illogically.

She leaned over and whispered to him.

"Are you sure?" he asked, a look of shock on his face. He lay back, staring at the roof of the tipi, and then without looking at her he blurted it out. "You want to try that?"

She nodded. They hugged each other and they began their experiment.

Spring came late to the prairies and even later in the shade of the spruces. And with it Rainbow and Joshua's idyll drew to an end.

Rainbow had built their honeymoon lodge close to their cherished spot near the creek. But the melting snows combined with rain to force the creek level higher. Joshua helped Rainbow dismantle their home before the river came up over its banks. Eagle Face allowed them to use his ponies to pull their lodge poles and their belongings away from the creek bank to higher ground where the entire encampment had wintered. Rainbow rebuilt their home up the slope from her mother's lodge and the tipi of Medicine Cow Lady.

When he returned to the main encampment, Joshua was surprised to see how Eagle Face had aged. He knew the man was old, but now his face had a grayish cast and his shoulders seemed more stooped than ever, as if the weight of the knowledge of what had really befallen Swift Bear and Big Elk was bearing down on him and would eventually break him. The three of them told no one at all—not even Crooked Bow, the war leader, not even Medicine Cow Lady, mother of them all. It was a heavy burden.

With the coming of spring the men began to congregate before each other's tipis and make plans for the spring and summer war parties. Some wanted to ride against the Peigan and drive them from the spruce forest. Others talked of raids on the Cree. Crooked Bow wished to see the lands of the whites and Métis near the Red River, especially once they received word that the whites and Métis were out on the prairie hunting the buffalo herd.

Medicine Cow Lady was consulted on all these plans.

She suggested that the men concentrate on the great hunt within the forest for deer so that all of the encampment could feast on venison for the summer. The meat would be dried into a venison pemmican for the winter. She also suggested that the women clear some meadow land and once again plant their seed corn. The men, without any resolution of their plans, immediately began making weapons both for war and for the hunt. The women went into the fields.

Joshua insisted that his wife remain in her lodge. Her belly had grown large, and he was certain that she would do great harm to herself and to their child if she had to do manual labor. Her mother disagreed and went through the camp denouncing her son-in-law for his strange ways.

Crooked Bow next announced his intention of leading a party of hunters to look for buffalo. Eagle Face disagreed and tried to dissuade him from entering the prairie. So vehement was Eagle Face that Joshua came to realize that the old man had actually convinced himself that it was venturing onto the prairies that had brought about the deaths of Swift Bear and Big Elk. He had told the lie so often that he had come to believe it himself.

Crooked Bow relented. His men continued to sit about and prepare themselves, although most were not sure for what. Already the women were beginning to make remarks about the length of this year's winter. Would it last to the season of the hot suns, they called out. Surely nothing but the length of the cold winter could keep their men sitting idle in the lodges of their wives. On their way to the cornfields that lay between the encampment and the river, the women began to make a ritual of calling out to the idlers, giving them female names and asking them to join them in the planting.

The men grew angry and looked to Crooked Bow. But deep inside, Crooked Bow feared going against the advice of Medicine Cow Lady and the elder of the tribe, Eagle Face. Joshua, much to his surprise, had discovered that Crooked Bow was a mild and gentle man.

One day Joshua sat before his tipi in the warm sun trying to make himself a proper bow. Eagle Face, who claimed to be the best bowman in the entire Assiniboine nation, had promised to teach him how to use it. He had worked on the wood for days now and still he could not see the shape of a bow coming from it. Rainbow sat inside. She busied herself with putting together things she would need for when the baby came. She sang a strange song in the minor tones that her people loved so much. Despite the unhappiness of the tone, he could tell from the rhythmic beat of the song and the few words of Assiniboine he now spoke that she was happy.

Joshua looked up from his work and saw Crooked Bow approaching.

"Is Eagle Face with you?" he asked.

Joshua pointed at the old man who trudged up the slope from Medicine Cow Lady's lodge to where they sat.

"My friend," Eagle Face greeted him, "you have come to argue with me again?"

The old man froze in his tracks. A scream pierced the quiet of the spring morning. There were several musket shots, more screaming, and then war whoops. They came from the cornfields.

Crooked Bow was on his feet instantly. He ran back toward his lodge. Joshua could hear the thunder of horses charging toward them. He darted back into his lodge. He yelled at Rainbow to get down. He grabbed the lance that Eagle Face had given him and he slipped his razor-sharp hunting knife into his belt. He saw horses ride past the flap of his lodge. Rainbow was terrified. She had fallen into the softness of their bed and had not moved.

"It is the Peigan avenging last fall's raid," she whispered. "Have you seen my mother or my father?"

Joshua ignored her questions. He moved cautiously toward the entryway. A war-painted Indian barged in. Joshua thrust forward with the lance. It entered the Indian's chest and pierced his heart. The thought crossed his mind that he had just killed a man and that he should be shocked by it but he was not. He would kill anyone who entered his lodge and threatened the woman he loved and the child she carried within her.

He picked up the musket the Indian had carried into

the lodge with him. He checked it. It was loaded. He heard some shooting on the other side of the encampment and he could smell smoke. He stuck his head outside. The Peigans had ridden through the village. They would already have the horse herd that some boys were watching by the river just below the cornfields.

Several Assiniboine men who had kept their favorite horses staked near their lodges were mounted. Joshua could see Crooked Bow's gelding and Eagle Face's stallion, their owners astride them, amid the confusion of horses and men swinging clubs at each other at the far end of the encampment.

Joshua looked down the slope toward his mother's lodge. It had been overturned. He ran down the slope. He found her trying to sit up amid the wreckage of her belongings. He pulled her to her feet and helped her back to his own lodge. He called to Rainbow.

"Hurry," he yelled at her. "I want you and Mother to be in the woods behind us before the battle swings back this way."

Rainbow, her face expressing sheer terror, came running as fast as she could from the lodge. Joshua grabbed her arm and pulled both her and his mother toward the cover of a thicket of young evergreens.

"Stay with us," Rainbow called out once she was safely hidden.

Joshua looked at his mother's face. It was clear she was fighting her own emotions.

"Fight for my people," she said finally.

Joshua nodded.

Rainbow called out to him, but he ignored her and ran the few steps back toward the encampment. A few tipis were already ablaze. Riderless horses ran amok through the village. Joshua saw Crooked Bow's gelding—rather Jamie McAlistair's gelding—standing with no rider. Joshua ran to it and swung up onto its back. The horse seemed almost to welcome his presence.

Joshua kneed the gelding's side and turned its head toward the end of the camp. The Assiniboine were being driven back by the far more numerous Peigans. Joshua was sure that far more warriors were here than could have been supplied by the village they had raided in the fall. The Peigans had sought aid from other bands of their own people.

He swerved to the right as a Peigan thrust his lance at him. It missed him, and Joshua charged right past his assailant. He saw Crooked Bow on foot fighting off about six Peigan warriors. It was clear they did not wish to kill, only to humiliate by counting coup endlessly.

Joshua aimed his musket at one of the tormentors. The Peigan's lance flew wildly up into the air as the lead ball pierced his back.

The gelding crashed into Peigan ponies, knocking two of them off their feet. Joshua used the musket as a club and swung wildly. He cracked the skull of one Peigan. The last tormentor had had enough. He pulled on the reins, turned his horse's head, and raced away from the battle.

Joshua reached down and pulled Crooked Bow up behind him on the gelding. The war leader patted his shoulder to acknowledge his appreciation for his assistance, but Joshua had already turned the horse back toward the fighting. The Peigans had driven the Assiniboine back in the direction of his lodge. He urged the gelding in that direction.

Suddenly he felt Crooked Bow stiffen behind him. The Assiniboine let out a low cry and slipped from the back of the gelding, a Peigan arrow protruding from his back.

It flashed through Joshua's mind that Crooked Bow had shielded him and that had he let him alone Crooked Bow probably would have survived. But Joshua had no time for regrets. He had to keep moving. He again charged the gelding into the Peigans. A warrior in front of him swung a war club, but he gasped as blood gushed from his mouth when an arrow entered his throat. Joshua twisted about when he felt someone else jump onto the gelding's back. The Peigan's face was painted in black and his eyes were outlined in red. He grabbed Joshua about the throat. His knife was out and he was ready to draw it across Joshua's throat. But he too slumped and fell off, the victim of a second Assiniboine arrow.

172

Both sides were taking losses. This was not a normal horse-stealing raid. Instead, both sides were satisfying long-standing blood lusts against each other. Finally the Peigan leader called his warriors away from the Assiniboine.

Joshua looked about him. There were only ten or twelve men of his encampment still ready to fight. He did not know if the others were dead or had run away. He still saw no sign of Eagle Face. A Peigan rode out from among thirty to forty men who faced the Assiniboine dozen. He called to them in their language.

"We end this fight, Assiniboine. There are a few of you left to remember us. We have taken your horses and your women. We leave you to each other like the man-buggers you are. Maybe now you will remember who your betters are and you will leave here and stay away forever from the sacred woods of the Peigan." He said no more—ever again. The twang of a bow was heard from the woods to the speaker's left, followed almost instantly by the thud of an arrow slashing into the Peigan speaker's chest, ending his speech.

Several of the younger Peigan warriors screamed in anger and started to charge forward, but their leader held them in check. What the speaker had said still held. The Peigans whirled their horses around and left to join those in their war party who had been given the task of taking the women and the horses. The battle had ended as quickly as it had begun. Only the crackling of burning tipis broke the silence. Then several of the Assiniboine began a wailing—a dirge.

Joshua kicked the gelding into motion. He rode anxiously back to where he had left his wife and his mother.

Elizabeth came out of the bushes holding Rainbow's hand. She looked about her in dismay. Within minutes the whole last decade of her life had been destroyed. Her people had been overwhelmed, scattered. She counted the dead with her eyes—well over two-thirds of the men of the encampment lay motionless in the dirt, and all the women were taken. They would be raped and eventually adopted by their captors. In time, they would lose their identity as Assiniboine while living in Peigan villages across the plains country.

There was nothing left. The surviving men sat dazed in a group singing a death song for their people.

Rainbow sat on the ground and began to weep. She could not see her father anywhere and she knew her mother's fate.

Joshua dismounted. He placed one hand on Elizabeth's shoulder and raised Rainbow off the ground with his other.

"Start to pack our things," he ordered. "We have had some small good fortune amid all this grief. We have not been burned out. Our possessions are intact. We have a good horse and there are some ponies running loose in the camp that we can take. Their owners will not need them any longer."

"Do we search for more of our people? We can find friendly bands of Assiniboine and wreak our revenge on the Peigans," Rainbow said.

"I will not go back onto the prairie and face mu-dra," Elizabeth said, shivering with fright.

"That is Medicine Cow Lady speaking," Joshua observed. "Not my mother, Elizabeth Stoddard Miller. She does not believe in mu-dra. What does that word mean in Assiniboine?"

Elizabeth looked at him. "It is not an Indian word. It is English. It is the Indian way of saying the word *murder*."

"And that's just what it is. I don't know who is doing the killing, but it is a who, a real person—a violent sick person, but a person nevertheless. Although Medicine Cow Lady must fear the spirit, Elizabeth Stoddard Miller must fight the person who kills in the night like the sick coward he is. No, Rainbow, we don't seek more Assiniboine. I want to take you to the land of the whites on the Red River."

Her eyes, which had been filled with grief, suddenly brightened. He realized she was looking past him and smiling.

Joshua turned. He saw the black stallion coming up the slope. Eagle Face, his bow swung across his back, rode

174

proudly. Behind him, and holding onto him with all her strength, was Eagle Face's Wife.

"Where were you? We thought you had died," Rainbow cried out in relief.

"Not dead, daughter. I covered the back of your man. Twice I saved him with my arrows. Then when the Peigan who spoke our language insulted our people, I sent him to the funeral platform. Only then did I go looking for your mother. She is such a good lay, the Peigan who took her could not wait. He tried to take her right in the cornfields."

The older woman blushed as her husband told her story. Then she brandished a Peigan scalp.

"Eagle Face's Wife has taken her first hair," the old warrior called out in pride. "From now on I shall call her by a new name. Now she is known to me as Warrior Woman."

The two old Assiniboine dismounted and looked about the camp. Their lodge had been destroyed. Eagle Face began to weep when the enormity of what had happened struck him. The band with which he had grown to manhood, the band with which he had become an old man, was no more. He would not die here as he had planned. The band was gone before his time had come. His tears were bitter and he cursed the Peigan's revenge.

"I want us to go live among the whites at Red River," Joshua said.

Eagle Face thought for a moment. "Perhaps that is best for you," he said. "Among the whites you may be safe from mu-dra."

"You must come with us, Father," Rainbow exclaimed.

Joshua could almost hear the grief in her voice at the thought of leaving her parents.

A group of seven of the remaining warriors had rounded up the ponies for themselves. They rode to within ten feet of Eagle Face.

"Old man," said one of the warriors; he was no more than a teen-ager. "It is our decision to form a new band. We will raid the Cree or the Blood." He looked at Joshua defiantly. "Maybe even the Métis or the whites. We will

175

get our own women. And when we are strong enough, we will come back and punish the Peigan for what they have done to our Assiniboine people. You are the last of the old men. We will take you and your women with us, but we wish no more of the medicine of the white witch." He said this last pointing at Elizabeth.

"I will not become a renegade—a man without a tribe," said Eagle Face.

"Neither shall we. We are Assiniboine," said the teen-ager.

Eagle Face sighed. He tried to reason with the youth. "If you are of the people then you will go find more of your kind and live with them. You must sit by the fire and hear the legends; you must know our history. Let the old teach the young. I go to find a new band, perhaps White Buffalo's band. This spring he camps on the Minnedosa. Warrior Woman and I go there."

"You are old. You could teach the young that the captured women will bear us," said another boy-warrior.

"Yes, I could, while their mothers whispered to them the tales of the Cree or the Blood. No, what you ask is too much. I go to look for White Buffalo's Assiniboine."

"Not only are you old, Eagle Face, I think you grow too old. Your stones have slipped up into your fat belly," said the first youth.

The old man glared at the teen-ager. "How many Peigan did you kill, Chipmunk?"

"You know my new name, old man."

"I do," he said, still ignoring the young warrior's manhood name. "But is there an answer to my question? I killed three today, and Warrior Woman, as I now call my wife, took the scalp of one who tried to rape her."

As if on command, the old woman raised her bloody hand and arm into the air, brandishing her trophy.

"I am sure all will go well for you as renegades," the old man said. "Unless, of course, you are confronted by mudra, and then all I can wish for you is that it be quick."

The fear that came into the eyes of all the young men was genuine. In their anguish and shame over the destruction of their people by the Peigans, they had forgotten the far greater danger.

176

"Mu-dra was made up by Medicine Cow Lady so that she might lord it over us," the boy asserted, but without much conviction. It was almost as if he hoped she would admit it and release his mind from the terror. But Eagle Face would not let it be.

"I have seen the work of mu-dra," he said. "Perhaps you have not. But if you go out into the prairie you will see it. I will tell you how to recognize him. The spirit must have teeth like hunting knives because he slices into the soft portions of the body, the belly in particular, the heart and the testicles and the breasts. But they do not even know what has happened to them because they die without terror in their eyes. Perhaps mu-dra kills only those who sleep. If you stay awake forever perhaps he will never touch you."

It was clear from the manner in which the others backed away from Chipmunk that they had abandoned his idea and turned to Eagle Face to lead them.

"We will be safe with White Buffalo," said Eagle Face. "He will protect us and help us plan to regain our women and our pride from the Peigans."

Elizabeth had listened to the debate in silence. When Eagle Face had finished, she touched his arm. "Good-bye, old man," she said.

Rainbow rushed into her mother's arms.

"It is not forever," the old man replied. "You will know where we are camped. We will never again know the peace of the years of your medicine," he said to Elizabeth.

She touched her cheek to his, then drew back from him, wiping tears from her eyes.

They parted in three groups. Chipmunk and three warriors who had not listened to Eagle Face's warning left first. They traveled light, carrying only their weapons, bedrolls, and enough pemmican to last them two weeks. They would be marauders on the open plains, a danger to anyone who came near them. They would attack without provocation, looking for women who would make lodges for them.

Eagle Face, his wife, and nine more young men carried their lodge poles and skins in travois tied to the backs of their ponies. The old man was dressed in the best clothing he could put together from the scattered lodges. He would come as a beggar to White Buffalo, but he must not look like one.

Rainbow had said tearful farewells to her parents. But now she stood, dry-eyed, as her father, splendidly feathered and mounted on the stallion that was his greatest pride, haughtily ordered his warriors to mount. Warrior Woman rode her own pony and pranced about scolding the young men for not knowing how to pack and load a travois.

Joshua, Elizabeth, and Rainbow watched the small party move through the recently planted cornfield. Rainbow waved at the disappearing back of her mother. Eagle Face signaled them to cross the river and enter the woods on the far side. He would ride due north to seek out more bands of his own people.

Joshua put his arm around his wife. "You'll see them again," he promised. "We will bring our baby to them to seek their blessings."

Elizabeth sighed as her friends were lost from sight.

"We have work to do." She began immediately to pack her own belongings on their travois. They would take one lodge and bedding for the three of them. Elizabeth would ride the travois pony and Rainbow another pony. Joshua rode the gelding, once again his after six months in Crooked Bow's possession. He turned to the east, following the course of the Assiniboine River out of the spruce forest and back into the open prairie.

VIII

Spring 1842

The rolling grasslands seemed to stretch on unbroken forever. Joshua felt a sense of freedom to be away from the confinement of the forest. He could see it in Elizabeth's face as well. Rainbow knew only terror.

Joshua and she rode together, with Elizabeth bringing up the rear. They made good progress those first days. They camped at the bend of the river where it turned to the north to begin its great arc before descending to the south and joining the Red. Tomorrow they would leave the river and travel due east to Fort Garry—about sixty miles. Joshua wanted to make the journey in one day, but he was not sure Rainbow could take a sixty-mile journey on horseback over unbroken countryside.

They ate pemmican in silence by the riverbank. No one suggested lighting a fire, and as soon as the dark descended they crawled into their bedding and waited for sleep to come. Joshua knew he should be posting a watch, but he was the only possible one. He knew his mother was capable, but Rainbow was not. A two-person shift would leave the two guards as weary as the pregnant girl and would slow their progress. They would all sleep.

Rainbow called to him before she fell asleep. He reached over and touched her. She asked him to join her. He rolled out of his bedding and snuggled close to her while she covered him with her fur.

"There is very little room for three of us in this bed," he teased her.

"I'm frightened, Joshua," she whimpered. "Please don't

179

tease me. I've never been on the prairies like this and I am afraid of mu-dra."

He wrapped his arms about her as closely as he could. "I will give you pleasure, if you wish it," she said.

"You give me pleasure just like this," he whispered to her. "Go to sleep."

She turned over and he snuggled his front comfortably into her back. He reached around and began stroking her breast. She sighed and then was silent. Before long he could feel the rhythmic breathing that told him she had fallen off to sleep. He was glad. She would need to be rested for tomorrow's ride. He heard a wolf howling at the moon. It sounded miles away. And then he too fell asleep.

The next day, they started riding at dawn into the rising sun. Joshua watched the look of pain grow on Rainbow's face. Elizabeth, on the other hand, seemed to blossom the longer she was in the saddle. Despite all the honor and wealth the Assiniboine had given her, she had been a prisoner among them. They had never let her out of their sight. Now she was free again. She longed to race ahead and once again feel the wind in her hair, but she knew she could not and so she continued to ride the plodding travois pony.

The sun grew hotter as it rose in the sky toward midday. Joshua checked Rainbow continually for signs of fatigue. Once, as he searched her face, he saw her lifting her nose into the air as if trying to identify some smell.

"All right," he confessed, "it's been two days since I have been able to wash. I am sensitive to the whole thing, but there is very little I can do about it."

She laughed at him. "I do not tease you, husband. It is not you who smells—this time. It is a strange smell but I have smelled it before."

Joshua sniffed the wind. He could detect nothing. They continued to ride east and Rainbow continued to complain of the smell. Finally Elizabeth agreed. There was a sweetish yet foul smell in the air. The wind came from the east and the smell was being blown directly toward them.

"In that case," said Joshua, "if we just keep forward we will soon discover what causes it."

"It smells like old buffalo meat that wasn't cured properly," said Elizabeth finally.

It was spring, Joshua thought, and they were within a day's ride of Fort Garry. Perhaps white or Métis hunters were out on the plains. Then he saw the birds circling in the sky. He remembered the last time he had seen that sight and suddenly he knew what the smell was. They rode to the top of the next hillock. Off on the flatland he could see ponies grazing not far from some bundles on the ground. There was movement among the bundles and then something rose and sailed into the sky. It was a buzzard.

Joshua halted the gelding. "Mother, you stay here with Rainbow," he ordered. He kicked the horse and it sprang forward. When he got closer he nearly gagged from the stench. They were boys, Indian boys, four of them. Their bodies were strewn all over the grass. Joshua covered his mouth and nose with his hand. The stench was overwhelming. The bodies were bloated and infested with ants. Joshua could not recognize their faces but he knew the ponies. It was Chipmunk and his companions. They could only have been dead for thirty-six hours at the most. But the heat was intense and they had been disemboweled and mutilated beyond recognition.

These boys would have been Rainbow's playmates as a child. He had no intention of telling her what he had found. One of the boys had had a musket. Joshua retrieved it. He rounded up the ponies and left the bodies of the young men to the birds and wild animals. He could not dig graves for them all and still make it safely to Fort Garry. He led the ponies back to where Elizabeth and Rainbow awaited him.

"A war party," he said. "They look like Peigans."

Elizabeth recognized the ponies instantly. She knew that Rainbow did as well. But it suited both of them to go along with Joshua's fabrication—Rainbow because if she did not, terror would blot out her sanity, and Elizabeth because it offended the Assiniboine part of her to leave "her children" unburied on the prairies.

They rode on. The terrain began to seem familiar to Elizabeth even after an absence of twenty years. The sun started its downward course and the air cooled. This far north the spring days were long, and they had extra hours of daylight to assist them. Just before sunset they arrived at the top of a large slope. Stretched out ahead of them was the land of the Red River rising from the territory south of the border and flowing into Lake Winnipeg. Like a little blot on the horizon where the Assiniboine River came down to join the Red was Fort Garry.

Joshua turned to the north. They forded the Assiniboine with a great deal of effort and finally were on the last leg of their journey to the McAlistair farm.

When they arrived within hail of the farm, Joshua boomed a loud call for Jamie. Although smoke came from the chimney of the house, there was no response at first. Finally the front door opened and Cree Woman, carrying a musket, appeared in the doorway.

"Cree Woman," Joshua hailed. The Indian woman studied them carefully. They looked like three Indians and she could easily identify them as Assiniboine, not always on friendly terms with her people. Then she recognized the gelding and Joshua. She waved to him. She was overjoyed to see him. She stared at the two women. One of them struck her as familiar. It was the way she rode. She seemed to dominate the pony. And then she remembered. That was the way Elizabeth sat a horse. Joshua had found his mother. The joy rose within her. She fired the musket into the air. Elizabeth leapt from her pony and embraced Cree Woman. Both of them began to cry. Rainbow hung back until Joshua pushed her gently in front of him.

"Cree Woman, this is my wife, Rainbow, daughter of Eagle Face of the Assiniboine." Then he patted her belly. "And this is our Assiniboine-speaking child, as yet without name."

Cree Woman smiled and embraced the girl. Then she turned to Elizabeth.

"It is like someone from the past coming back to life to see you again, pretty one. It reminds me of Rowand, my first husband, and my babies. Tell me how it is that you return to us. But first come to my house. We must feast."

Elizabeth smiled. "And Jamie?"

"Oh, he will be delighted to see you. He is off with the hunters. You remember the spring buffalo hunt."

"How could any of us forget it," Elizabeth responded. "So much suffering."

"I refuse to go with him. I may be the best skinner of hides in all of Rupert's Land but I will not return to the graves of my children until I join them. And you, Joshua, that was a long ride into the prairie."

He laughed aloud.

"And my husband will be glad to see the return of his favorite horse. And look at the ponies. By the standard of an Indian brave you are a wealthy man, Joshua. You left our home on a borrowed horse, not even taking your musket, and you return with your mother, a pregnant wife, and six more horses."

Joshua looked at the ground. He did not wish to tell her that they were the two surviving remants of a once proud and prosperous Assiniboine encampment.

She brought the women into her house while Joshua unloaded their things and stabled the horses.

"I have some bread baking and some honey." She produced a bottle of whiskey from the wall cabinet. "And I have so much to show you. There are white men's writings that came here to us from the fort. I have opened them but I cannot read them. You must read them for me."

Cree Woman busied herself about the hearth, dishing out plates of pemmican stew.

"I'm sorry," she apologized. "If you had returned a few days later Jamie would have returned with our fresh meat."

Joshua watched her in amazement. She was almost gleeful and had said more in the past ten minutes than she had spoken in all the time he had been with her and Jamie.

Joshua looked down at the first letter. It was from Michael Brant, addressed to him at Detroit and dated two years ago from Boston.

"It's from your brother," he said to his mother.

Elizabeth slipped behind his stool to read over his shoulder. To her shock she could barely see the page. Her

183

eyesight had weakened and she had not noticed it. Now she understood the difficulty she had in threading her needle recently.

Joshua read in silence.

"Read aloud," Elizabeth said.

Joshua looked up at her.

"For the sake of the others," she explained.

Dear Joshua:

I hope this letter reaches you. The latest I received from my mother said you were trapping in Michigan. I assume that if you are reading these words you have come back to Detroit.

I am living in the Breed mansion in the village of Charleston near Boston. It was made available to me by family—your Aunt Margaret. She is now the most proper lady in Boston society, also cultured and very wealthy. She owns this house but will not come near it. I enjoy being here. The whole family began here. Although the architects of Boston tell me this is not the original eighteenth-century house, nevertheless, I feel the presence of our ancestors all about me. Here Sarah Nowell gave birth to Stephen Nowell. He was my grandfather and your great-grandfather. I visited the Charleston burial yard and saw the tomb of Jonathan Breed, my great-great-grandfather. It says he was born in 1675. Can you imagine back that far? I have been puzzled by two graves with the same name, Matthew Nowell, one dated 1766 as a birthdate and 1775 as his death date. And then there is another Matthew Nowell, a much newer headstone with the same name birthdate 1766 and a death date of 1812. Cousin Margaret will not talk about Matthew Nowell (The one who died in the last war—1812). We all knew about some scandal there. And she would not explain the earlier stone. She merely deepened the mystery by saying "he should have stayed dead."

I have broken with Will Mackenzie. Even now he sends raiding parties of Irish rowdies across the lakes to damage our beloved homeland. He must be made to stop. Until he does, men like myself, who joined the rebellion reluctantly and who long to return home in peace, will be kept in exile. Boston treats me well but the Nowells, Brants, and Millers made their choice of a home almost three score years ago and I want to return there.

I have asked Willie Mackay to become my wife. She has lived with me here on Breed's hill since I arrived. She has been mistress of this household and companion to me in my loneliness. I know she loves me but it is the love she transferred from her dead father. I am an innocent in matters of the heart but I am no fool. I know also that she will always be deeply in love with you. Even when you were children she loved you. That will surprise you because she expressed her love by throwing green apples at you. But for a child there is no more appropriate way to show affection than to shower you with green apples. I love her, she loves you. I envy you. By the time you will have read this she will be my wife and true mistress of this house. I will do everything I can to make her as happy as I know you would have.

Your Uncle, Michael Brant

Joshua looked up from the letter in amazement. Willie Mackay loved him. That was indeed difficult to believe. Elizabeth was crying softly. But Rainbow had a mean-looking scowl on her face.

"Who is this Will-ie?" she asked.

Joshua looked uncomfortable under her glare. Then he started to laugh.

"Well, if you must know, my pretty, the only other girl I knew in my youth whom I loved is now my stepmother. You see, Rainbow, I was always intended for you and no one else."

She relaxed slightly, but she did not like the sound of his laugh. There was a tinge of bitterness in it that frightened her.

Joshua picked up the second letter. He could barely make out the script. It was faded and the paper was worn and dirty. "It's addressed to Jamie McAlistair. My God, it's six years old!"

He started to read aloud. "From Edmonton House on the North Saskatchewan to Fort Garry."

I am safe and living at this piss pot fort. Sometimes in a loge of one of the fort squaws sometimes in the jale, when I get drunk. Kis Kre Woman for me. I hope you have many babes and that you call a girl Elizabeth.
Your friend, Stephen Miller

Elizabeth reached down and took the letter from Joshua and pressed it against her lips. Cree Woman had stopped working as she listened to Joshua read. Her face lit up with a smile.

"Elizabeth, both of you have returned from the dead and in the same day. I cannot believe this. I am so happy. This must be the best meal we have ever eaten together."

She opened her stove and reached into it with a large flat-bladed skinning knife. She pulled out a loaf of wheat bread and then a second. The cabin was filled with the delicious smell of baked bread. She uncorked a bottle and poured four cups of whiskey.

"At last we are almost together again. We lived here in this home in happiness. Terror struck at us but we survived—you, Stephen, Joshua, Jamie, and myself. We were the ones who lived. Soon we will all be together again. Stephen lives. We must bring him back. Jamie will do it. I will ask him."

Cree Woman sliced the bread neatly with her knife. Then she put out the bowls of stew. The travelers were hungry and Cree Woman refilled Elizabeth and Rainbow's bowls. Joshua ate even more.

Darkness had settled upon them much earlier. Cree Woman set candles out on the table. It was an extravangance, but it was a special occasion.

Joshua could see Rainbow's eyelids getting droopy.

"I am going to let you and Cree Woman reminisce, Mother," he said, "but my wife is exhausted and I'm going to put her to bed. May we use the loft?" he asked.

Cree Woman nodded. She went over to Rainbow and touched her cheek with her own.

"Good-night, child," she said.

Elizabeth smiled at her daughter-in-law and wished her a good-night as well. The two women intended to sit up far into the night talking.

Joshua helped Rainbow climb the ladder to the loft. He had hauled their favorite wolfskin up behind him. He found his bedding of six months ago untouched. He spread out the skin and then helped her to lie down. He took off his clothes and dropped down beside her. She whispered in his ear.

"Did you love the girl in the letter?" she asked him.

"No," he whispered back to her.

"Good," she responded. "Did you ever love anyone other than me?"

He did not respond immediately. God knows he thought he had loved Allison Winslow, and if love was the feeling of your stomach turning over every time the girl looked at you, then certainly he had loved her.

"No," he said. "I have never loved anyone but you." And he knew he spoke the truth.

The morning seemed to come upon them so quickly. Joshua heard Cree Woman at the stove. She hummed an Indian song to herself. Rainbow still slept the deep sleep of the exhausted, and Joshua decided to let her sleep on.

He climbed down the ladder. "Where is my mother?" he asked Cree Woman.

"Oh, she could not resist going back to the farm. She is walking along the river. There is nothing there anymore. I told her, but she wanted to go anyway."

Joshua was nervous about letting her roam alone.

Cree Woman picked up his tension. "Your mother shoots better than any man I know and she can take care of herself. She always could. Did she not survive twenty years on the prairie without your help?"

Joshua relaxed. "Nevertheless," he said, "I'm going to find her. I think I would like to see her farm. Was I born there?"

"No, here in this house. The Métis had burned out your parents' house and Jamie's house. They came here for refuge."

Joshua stepped out into the morning. The air was brisk. He could see his own breath. Across the river the sun poked its head above the hills and turned the waters of the river the color of its name, red.

He went to the barn and let out two of the ponies after feeding them. He hopped on the back of the one and led the other. He allowed the horse to move at a slow pace along the riverbank.

He found Elizabeth sitting on the grass in front of a mound of dirt. There were some heavy wooden beams protruding through the grass that covered the mound. She looked up when she heard him coming.

"This was my home. Your uncle and I lived here."

He dismounted and sat down beside her. "Not much left, is there?"

She shook her head. "But, Joshua, he is alive and I am free to go to him. Cree Woman and I spoke of it in the night. Jamie will give me the gelding and I will ride west along the Saskatchewan until I reach Fort Edmonton."

"How far?" he asked.

"I don't know. Cree Woman says maybe a month's journey by horse going at a steady but not fast pace."

"Mother, the letter was six years old. Even then he did not sound like he was living the kind of life that leads to a healthy old age. My God, I don't want to deprive you of hope, but I don't think you can make a journey of what sounds like eight hundred to a thousand miles on the basis of a letter that is six years old."

"I am going to find him, Joshua. So help me God. If he is alive, I am going to find him."

She rose and walked over to the ruins of their house. She placed her hand on one of the protruding beams and was lost in thought.

The pony Joshua had brought for her snorted. She turned and smiled at her son. She climbed up onto the pony's back.

"I'd like to ride south before we return to Cree Woman's

elaborate breakfast. I'd like to see the old McAlistair homestead too."

The two of them rode a few hundred yards south upriver. The ruins of the McAlistair farmhouse still stood. It was sagging in the front, and some of the outside walls had collapsed and burned, but the roof almost looked as if it had been repaired.

Elizabeth dismounted in front of the ruins. The door to the cabin was missing. Joshua dismounted and waited for her. She walked through the empty doorway and disappeared into the gloom.

"Joshua, come in here," she called nervously.

He moved swiftly through the doorway. She stood in the center of the room. Sunlight beamed through some holes in the roof and more of it poured through the holes in the walls that had once been windows. In the far corner was what was left of an old bed and mattress. It had been burned years before but there were rags on the bed, men's clothing and an ancient gingham dress. In the corner on the floor some dolls were carefully arranged, and in the other corner there was a wooden top, a little boy's toy. The whole room was free of dust and dirt.

"This is very strange," Elizabeth said. "Someone has arranged these things. Someone comes here and tries to make it like it was."

Elizabeth said someone, but they both knew she meant Jamie. "He was young when it happened. When Chris Douglas..." she had some difficulty mentioning his name, "when he and his Métis henchmen came here and murdered the whole McAlistair family, all but Jamie. He was so young, but he suffered. This is a private place, Joshua, we should not be here."

Suddenly the sun that poured through the doorway was cut off. Joshua turned and made out the form of a person outlined by the bright sun behind them.

Elizabeth gasped.

"This is my husband's place," Cree Woman spoke.

Both Joshua and Elizabeth relaxed and breathed easier.

"He comes here often to be alone. I have never been here before. I do not wish to invade his private world. Let us go home for breakfast. Joshua, your woman longs for you. She is awake and misses you."

Cree Woman had made enough corn bread to feed a war party. It was still warm, and Joshua poured liquid honey over it and allowed it to seep into the yellow cornmeal. He ate enormous quantities of it. Rainbow shook her head in disbelief at his appetite.

"I am the one who is feeding a little one inside me. I should be eating for two but Joshua eats as if he ate for four."

He started to laugh but his mouth was filled with the bread.

"You're going to choke, Joshua, if you keep stuffing your face."

Finally he pushed his chair away from the breakfast table. "Enough," he said to Cree Woman, who cut him piece after piece of the bread, gleefully watching it disappear into him.

"I wish Jamie had your appetite," she said. "He is so skinny now. As a boy he showed promise of being a man with large muscles, but it did not happen. He slimmed down and has remained wiry ever since."

She reached up to the shelf above where she kept her earthen jug of honey. She stopped and stared.

"I had almost forgotten. I have another long-lost item to give you. Jamie found it out on the prairies long after you had disappeared. He found it in the possession of a dead Assiniboine."

She held the Nowell locket in her hand.

Joshua stopped chewing his food.

"But how?" asked Rainbow.

Elizabeth placed her finger on the girl's lips.

The three of them stared at Cree Woman. The full implication of what she showed them sank in.

"Mu-dra," Elizabeth mumbled. "My God, how else? Jamie—poor Jamie."

"What is it?" Cree Woman looked at their shocked faces.

"It's nothing," said Joshua, rising and walking over to her. He took the locket in his hand. He had never seen

Swift Bear wear the locket, but it was a prized possession. He would never have lost it. Whoever had it would have had to take it from Swift Bear, and whoever took it from Swift Bear was the murderer, the night stalker of the innocent and guilty alike—a homicidal maniac.

Joshua thought back to the first time he had seen the victims of mu-dra. But Jamie had been with him all the time. Then he remembered that Jamie had slipped away at night and returned struggling with the buttons of his pants. Was his call of nature a charade played out to convince an easily fooled boy? It had to be. He felt sick. He looked at the locket in his hand. The vague outline of the gothic *N* could still be seen if held up to the light. The chain was broken and so he slipped it into his pocket.

"Thank you, Cree Woman," he said and returned to the table. He caught Elizabeth's eye. "I need to walk off that breakfast," he exclaimed. "Rainbow, how about a little exercise. We'll check on the horses and then take a walk." He took her by the hand and led her out of the house to the barn.

"What has happened, Joshua? That white man's metal, Swift Bear took it from you. How could this Jamie, the husband of Cree Woman, get it?"

"I think he took it from Swift Bear," Joshua said.

The full import of what she said hit her. She gasped. She had seen Swift Bear. She had seen what mu-dra had done to him. It meant that mu-dra was a man—Cree Woman's man. She grabbed Joshua in fear. He held her tightly in his arms.

Elizabeth entered the barn. "We must act swiftly. Cree Woman is no fool. She knows we have all been shocked by the locket. She knows something is very wrong. We must make our decisions quickly."

Joshua was at a loss. His idea of coming back to the white settlement had backfired.

"We could confront Jamie," Elizabeth continued, "with what we know. He could deny it or he might simply kill. From what I saw at his old family homestead this morning and from what I know he is capable of, I know he is the murderer of the prairies, the mu-dra. He is beyond our

191

power to stop. Joshua, you are a brave and strong young man. You are my son. You are no match for Jamie McAlistair. The man is obviously dangerous. I think we must leave here."

"To go where? Rainbow is seven months pregnant at least. She is in no condition to ride."

"We are in grave danger, Joshua," the Indian girl said. "My baby is threatened. Jamie will kill me and spill my unborn child, our unborn child, out onto the ground. I will make myself ready to travel."

"Good," said Elizabeth. "It is decided, then. We go west. We will find Eagle Face and then I will go on to Fort Edmonton. Joshua, we travel light and we travel immediately. Tell Cree Woman we are riding to Fort Garry to seek news of the hunt. It can't last too much longer. Jamie will be home in a day, perhaps even less. Take some pemmican, take some bedding. We will ride the gelding and two of the ponies. The rest we leave behind in payment for what we have taken. Quickly now, we must hurry."

Cree Woman sat by her fire the whole of the night. She knew when they left that their story was a false one and that they never planned to return. She had been wrong to think of yesterday as the beginning of new times. Once again it was Jamie. He had brought her back from her death song so many years before on the prairies when she had finished burying her husband and children after the Métis had killed them. She had taught him to make love, and perhaps it was her punishment for not dying when she should have.

He had learned too well. He now made her do things in the bed to which no daughter of a Cree chief should have been submitted. They had no children by design. It was impossible to have children his way. And now after so many years with him, years of loneliness, years of pain, her friends of the past had returned. But Jamie had done something that caused them to flee in terror. She should have done the same. For the first time she realized how brutally the past had affected his mind.

Suddenly he stood in the open door looking at her.

"Who was here?" he asked without greeting.

"Joshua returned with his new wife and then left again."

His eyes darted about the cabin. He walked to the shelf and reached for the locket. "You gave it to him?"

She nodded. He smacked her in the face. She stood impassively.

"It was his, was it not?" she asked. "What did you do, Jamie? Did you kill for it?"

He smiled. "I kill constantly," he said. "I roam the prairies at night when I am away from you and your filthy Indian body and I cleanse the bodies of your people. I open their bowels and I let the air, the fresh night air of the plains, bathe them. I cleanse the filth of the men by taking away the possibility of their doing the dirty things that men want to do."

"I never knew. How could you have kept all of this from me and live with me? They were right to flee."

"There were three of them, Cree Woman. Who else was with Joshua?"

"An old lady, the girl's aunt," she replied. He stepped up to her and looked into her face. The mark of his hand was clearly visible on her cheek. He stared into her eyes.

"You're lying to me," he cried out, and struck her again.

He saw the look come into her eyes. He could beat her from now until morning and he would get nothing from her. He would try a different tactic. He went over to the bed and sat down upon it. He removed his boots and lay down. She turned her back on him and pretended to wash some dishes in the tub atop the stove.

"Woman," he called out, "I have a need for you."

She cringed. He was going to use her once again. She slipped the bread knife into the sleeve of her tunic. She could take no more of the humiliation. She walked mechanically to the bed. He had slipped out of his clothes and lay naked before her. How he had changed from the muscular, handsome boy to this sinewy, almost bony man. He pointed to his feet. "You may begin there," he said.

She was quick. The knife slipped from the sleeve into her hand and she plunged it downward. But it never made it to his heart. His hand caught her wrist in midair, snapping the bone as her force met his. She dropped the huge weapon on his chest. The point stabbed him lightly, drawing a small drop of blood to the surface.

He was in a rage. His face turned ghastly pale and his eyes seemed to register nothing, although they clearly saw. He took the knife and plunged it to the hilt in her belly. She screamed. It was as if her scream awoke him from a trance. He saw her staggering backwards.

"Cree Woman," he yelled in anguish when he saw her. He reached for her but she pulled away. She took the knife handle and pulled the blade from her stomach. She groaned and the blood rushed to soak the front of her tunic.

He caught her as she started to fall. He carried her to the bed.

"I am sorry," he said pathetically, like a boy who had just done something naughty. "I didn't mean it."

Her face looked peaceful. He placed his head down on her chest.

"Don't die, Cree Woman," he pleaded with her. "If you do I'll be alone. Who'll take care of me? They all die; they are all taken from me. You promised you wouldn't die out on the prairies that night I made you stop your death song."

Her lips moved. He bent down to hear her.

"Leave them be, Jamie. Joshua has found his mother. She looks for Stephen. They deserve peace together after all these years."

"I'll leave them be. But you must keep your promise to me and live."

She mumbled something he could not understand. Her eyes flashed open and looked into his tearful face.

"It is you who have killed me," she said almost as if startled by the truth of it. "You were the only one who could release me. You drew me from my death song. Now you allow me to renew it. Rowand, my husband, my babies—I join you. It has been so long. Mother has been held from you so long, my babies, my beloved."

Her eyes closed. Her lips moved. She was singing. It was a song he had heard once before.

She was leaving him. His rage returned. How dare she desert him? He stood and screamed at her not to leave him and to stop singing, but she could not hear him. He picked up the knife again. She would not sing her death song. She would not leave him. He plunged it into her heart.

Jamie stepped back from the bed. He dropped the knife on the floor. He looked in horror at what he had done. She was not like the others. They were Indians and Indians had killed his parents, his brother, his sisters. Indians had killed everyone he had loved. Indians had killed Ian Rowand and Elizabeth and Stephen and Joshua and Christopher Douglas and Père André. All of them had died at the hands of the Indians. Some had tried to fool him and to blame the Métis or even the whites. And some had even suggested that he was responsible, but he had seen them do it all. He had seen his little sisters clubbed, his brother's throat slit, and now the Indians had come here. They had found Elizabeth here. Elizabeth was the most beautiful woman he had ever seen, his friend Stephen Miller's wife. They had captured her. They would rape her and put their filthy seed in her body and blow up her belly again like it had been that first time. He hated women when they were large with child. He and Cree Woman would never have children. He would see to that.

He fell back against the chair and raised his hands to his face. They were covered with blood. He stared at them in horror and screamed. He ran to the bed again and called out her name. But she was dead.

"Cree Woman," he called out in anguish. But the Indians had been here already. They had killed her. He picked up the body from the bed. He was naked but he was unaware of it. He went out into the front yard and walked down to the edge of the Red River. He followed its silent twist past Stephen's farm until he came to the home of his mother and father. He walked up the path from the river toward the front door and carried his bride across the threshold. He had to find a place for her. Mum and Dad were in the bed. Maybe he should not disturb them. Andy played in the corner with his top. His sisters were fighting over who would get to play with which doll. His bed was in the loft. The ladder was broken. He took her to the only unoccupied corner and laid her down.

"Rest awhile, Cree Woman," he said softly to her. "I must find Stephen and Elizabeth."

IX

Spring and Summer 1842

They raced across the open prairie, following the north bank of the Assiniboine River. They stopped only twice to rest the horses. Sometime before dawn, they stopped to eat and sleep. They were somewhere west of the Métis settlement at Portage la Prairie.

Rainbow fell into a deep sleep. She had not complained the whole night. Joshua sat beside her, stroking her and looking down at her. Elizabeth walked over to him.

"Son," she said. Once again she seemed the shaman woman of the Assiniboine preparing to give orders. "We must have a plan."

"I have one. Get rid of Jamie McAlistair."

She shook her head in disagreement.

"I think I am more capable than you give me credit for."

"Perhaps you are, but I have little to go by. Please don't misunderstand me, Joshua. I know you are brave. I saw you in the fight with the Peigan."

He sat silently for some moments. "Do you have a plan?" he asked his mother.

"We must assume that Jamie will be able to track us. The trail of two Indian ponies in the company of a shod horse will not be hard to follow. We must stay ahead of him. It will be hard on Rainbow, but she is determined to keep up with us and not to hold us back. She too has much courage. Your child will be brave. We must make it as quickly as possible to White Buffalo's encampment on the Minnedosa. Once there we can turn Rainbow over to

Eagle Face and Warrior Woman. Then you and I will go on to Fort Edmonton."

Joshua looked at her as if she had gone mad. "I'm not leaving my wife. She is pregnant, about to give birth to my child. What kind of man do you think I am?"

"As I said, you are a brave man who needs to do what needs to be done to protect his wife and his child. Listen to me, Joshua. You don't know what Jamie knows about us or even if he will follow us. But if he does, he will look for those he can recognize. You, possibly me. He might not know me, as I might not recognize him. It has been a long time since we last saw each other. But the point is that he has never seen Rainbow. In a large Indian encampment she is only one pregnant girl among many. She will be safe. But if you and I remain with her she is targeted."

"You are so sure he'll follow us?"

"I am certain of only one thing. Jamie McAlistair is mu-dra, the murderer. We know it, and he knows we know it. He will follow us."

Joshua looked down at his hands for a moment. "Mother, I can't leave her."

"You must. We must draw him away from her. We will make sure he follows us and then your wife and her child, my grandchild, will be safe."

"What will we do then?" he asked.

"Once we are sure he follows we will try to lose him, or at least stay ahead of him to Edmonton. Then I will find Stephen Miller. We will lure Jamie into civilization and then we will confront him."

"We'll have to kill him, you know," Joshua said fatalistically.

"You're probably right, but that will be easier to do in the settlement than out on the prairie. He is mu-dra. He is better in the Indians' world than the Indians themselves."

Joshua looked down at his sleeping wife. "How will I tell her? Will she ever believe that I have left her alone in her hour of pain in order to save her?"

"She had no intention of having you with her in labor, my son. She intended to have her mother. When she left to go to White Buffalo she asked me to be with her. You were to be sent away."

"Not as far as you're sending me."

"No, not that far."

That afternoon they remounted. Elizabeth estimated they had a fifty-mile ride to the Minnedosa river. They rode in the heat of the afternoon and kept on after sunset, eating while in the saddle.

Joshua could see the weariness in his wife's face and feared for her.

"We have to slow down," he called to Elizabeth.

She reined in her horse and rode up to Rainbow.

"Where does it hurt?"

Rainbow spread her hands about her midsection and all the way to the back. Then she pointed to the blanket on her horse's back. Joshua touched it.

"The horse sweats," he said.

"No," she said, biting her lip. "I have wet myself."

Joshua looked at his mother. Perhaps her trouble came from the way her belly was swollen.

"No, Joshua," Rainbow said, "it rushed from me. I had no control."

"Her water has broken," Elizabeth said. "It is a sign that labor is near or already begun."

"Shall we stop?" he asked her.

"Shall we die?" she replied. "Can you ride, Rainbow? I think we have ten miles more to go before we reach the river. The trail sign will tell us where to find them."

Rainbow looked at Joshua. She wanted to say no, to plead with him to intercede with his mother, to do something to stop her pain. But she knew within her that had Medicine Cow Lady been in her place she would have continued to ride.

"I am better already," she lied. "Let's ride on."

Elizabeth smiled at her. She knew her courage.

They came to the river before dawn. Rainbow climbed down from her pony with Joshua's help. He spread the wolfskin on the ground and let her lie upon it. He sat by her side with his musket across his lap waiting for the sun and some indication of where White Buffalo's encampment might be. Elizabeth followed the stream further south and saw nothing.

At sunrise Joshua woke Rainbow up. She had fallen into a fitful sleep and had cried out several times in pain. She smiled at him when he shook her to arouse her.

"In pain?" he asked.

She hesitated a moment and shook her head. In fact, she did not lie. The rest had helped her.

Elizabeth rose to join them. "I've seen the signs. Many Indian ponies have come this way over a long period of time. White Buffalo's lodge is south of here and not far."

Rainbow's heart soared. Soon she would be among her own people—with her father and with her mother. Here she would have Joshua's child. For the first time since before the Peigan raid in the spruce forest she was filled with joy.

Eagle Face greeted them with a wild war whoop. He had set up his lodges in the midst of the encampment. Normally a newcomer would have been placed on the fringes. But White Buffalo was a good and sensitive leader. He listened to the spruce forest survivors and realized they would need a sense of being surrounded and protected by their own people. The encampment was large; several hundred people lived on the banks of the Minnedosa.

Warrior Woman ran to her daughter and held her as if she had not seen her in months rather than in days. Rainbow whispered to her mother. The older woman nodded and the two of them slipped quietly through the crowd. Joshua followed them with his eyes. He wanted to go with her, but Elizabeth signaled him to stay where he was.

White Buffalo himself came to greet the Medicine Cow Shaman Lady of the spruce forest Assiniboine. He had heard much of her. All the elders of the tribe came to pay their respects.

Medicine Cow Lady greeted them all solemnly. She had news for all the Assiniboine, she announced.

White Buffalo invited her to a council outside his lodge. She agreed to come if it were held immediately. Her news could not wait.

The chief and elders, the curious, the children, dogs, all

surged across the encampment to White Buffalo's lodge. They had no time to fix food. White Buffalo's three women had to serve whatever was in their cooking pot. But the women of the elders donated their dinners as well. Soon they had all settled down. The children had been hushed. All sat quietly in a giant circle. Only the tent hides flapping in the prairie wind could be heard.

White Buffalo stood. He took the fancy ceremonial pipe and puffed it and passed it along the long route around the circle. When it returned to him he began a loud chant. The others picked it up and the single drum began to keep a beat.

Then White Buffalo called out and all the noise again stopped.

"The circle is complete," he said. "The great shaman lady of the Assiniboine wishes to speak to us. The Peigan have destroyed most of her people." He turned to Elizabeth.

She stood up. "It is not of the Peigan I speak to you," she said.

There was a murmur of surprise in the council.

"Instead I speak of mu-dra."

Now there were gasps and then silence.

"I am followed by mu-dra to this village."

There was a roar of anger now from the crowd.

White Buffalo, clearly shaken by her words, ordered his people to silence.

"Right now he waits for me outside this village. I am sure of it."

Again the crowd was in an uproar.

"But now—but now I know what mu-dra looks like. He is not a spirit. He is a man. A white man."

There was shocked silence.

"He follows me, my son, and his wife, Rainbow, who is heavy with child. He wishes to make us the victims of his knives. But I will draw mu-dra away from the village and away from the land of the Assiniboine forever. My son and I will ride from here and draw mu-dra farther and farther to the west, farther even than the lands of the Blackfoot. There he will be powerless and unable to turn back. There I promise you he will die."

A roar of approval went up from the Assiniboine.

"Then, and only then, will the bull calf return for this woman and the child she will have borne him. I beg you to protect her for me and for my son. I ask of White Buffalo that his men watch the trail of Medicine Cow Lady and her son. If a sole white man does not follow us, signal to us with the smoke. If we see no smoke we will know that mu-dra has come for us and we will continue. But whatever you do, White Buffalo, do not try to stop mu-dra. He will escape you, and you and your people will suffer for it."

There was a great shouting from all the council members and bystanders. Several sang the praises of the great shaman lady.

Joshua left the circle as soon as he was able. He had to find Rainbow. He found Eagle Face's lodge but Warrior Woman was blocking his path. He tried to push past her but she stepped again in his way.

"Rainbow," he called out.

"Joshua," she responded. "Stay out. The child comes. It is early but I cannot help it. This little one seems to have a mind of his own."

"I have to speak with you." He turned when he felt someone touch his arm. It was his mother.

"Do not burden the child with your news. It is not happy news. She will have to endure much in the hours ahead. Let her suffer one thing at a time."

She held the reins of the gelding and Eagle Face's black stallion.

"At least we head west well mounted. I will ride the black. Come, my son. The sun is already high. McAlistair will soon be approaching this village. We have no time to lose."

Joshua looked at Warrior Woman, who blocked his path, and his mother, who summoned him to his duty. He sighed deeply.

"Rainbow," he called out to her, "know always that I love you."

She cried out in pain and did not respond to him.

*　　*　　*

The black stallion took the lead from the very beginning. He strained his high neck, searching for danger to the right and the left, always alert, much like his rider. Behind Elizabeth, Joshua searched the sky for signals. There were none. Jamie had been spotted by the Assiniboine and he was following their trail.

They crossed the Assiniboine River once again as it swung to the north across their path. They followed the Pipestone River for days into hill country. The pace they set was killing. They slept only three hours each night. They ate the pemmican the Assiniboine had given them as they rode, and they rested the horses every two hours. They never caught sight of McAlistair. Once they heard a musket shot and knew that he hunted for food. He was still behind them, even if he was not as well mounted as they were. As long as they kept going, as long as they remained alert, he would have trouble reaching them. If he made a mad dash forward and they escaped him, he was finished. His horse would be played out and he would lose his chance. Elizabeth was sure he would stay behind and wait for them to make a mistake, and she was determined not to play into his hands.

The Pipestone rose in the hills. They crossed the hills and descended on the other side. They kept moving onward until they reached the Qu'Appelle River. In one form or another they would follow it all the way to the Saskatchewan.

At night they rested and took turns watching and sleeping. They hobbled the horses. If Jamie came on, he would come at night and he would strike at the horses. Each of them had a musket and each of them was determined not to allow mu-dra to strike again—ever.

At dawn they remounted and pushed on farther into the prairies. There were buffalo herds all about them. There were signs of the Blood. But they encountered nothing but signs.

They followed the Qu'Appelle out of the rolling hills and out onto the flat prairies again. Ahead of them lay the South Saskatchewan.

Elizabeth was quiet that evening as they camped.

"What is it?" Joshua asked.

"I don't know," she said. "Maybe it was my years as a woman of magic. I have a feeling he has had enough. I think we have drawn him too far from what he knows. If I were him, I would strike now. I would go on no farther."

"What do you suggest?"

"That we wait for him tonight."

The moon was full. Joshua was sure that Jamie would try nothing with that kind of handicap. They had stuffed their bedrolls with the rest of their equipment and retreated to a rise overlooking the camp. There they sat with their muskets trained on the dark forms that were their surrogate selves. The horses were well hobbled.

Both of them would give up their sleep this night. They sat side by side in silence. They whispered to each other to make sure that one or the other did not drift off. At one point the stallion cried out in warning. Joshua froze. He nudged Elizabeth. She was alert. A dark form had entered their camp. It nosed around the bedrolls, pawed at them trying to unroll them and get at the food.

"It's either a wolf or a coyote. But then it behaves more like a bear. What a strange place to find a bear," Joshua whispered. "I don't dare fire. It would surely alert him."

"Don't fire," she ordered. The animal could not get at the pemmican. Discouraged, it left the camp. The horses calmed down. The night wore on without any further disturbances. Before sunrise they gave up and crept back to the camp. Joshua was anxious to see what damage the marauder had done. He pulled down his wolfskin bedding and stared in disbelief.

"Mother," he croaked as his voice broke with strain.

"What is it?" she asked, joining him. She too stared in shock. There on the wolfskin was Cree Woman's bread knife. There was no mistaking it.

"He's toying with us," Joshua said angrily. "This is his way of telling us he can take us any time he wants."

Elizabeth remained silent. "It was his biggest mistake," she said finally. "He had us, he should have killed us. He left us alive. He will not get a second chance."

If McAlistair had hoped his exploit would panic them,

his hopes were dashed. They mounted their horses and continued their journey just as they had before.

White Buffalo had warned them about the point where the South Saskatchewan swings back toward the northeast. They must leave it there and strike across the prairies to the northwest. Some thirty miles later they would strike the north branch of the same river. They were to follow it all the way to Fort Edmonton—three hundred miles to the west.

Every night they continued to sleep three hours and watch three hours. Every day they rode at the same pace, resting their horses at precise periods. McAlistair never came into sight even on those sections of the prairie that were flat and where one could see everything all the way to the horizon.

The North Saskatchewan twisted and broke off into branches heading nowhere. But they were never lost. They kept riding west.

Elizabeth was growing weary. Joshua could tell from the slump of her shoulders as she rode the stallion. But nothing and no one could break her will. Her body ached with saddle sores. It had to; his did. He tried to keep up small talk with her but she was in no mood. Her lips were like straight lines holding back any cry of pain or complaint.

"We can stop earlier tonight, Mother," he offered.

She shook her head. "In fact, Joshua, I suggest we push on a little longer tonight. If we do, we add a few extra miles between us and him. And if we leave an hour earlier in the morning, a few more miles between us. When he catches his first glimpse of us he will be farther away than he anticipates. This is new country to him. He does not know how far it is to a settlement. He will push forward a little harder and his horse is not as good as ours."

They followed this new schedule for three days in a row without knowing if it had any effect. But on the fourth day they knew at had. They saw him for the first time. He was miles behind them. Ahead of them was hill country again. He was clearly afraid of losing them in this new terrain.

Elizabeth urged the stallion to a faster pace and Joshua caught up to her.

"Is it wise to increase our pace?" he asked.

"We have not yet pushed these animals to the extent they are capable of. He has. His overconfidence has gotten the best of him, Joshua. If we push a little harder, he must push very much harder."

The gelding and the stallion moved side by side. They did not see McAlistair again that day, but after sunset they rode two more hours despite the darkness. Both animals were surefooted, especially after they slowed the pace at dusk. They made camp and prepared to sleep and keep watch.

"Where are we? Do you have any idea?" Joshua asked.

"The river turns to the south again. White Buffalo has been to Fort Edmonton only once as a youth. He said, however, that when it bends we are close."

Elizabeth walked away from the bedding to take up her watch. Joshua lay down and was soon asleep. He bolted upright when he heard the musket roar. A second musket discharged right after the first. He reached for his gun and searched in the immediate area for his mother.

He heard a sound. He moved cautiously toward it. Then he heard the sound again. It was weeping.

Joshua saw the animal. It was down. It struggled to get to its feet and then collapsed again with a shudder. It was his gelding. Elizabeth sat beside the horse, which died just as Joshua reached it. She was crying in anger, frustration, and sorrow for the animal.

"He must have ridden all night to come to us. Tomorrow he plans to finish us off. We have only the stallion left and there are two of us. He would have shot the stallion too had I not shot at him. I suspected he was going to try again tonight."

Joshua sat down beside her. "Do we sit here and wait for him?"

"Never," she said vehemently. "The river has bent. That means the settlement, the fort, is a day's ride. It's a night's ride too. Forget the saddles, Joshua. I'm going to show you how a woman can ride. No one can stop me now."

She cut the stallion's hobbles. Joshua grabbed his musket and walked in front to warn her of any pitfalls or holes in the trail. They walked through the night. At first light Joshua searched the horizon behind them. There he was. He had done precisely what they had done. He had walked his horse.

"Now we ride," Elizabeth called out. Joshua jumped up onto the horse behind her. The horse protested the extra burden and then broke into a gallop.

Elizabeth drove him and soon left McAlistair far to the rear. But Joshua worried that she went too fast and that the stallion would give out. But Elizabeth kept driving, forcing the horse to run to its capacity. It could not last. The horse had broken into a heavy sweat. It was beginning to show foam at the mouth.

They came to a bluff above the river. Once again Joshua could see Jamie, but now he was far behind them, too far behind to catch up. McAlistair realized it himself and halted his horse. Still Elizabeth drove the stallion. The horse no longer needed her to urge him. He raced forward on his own. Nothing could stop him. He tore up the bluff and down the far side.

"Mother," Joshua called out in joy, "we've won. He has given up."

He hugged her, and she threw back her head and yelled at the top of her voice. Her hair had come loose and it flew straight out behind her into Joshua's face. She was laughing and crying out loud.

"We've won! We've won!"

Ahead of them, sitting perched on the bluffs of the Saskatchewan River, was the trading post and settlement of Fort Edmonton.

Rejean LaMotte listened with a certain amount of indifference to Joshua's story about a madman wreaking havoc and mayhem among the Indians.

"He followed you into Edmonton?" he asked Joshua.

"I don't think so," the boy responded. "At least I hope he didn't." Joshua looked about the store nervously.

It was clear to LaMotte that this McAlistair had truly frightened the young man. Well, as the Hudson's Bay factor here in Edmonton, he was the only symbol of law and order in the fort. Men turned to him on the infrequent occasions when they felt a need for law.

"If he comes into the fort, you just come to me and we'll set the fellow down and begin asking some questions."

"You mean you're not going out after him?" Joshua asked with some anger.

"Where do you suggest I look for him?"

Joshua was crestfallen. "The man's a maniac," he shouted. "He can't be allowed to roam freely out there."

LaMotte glared at the young man. "It's not my responsibility," he said finally. "I'm only a storekeeper. I'm not a constable. I'll protect the property of the Hudson's Bay Company and I'll stop your man from hurting anyone in this fort. But I can't police the plains. Besides, killing Indians ain't nothing that's going to get this community angry enough to do anything to your murderer."

Joshua knew that LaMotte spoke the truth. He started to walk away, but realized that in his anxiety over Jamie he had forgotten his most important task. He turned and faced LaMotte, who had already risen from his desk and walked to the counter, which was piled high with furs and skins.

"I almost forgot," he added. "I'm looking for a man."

"Not another maniac, I hope," LaMotte moaned.

"Stephen Miller."

"I was right," LaMotte responded. "Another maniac."

"You know him?"

"All Fort Edmonton knows him."

"Then he's here!"

"No." LaMotte shook his head. "And thank God he's not."

"Where, then?"

"I don't know," LaMotte said. "Some say he went west."

"He just disappeared?"

"Why do you ask?" LaMotte questioned.

"My mother is looking for him. Many years ago they were husband and wife."

"Etienne Miller never mentioned family. None of us suspected he would have any relatives who would wish to find him. He was too wild even for this town. He was asked to leave last year."

Joshua was close to tears of frustration. He wanted his mother to find Stephen and he wanted to go back to his wife and his child—to protect them from the horror of a Jamie McAlistair. But nothing seemed to work out. He had to find Elizabeth and break the news to her. He turned and left the store.

LaMotte watched the boy leave. He had given away nothing. Etienne had always warned him about people coming from the east looking for him. When he was drunk, he spoke of dragons coming after him from the rising sun. Then and only then did he show fear. But even a frightened Etienne Miller was worth any ten other men. A drunk Etienne was worth twenty. He would send the message about the woman and the boy—maybe they were the dragons, maybe not. But he would watch this newcomer to judge if he was friend or foe.

The livery man could not believe the condition of the stallion. "Shit, ma'am, if you'll excuse the expression, you damned near killed this horse. Probably took the heart right out of him."

Elizabeth helped him brush the stallion.

"Oh, no," she exclaimed, "nothing can break this horse." She rubbed him lovingly, and when she was sure he was ready for it, she gave him some water and some oats.

"This horse just saved my life," she said to the livery man. "Take care of him."

She left the stable and went looking for her son. She walked toward the store. There were men on the porch who gave her the once-over. It was clear that they did not know what to make of her. She looked like a white woman but she was dressed like an Indian.

Joshua came down the steps from the store to meet her. He took her by the arm and led her away, back toward the stables.

"I don't quite know how to tell you this, Mother, but we are too late."

"He's dead?"

"No, not that. They think he went across the mountains, last year."

"How far?" she asked.

"I don't know. They say it's another two hundred to the mountains and then maybe another six hundred over the mountains to the sea."

Elizabeth walked away from him. She sat down on some steps across from the porch. She put her head in her hands and began to cry. He sat next to her. He put his arm around her shoulder.

"I am sorry," he said.

"Why?" she responded. "What did you do?"

"Nothing. I just feel bad for you."

"I can tell your father raised you, Joshua. He did a poor job. You're without doubt a strong and brave man, but you lack confidence. Never apologize unless you have reason to. You rode by my side through it all. You never complained. You left that lovely child back on the prairies in the middle of giving birth to your own child. You don't know if you sired a son or a daughter. You've never seen the child. You don't know your own child's name. All because I told you we had to leave to save her, to save the Assiniboine. That was done at my command and you obeyed. You have no reason to be sorry. You have reason for pride."

She wiped her runny nose on her sleeve. "Oh, God, I wish my nose didn't run every time I cried," she burst out. "I'm sad, Josh. I'm sad because I've missed him. You're days away from Rainbow. I'm twenty years away from that brawling drunk. If I don't get to him soon to straighten him out again, I'm afraid there will be no straightening out."

Joshua smiled at her. "Well, now do we go across the mountains?"

"Of course we do," she responded. "But not now. We have nothing left, Joshua, except the stallion. We have no food, no money to buy our own dinner tonight. We are going to have to find jobs. We are going to have to save our money. We get ourselves some supplies and we go another eight hundred miles. What is another eight hun-

210

dred miles to the two of us? We've just come eight hundred to get here to begin with."

Joshua found a job washing dishes in the local saloon. Elizabeth made extra money helping out in the livery stable. The livery man realized she was a wonder with horses and he had hopes that she might not mind a little ride with another stallion—namely, himself. But he had to admit after a few days' chase that she was a wary mare. He had not yet cornered her.

One Friday afternoon when the late August heat was oppressive, he told her she would have to come into his office in the back of the stable to get a few coppers extra she had earned over and above the feed and stable bill for the stallion. The office was tiny and sweltering. The livery man had already removed his shirt because of the heat. He shut the door behind him after she stepped into the room. He reached into his pocket and handed her the money.

"Now," he said, "I've paid you. How's about you pay me?" He started to reach out to grab her breast but reached instead for his testicles when her knee came crashing into them. He screamed in agony.

"Don't try that again," she said, looking down at him as he stooped, heaving on the floor. "Next time I'll really hurt you."

She went directly to the shanty that she and Joshua shared at the back of the saloon. This was not going to work. They would be here all fall and winter before they could save enough to buy their supplies for a trek over the mountains. She had to come up with another scheme. But in fact it was Joshua who came up with the solution.

The saloon at Fort Edmonton was filled every evening in the summer. Those who worked there for some time told Joshua it was filled evening and daytime in the winter. It was too cold to be outside and so everybody stayed indoors, preferably in the saloon, and did nothing but get drunk.

The champion drunk of Edmonton had definitely been Stephen Miller. He was also the champion whoremonger,

211

the champion card cheater; he had been in jail seventeen times in the past two months of his stay. Joshua learned all this from customers in Rejean LaMotte's saloon. After a while Rejean himself began to open up. He was a large, big-boned French-Canadian with dark black hair and a great moustache, which he waxed at the ends.

"I cannot understand why a quiet good boy like you, Joshua, would want to find Etienne Miller. He is the wildest man I have ever known. He cares not a sou for his own life. I have seen him kill three men in fights. It is almost as if he regards himself not at all. He loves his pleasures and he indulges in all of them but with no sense of moderation."

"But you liked him, didn't you, Monsieur LaMotte?" Joshua interjected.

"What was there not to like besides violence and drunkenness and whoremongering?" He laughed. "Yes, I did, although I think I was the only one in all Edmonton who missed him after they drove him out. And he did leave by popular request."

"But why across the mountains?"

"Why not? He had never been there. The company was scheduled to open a new post on Vancouver Island. He wanted to be there at the beginning."

Joshua's attention was pricked. This was the first time LaMotte had been specific about Stephen's whereabouts.

"I want to find him, Monsieur LaMotte. How can I get across the mountains?"

"The same way your uncle did. You get on your horse and ride west until you reach them. Then you find the pass through them until you reach the river, the Fraser or the North Thompson, and that will take you to the sea."

"That is easily said. My mother and I, alone, could not do it."

"True," said the Frenchman, "but you would not have to be alone. I have one more party to set out before winter. It will be small, so it might move rapidly. It will not be able to leave until September, which is too late for a large, heavy-burdened party. I am to bring provisions to the mouth of the Fraser River. It is said that they need these

212

provisions to guarantee that the village on the island survives. The Hudson's Bay Company takes no chances."

"We can go with your caravan?"

"You may," said the older man.

Joshua let out a whoop of joy, startling several of the drousy customers of the oppressively hot saloon.

"I've got to tell my mother," he said excitedly, and raced toward their quarters.

LaMotte smiled. He hoped Etienne knew what he was doing. The return response had been short and sweet: "Say nothing, but send them on!"

the . . . and the changes of a singular . . .
was fixed with you . . . the . . .
. . . and the older e . . .
. . . of the end of the smoke . . . were . . .

. . . might appear . . . and eat . . . have . . .
. . . care received.

. . . . B . . . when they found a . . .
. . . the name has long been short and quick
. . . . had not been felt of . . .

Part Three

THE MOUNTAINS

X

Rocky Mountains, Fall 1842

They loomed out of the earth like giants cloaked in green fur. In contrast to the flatness of the prairies that stretched on unbroken and endless, they assaulted the eye. Even the hills of the Moose Mountains, the foothills that swept up toward the Continental Divide, had done nothing to prepare Joshua and Elizabeth for the grandeur that surrounded them.

The wagon train consisted of five Conestoga-type wagons drawn by mules. Elizabeth had signed on as a cook while Joshua was hired as a driver. In fact, they would each have done better if their positions had been reversed.

The leader of the train was John Cabiney, an old-line York boatman from the days when the Hudson's Bay Company men sailed and rowed from York Factory on Hudson Bay to Fort Edmonton. He was originally from Cornwall or Devonshire. He could no longer remember which, since he was brought as an infant to York Factory. He had grown up in the company and he would die in the company and the company trusted him. At least he thought it did; why else would he be ordered to take a mule train, even a small one like this, up Yellowhead Pass? All of this with autumn upon them. He knew they had asked him because he was the only one who could do it.

A small man, he was now fifty years old, with not an inch of fat on him. Hard work kept him that way, and he drove himself hard. What was good for him was good for those who worked for him. He would drive his men—or rather, his men and one woman—as he drove himself.

He had fought with LaMotte about taking the woman over the mountains. It was only when LaMotte told him of her relationship to Stephen Miller that he relented.

Cabiney disapproved of Stephen Miller more than any other man he had ever met. He personally had helped LaMotte pick the drunk up off the saloon floor and dump him in the back room of the company store, which served as a temporary jail, on numerous occasions. He had stitched Miller's face after fights, most of which he himself had caused. He was not a man fit for civilized society. But Stephen Miller had also ridden through a Shoshonee village at breakneck speed and put a bullet in the head of a warrior who was about to lift the scalp of John Cabiney. Neither one of them would dare set foot in the Shoshonee country ever again. He owed Miller his life. If this was his lady, he owed it to Miller to get her to him. Though God knows why any woman would want him on a permanent basis. True, the squaws loved to flock around him. But they did not have to live with him.

The shadows of the mountains lengthened. It was time to camp and get some grub. Cabiney raised his hand. Baker, the lead driver, yelled out to his mules. Young Miller had difficulty holding his place in line behind Baker. The boy had a lot to learn, Cabiney thought, but he was a willing hand and worked hard.

"Circle those wagons," Cabiney called. They were not in danger from hostiles of any kind, but Cabiney had been a cautious man all his life and he had no intention of changing now.

The wagons were circled in an open meadow. The mules were hobbled and herded into the circle along with Cabiney's bay horse and Elizabeth's black stallion. A watch was posted.

Elizabeth struggled with the giant pots while Joshua started her campfire for her. It would be pemmican stew again tonight. Cabiney had sent out a hunter earlier in the day for fresh meat, but he had not returned.

They had kegs of rum for trade and they were allowed to use one of them for themselves. But Cabiney had insisted they wait until the weather warranted it.

The water was boiling before long and the pemmican slices were dropped in. Elizabeth stirred the stew with a long ladle. Joshua hoped the leader would give the word on the rum, but he remained silent. The nights were cold in the high country, especially on the late watch.

Joshua helped his mother clean up after the men were fed. Then she left him to sleep. She was tired after a full day's ride and would have to get up early the next day to make breakfast.

He had said nothing to her, but LaMotte had sent word to him by special messenger to the wagon train that a man fitting the description of Jamie McAlistair had been sighted near Fort Edmonton the day after the wagon train left. Joshua was shocked, not that McAlistair had tracked them to Edmonton—he must have known all along where they were headed once they took the north branch of the Saskatchewan—but that he had waited for them to leave and was following them once again. He had been so sure that, failing to kill them on the way to Edmonton, Jamie would go back to his wife and to his farm at Fort Garry. Instead, he had waited until they were again on the prairie. Every night Joshua waited for him to strike. He slept with his musket. When on watch he guarded his mother more than the wagon train.

Maybe it would end soon. Maybe McAlistair would put himself in Joshua's gunsight by mistake and it would all be over. He thought of Rainbow and the child he had never seen. He thought of his wife's face, her warm smile and white teeth, of her body so alive and so inviting, her breasts so brown and so soft.

Cabiney interrupted his reverie. "Your watch, Miller."

"Yes, sir," Joshua responded. He rose from the low-burning campfire and moved outside the perimeter of the wagons. He picked a spot up the slope where he could see the whole encampment and the sweep of the meadow as it flowed away toward the foothills and prairies below.

He pulled his Indian blanket about his body tightly and sat watching the night and the sleeping wagon train. The mountains were outlined in black against the light night sky.

Joshua's attention was drawn by a motion beyond the wagon train. He rose to a crouching position and trained his eye to the spot where he had seen the movement. There it was again. It was four-legged, a wolf, a coyote, perhaps at this elevation a bear. It drew closer. He remembered another night, another wolf. Joshua fired. There was a yelp as the animal rose into the air and then collapsed.

There were some shouts in the sleeping camp. Joshua ran down to the circle of wagons where his mother lay. Cabiney joined him carrying an oil lamp. It was a stray wolf. He had shot it in the head.

"That's a mighty fine shot, boy," the leader complimented him. "If you skin him, you might make a decent robe. I don't know if I have ever tasted wolf meat, although I have eaten dog, stringy stuff. I guess wolf will be the same. Damn wolf wouldn't have hurt anybody though, Joshua. You could have saved yourself some powder and shot. You get the job of skinning him and we all get to go back to sleep."

Elizabeth looked at her son quizzically. When the others had left to go back to sleep, the two of them dragged the carcass outside the camp. She pulled out her knife and began to skin the wolf.

"You were thinking of our ride to Edmonton, weren't you?"

He said nothing.

"You are sure he still follows?"

He tried to ignore her, but his very silence was an indication of his fear and an admission of his knowledge.

"He comes," she said more to herself than to him.

"I don't know that," he spoke finally. "All I do know is that he was seen right after we left. That means he hung around out on the prairie until we left and he didn't go back home because we beat him."

"You were right to shoot. He has a devil."

She finished skinning the wolf. "If you cure this fur properly, you'll have a match of your favorite robe. Help me with the meat. I want to get some sleep before morning is on us."

They continued to climb into ever higher elevations. Cabiney's eyes never left the peaks of the mountains. He was silent, but every one of the veterans of mountain crossings was doing the same thing. They searched for the white, the onset of winter on the peaks of the highest elevations.

It struck them without any warning. The day before had been sunny and brisk but when they awoke to get under way in the morning, the clouds, heavy with moisture, came from the west pushed by winds that roared and at times almost wailed through the mountaintops. White flakes, heavy and large, blew into their faces. Cabiney gave the word to give up any thought of more forward motion. By noon, there were eighteen inches of snow on the trail.

Joshua and Elizabeth climbed into Joshua's wagon. They rearranged the boxes of trade goods to block off the wind, and although the canvas cover flapped and frequently seemed on the verge of being torn off the frame, they remained relatively dry, if not warm.

The snow swirled about them and piled in drifts against the wheels. The mules stood dumbly up to their knees in snow. They bowed their heads before the wind and awaited better times.

"How much farther do you guess?" Elizabeth asked.

"Five hundred miles maybe. We were supposed to have weeks more without snow like this," he responded. "This is very dangerous. If we are trapped here we are stuck until March, maybe April."

"If we are trapped here," Elizabeth corrected, "we are dead."

The wind howled even more, as if to accentuate the finality of her statement.

"I am glad we have the new wolfskin," he said, shivering.

"It's not quite ready yet," she observed. "It still stinks."

"You know something, Mother?" he retorted. "Somehow tonight I don't think I'll care."

It snowed through the night and into the next morning. At dawn Cabiney called the whole party together. The mules stood chest-deep in the snow. Even Elizabeth's stallion snorted and thrashed about, trying to free himself from these strange hobbles.

"There are six men and a woman in this party, five mules and two horses. We got food for a month's trek across these here mountains and we got boxes of dried pemmican."

"Shit," said Baker, "we got enough food to sit out here the whole winter if we can keep warm."

"It ain't my job to sit here the whole winter and rot. We were supposed to meet the canoe team at Moose Lake just across the Divide. There will be about twenty men there. We've got to dig these mules and wagons out of the snow, load the mules with the provisions, and lead them to Moose Lake. But we will need more manpower to do it all. I want those twenty company men on the other side of the Divide. They can't be more than fifteen miles from here."

"How do we get them here?" Baker asked.

"I'd go for them myself," Cabiney said, "except that would leave an asshole like you in charge, Baker, and I'd never get out of here. And I couldn't send you. I hate to admit it, but you are the best man in the company when it comes to handling mules. I need you."

"What are the chances of getting fifteen miles through three feet of snow?" Joshua asked.

"It can be done," Cabiney responded. "This was just a freak storm. It should warm up now and the sun will melt some of it. So long as it doesn't snow any more, a man can make it there and back with the canoe men in two days, maybe three."

"And what if it snows some more?" Elizabeth asked.

"If it snows, we move the wagons and mules into the fir trees. We cut some trees down to build shelter and fire and we are here to spring, like Baker said."

"My son and I will go for the help," she volunteered.

"Wait a minute," said Baker. "I don't believe in sending no woman on a man's job."

"Mister Cabiney." Elizabeth ignored the wagon man. "My horse is ridden only by me. If any animal can make it through the snows, he can. He can clear a path for my son—that is, if you lend him your horse. We are the two most expendable members of the party, and I suspect I'm the best horseman here. I'll make those fifteen miles and I'll get you your help."

Cabiney looked over at Joshua. "Is that all right with you, son?"

Joshua wanted to scream that it was not. Once again she was giving orders that put his life in jeopardy.

"She's the boss," was all he said.

The stallion seemed almost grateful to move against the white wet snow. At first he tried to leap over it, but Elizabeth held him in check and forced him to use his strength to push it aside. Joshua followed on Cabiney's bay horse. After a time, he turned in his saddle. Far down the slope he could see the wagons and mules. They were making good progress. Elizabeth called to him and pointed to the sky. The sunlight had been obliterated by a new bank of clouds.

"I don't like the looks of that," she said.

Elizabeth bent low on the horse's back, leaning her head against his neck and whispering in his ear, urging him forward. He showed no signs of wanting to give up the struggle, but Elizabeth took no chances with him. They climbed higher and higher. Icy pellets of snow began to fall, and the cloud cover swirled about them. It was difficult to see the trail ahead. Again Joshua twisted in the saddle. They were cut off now from the view of the wagons below. Suddenly the trail had evened out. If anything, the slope was now downward. They had crossed over the Divide, the point from which all waters now would run toward the sea—the Pacific.

Elizabeth left the trail. At first Joshua thought she had become disoriented, but then it was clear that she headed for a half-buried clump of Douglas fir trees. Joshua followed her. When they reached it, she dismounted. She held the bay for Joshua as he jumped down into the snow.

"We've crossed the Divide. Soon the trail will swing to

the north toward Moose Lake and the comapny station there. We'll miss the trail if we keep going like this. Cabiney was specific. Once you're over the Divide you head north."

"We're going to wait out the storm?" he asked.

"We've no other choice. Let's make a shelter."

They dug the snow away from the base of the fir tree and piled it high as a windbreak. Soon they were sweating despite the cold. Joshua hacked down the lower branches of the tree with his knife as he uncovered them from the snow. Elizabeth led the two horses to the shelter once it was complete. They would give off some warmth also. They broke out some pemmican and shared it. They had not taken much food. They had hoped to be all the way to Moose Lake by now.

Elizabeth fed the horses the last of the oats. They had worked hard, especially the stallion, and he complained about the poor fare. Elizabeth sat down on the floor of snow mixed with the fir tree's dry needles. Joshua collapsed beside her.

"You've been quiet," she said. "Are you angry with me?"

He smiled. "How could I be angry with you? You have more strength, more courage, more stamina than anyone I know."

"You keep up with me."

"Yes, I do, and with no small effort. But I would never try to do the things you do. I'm not even sure I know why you do them. This advance to Moose Lake. I listened to your explanation to Cabiney but I was not sure that the reasons you gave him were your real reasons."

"You are becoming shrewd, Joshua." She laughed wearily. "The real reasons had to do with your news about Jamie. I want to keep ahead, always in the van. If we lie still he will pick us off and destroy us."

"I thought it might be something like that. Will we ever escape him? I feel I have been fleeing from mu-dra for so long."

She nodded and leaned her head back against the trunk of the tree. He threw the new wolfskin over her.

"You sleep," he said. "I'll watch."

"Wake me if it clears," she mumbled to him.

The wind continued to howl, and more and more snow piled up against the windbreak until it reached the top and then started to spill over. Joshua kept awake and allowed his mother the rest he knew she needed. He tried to keep awake by thinking of Rainbow. He tried to remember the number of times they had made love but the number evaded him. He tried to remember the actual details but each event tended to become blurred. He remembered the first time, actually the first three times, on that one day by the creek. He smiled. He felt like an idiot when he realized Elizabeth had awakened and caught him smiling to himself.

"Your turn," she said, "and I hope your night dreams are as pleasant as your daydreams."

Joshua laid his musket on the wolfskin to make sure it stayed dry. He put his head down. Despite the snow and the cold he still smelled the odor of the fir tree, a strong perfume mixed with the pungent odor of pitch.

The sun was shining when he awakened. Elizabeth had fallen asleep as well. The horses had messed the inside of the shelter and steam rose from their droppings. He shook his mother, who awoke with a startled look on her face.

"I fell asleep!" she said, clearly embarrassed.

"You *are* human, after all," he laughed. "Now, if you would turn the other way, I must demonstrate my own humanity and add to the untidiness of our little shelter."

"I'll follow you," she laughed. She started to clear the path outside for them. Joshua held the stallion and the bay by the reins until Elizabeth joined him. She mounted and followed their path back to the main trail. They found the spot where they had left it. It was difficult to determine just how much snow had fallen. They continued, this time with greater difficulty. A crust of ice had formed on top of the snow. It cut the legs of the stallion, and each step left a pink tinge on the broken white snow. They had moved about half a mile when Elizabeth pointed to the north.

"I think the trail turns here," she called out. The jumble of fir trees directly ahead and to the left of them caused Joshua to agree.

"How much farther?" he asked.

"Seven or eight miles, Cabiney said."

"You want me to take the lead?"

"No," she said vehemently, "we can do it." Again she urged the horse forward. This time he protested. She leaned forward and stroked his neck and soothed him, whispering, telling him how strong he was. Like a seductress, she lured him on, made him want to try just a little bit harder, a little bit further.

They rode for another two hours—slowly, painfully slowly. Then they came around a bend in the trail. Below them the sunlight hit the blue waters of a large lake. It was not yet frozen, and it appeared almost like a sapphire set in the snow. Beside it they could see a cabin with a barn. From the cabin's chimney, smoke curled upward into the cloudless blue sky.

The next two miles were every bit as difficult as those that had preceded them, but it did not seem so for the two riders. Even the horses seemed to sense the end of their suffering. The bay surged forward for the first time since the journey began, and Joshua had to rein him in.

They struggled down to the shore of the lake and entered the empty fenced-off area in front of the cabin.

"We're from Cabiney," Elizabeth called out. "He's marooned on the east slope and needs help."

She jumped from the black horse's back into the deep snow. She swung open the cabin door and stood in the doorway. Joshua stepped in behind her. There was a warm fire in the hearth and the wood in the fire crackled as it burned. But the room was empty. She turned and looked at Joshua in amazement.

"There are supposed to be over twenty boatmen here. Where have they gone?"

"Let's try the barn," he suggested. They left the exhausted horses in front of the cabin and walked to the rear where the small barn stood. They struggled through snow that was almost waist-deep. The doors of the barn opened inward, Elizabeth noticed with thanks. It would be next to impossible to open them against the snow. Joshua stepped ahead and pushed open the door.

Elizabeth's scream of fright shattered the silence of the valley. Joshua stepped back in horror. Just beyond the entryway, there was a man hanging from the ceiling, impaled on a meat hook. He was naked. Some of his entrails hung from his open stomach cavity, while the rest had oozed down to the barn floor. His eyes were wide open and registered nothing.

Beyond the man's body, sitting on a pile of last fall's hay, his musket pointed at both of them, was Jamie McAlistair.

"I've been waiting for you, Elizabeth and Stephen. I've been waiting for you for twenty years. Why do you keep running away from me?" he said with a whine in his voice.

Joshua's eyes flickered around the barn.

"If you're looking for the others, Stevie, I've sent them all away. They were happy to hear that the company officers, especially Rejean LaMotte at Fort Edmonton, had come to their senses and decided to hold the supply train until spring. Some of them were real friendly when I brought that news. They got them canoes in the water and headed for the Fraser before the cold winter and storms struck. Now, Mr. Buttle—he's the fellow hanging there—he lives here all year round. He didn't want to leave, so I had to help him on his way. It's just you, me, and Elizabeth, Stevie. Just like it used to be."

Elizabeth was shaking with fright. Joshua put his arms around his mother to steady her.

"I remember that, Stevie; you always took good care of Elizabeth. I tried to do the same thing with Cree Woman after we took up together."

"Jamie," Joshua said, "let's go into the house. Why don't you put the musket away?"

"No," he shouted, "don't touch the musket. You can't tell when them fucking Indians are going to strike. You gave yourself once before, Stevie, without fighting, and those Indians just slaughtered everyone. I hate those red-skinned bastards. They killed Mum and Pa, Andrew and my little sisters, and now they have even killed Cree Woman."

Elizabeth's heart sank. She knew instinctively that he

spoke the truth, that Cree Woman was dead, but at Jamie's hand.

"There's a fire in the house, and food, Jamie. That's where Elizabeth and I are going."

"Not a bad idea, but you go first," he said, turning the musket on them.

They turned and started to go back out into the snow with Jamie following them.

Suddenly Joshua grabbed the legs of the corpse hanging from the ceiling and swung them viciously at McAlistair. The gun went off and the ball struck the barn ceiling. The corpse tore from the meat hook and collapsed onto Jamie, who began to scream. Joshua grabbed Elizabeth's arm and pushed her ahead into the snow. He ran, stumbling, reaching for her, pulling her along until they made it to the front of the house and the horses. Jamie had stopped to reload.

"Inside," Joshua called to his mother. She opened the cabin door and stumbled through. Joshua grabbed the reins of the stallion and bay and forced their heads down and pulled them through into the cabin.

Elizabeth slammed the heavy bar, bolting the door. She ran from window to window slamming the shutters and bolting them.

Joshua pulled the horses through the room. Furniture was kicked and shattered. In the back he found the woodshed and pantry and lean-to kitchen. They would make acceptable stalls for the horses. He put them there and bolted the back door off the kitchen and returned to the main room. He placed a heavy wooden bureau in the back doorway to hold the horses in their new home.

He looked over at his mother, who stood with her back against the bolted door of the cabin.

"What now?" he asked.

She said nothing.

"Mother," Joshua called out.

"I froze," she said. "He has so terrified me that I couldn't think. I couldn't do anything." She slid down until her bottom touched the floor. "He is insane. He is beyond communication."

There was a banging on the front door. Joshua imagined that Jamie used the butt of his musket. But the door was a solid one. Suddenly there was a roar of a gun, and a lead ball penetrated the door and slammed into the bureau Joshua had moved to keep the horses in the back room. If Elizabeth had remained standing, the ball would have entered her.

Joshua waved her away from the door. He returned to the rear room on his hands and knees. He slipped behind the bureau into the kitchen. Both he and Elizabeth had left their muskets with the horses. He took powder, shot, and ball back with him along with the muskets. He gave Elizabeth her gun. She took it mechanically from him. Joshua heard thumping on the roof of the cabin. The snow was deep and the weight added by a man made the beams creak. What would he be doing up there? Joshua glanced over at the fire that burned in the open hearth. He walked over to it. There was a kettle of water as if someone was intending to prepare a meal. Joshua poured the contents of the pot onto the fire. The wood hissed and billows of steam rose up the chimney; some of it came forward and filled the room with the smell of wet ashes. They heard a shout of frustration as Jamie realized the fire had been extinguished and that his plan to smoke them out had been thwarted. There was more creaking of the beams and then a thud as Jamie jumped down into a snowdrift.

"Stevie, please let me in," he called. "It's cold out. And it's going to get colder. I've got no place to stay. I've got no food."

Joshua went back into the pantry. The bay stood there stolidly but the stallion still kicked its feet out at anything within reach. Joshua waited until he thought he heard the heavy breathing of someone trying to work his way back to the barn through the heavy snow. He pulled open the back door a crack. He saw Jamie already halfway to the barn. He had him in his sights. He started to squeeze the trigger when the stallion reared and kicked out at the musket. The gun went off, but the ball went whizzing over the head of McAlistair.

Jamie turned, a look of surprise and anger on his face.

He shook his fist at the house and proceeded toward the barn.

Joshua rebolted the back door and returned to the main room. He saw the look of anticipation on his mother's face. He explained what had happened. She started to laugh bitterly. "The horse saves lives—yours, mine, Jamie's. He's indiscriminate."

"Mother," Joshua said, "we are stuck here, God knows how long. Let's make the best of it."

"What about Cabiney?" she reminded him. "A few days of warm weather and melting snow and he'll make it to us."

"We were supposed to get help for him. Don't you remember? It will be days before he gives up on us and thinks of some other tactic. I think he'll go back down to the lower elevations."

"And we spend the whole winter in the company of a madman."

Joshua didn't want to think about it, much less talk about it.

"Let's make an inventory of what we have here," he suggested.

He searched the pantry. He found bags of cornmeal and three kegs of rum. There was enough pemmican for a month. He returned to the main room of the cabin. Elizabeth continued to sit on the floor where he had left her. His attention was drawn to the floor. As she had slid down against the back of the door her foot had dislodged a rug. The small rug had covered a trapdoor. Joshua lifted the trap up. There was a stairway down. He wished he had a lamp, but he descended anyway.

Elizabeth watched him disappear again. She had to stir herself. She could not continue to just sit there watching Joshua work. But she felt defeated. She had driven herself and him only to find Jamie awaiting them. She had brought Joshua to what would have been certain death had it not been for his quick thinking and quick actions. She should be helping him or death might come anyway. But all she really wanted to do was cry.

Joshua came out of the cellar holding an oil lamp. He had gotten his wish.

"From what I can see, there is a cold cellar loaded with apples and onions and potatoes. I wonder if the horses will eat them?" he asked.

"They will if they get hungry enough," she responded. "God knows what it will do to them, but it couldn't be worse than starving."

She rose to her feet at last. He handed her an apple. She bit into it. It tasted sweet.

"Joshua, you feed the horses," she ordered. "I'll get some pemmican stew. We've got to keep up our strength. Tonight we take turns keeping watch. In the morning I'll feel better and we can work out a plan then."

He smiled. Things were back to normal. Now he was convinced they would work something out.

That night during Joshua's watch, Jamie slipped out of the barn and tried to set fire to the cabin. But the heavy snows banked against the house melted when the blaze started and quickly extinguished it.

They saw nothing of him the next day. But they heard him. He sang a strange song over and over again. Neither Joshua nor Elizabeth could recognize the tune, and neither could tell the language he used. In reality it was a Scottish lullaby.

That night he raged, screaming most of the night. His incoherence forced Joshua to conclude that not all of the rum had been in the house.

Late the next day he opened the barn door a crack and called out to them.

"Elizabeth, Stevie, I'm hungry. I got no damned food in here. I want something to eat. Come on, we're friends, aren't we?"

They did not respond to him. That night they smelled meat roasting over a fire in the barn.

Joshua said nothing about it but it disappointed him. He had hoped that starvation would eventually drive Jamie away. Now he had slaughtered his horse. He couldn't go if he wanted to.

The laughter that came from the barn was crazy and terrifying. He came at them again that night. This time he found a wood ax. The first they knew of his assault was the cracking of the ax through a window and the smashing of a shutter.

Elizabeth had the watch. She fired the musket into the broken panel of wood. Her shot produced another squeal of wild laughter.

"My belly is filled," he yelled out, "but the winter is long so I may be calling again."

Joshua sent his terrified mother to bed and took over the rest of the shift. He watched for Jamie to go back to the barn. Sometime before dawn he saw his dark figure open the barn door and go inside. He knew he should follow, that he should follow Jamie into his own lair and kill him. But if something went wrong he would leave his mother to face the madman alone. Or so he told himself. He also realized that Jamie McAlistair terrified him as well. He thought he could face almost any danger, but he could not deal with homicidal lunacy. He was no coward, but neither could he face Jamie.

The next day Elizabeth and Joshua shared some tea and corn bread she had baked. They were startled to hear the cry of Jamie's horse. He was drinking again and he was beating it.

If the horse is alive then what is he eating? What is he roasting? The realization of just what he was doing came to Elizabeth. Joshua saw it in the horror that flooded her face. She cupped her hands over her mouth and tried to stop her stomach's reaction, but she became sick anyway. Joshua could think only of his words of last night—that the winter was a long one and that he might be calling again.

They could not go on like this. Joshua stood up and reached for his musket.

Elizabeth looked at him, her face pale from nausea.

"Where are you going?"

"I've got to go take him," he said. "I can't sit here and wait any longer."

"He's too good for you, Joshua. Please, we can wait him out."

"He's absolutely crazy, Mother. He is thinking of us as future food supply. He has no problem at all with keeping us alive. It suits his purposes. He's better at mayhem than I am. I suspect he's better than anyone at that. But he drinks, and maybe that is the equalizer. You take the horses out front and down the trail toward the lake. If you hear a shot and I call all clear, then he's dead and you return here. Anything else and you keep riding back to Cabiney's last camp, because I'll be dead."

"Joshua, please don't do this." She threw her arms around his neck.

He pulled away from her.

"You did what you do best to try to save us. You and the stallion. Now I must help us."

His lips trembled and she knew he was frightened. But she knew also that he was right.

At nightfall she filled the saddlebags of the two horses with as much food as they could hold. She grabbed her own musket and led the horses through the cabin. The front door bolt was thrown out of place for the first time since they had arrived days earlier. She led the horses out into darkness, then leapt on the stallion and began the slow journey down the road toward the lake.

Joshua slipped out the back door at the same time. There was a commotion coming from the barn. He raced toward it as fast as the snow would allow him. There was only one entryway into the barn and there were no windows. It would have to be a frontal assault. He flung open the barn door and rushed inside, his musket at hip level. His eyes darted from side to side seeking out McAlistair. It had to be quick. Where was he? But there was no sign of him. Joshua's heart seemed to stand still. He felt the knife begin to enter his back. He cried out. He had failed. Then came the blackness.

Elizabeth waited as long as she dared. There was no musket shot. No call from Joshua. She knew he had failed. Why had she let him do it? She was sick. She did not know what to do. Maybe Jamie would keep him alive. Maybe if she rode on she could bring help and rescue him. When she saw the flames rising from the cabin she panicked. She had no choice now but to ride. To ride had always been the answer. To ride and get help.

She dug her heels into the stallion and let go of the bay. He could fend for himself. He would only hold her back. The stallion plowed through the snow, following the path he had made days before. Elizabeth reached the shores of the lake. The horse fell for the first time and threw her. She landed safely in a snowdrift. She pulled herself to her feet. The stallion had stopped in the cold water and was drinking freely. She approached him. He shied off. He held his foot strangely. Elizabeth reached his side and calmed him down. She started to walk him and realized with horror that he had gone lame. Even the stallion had now failed her. Tears came, running down her cheeks. Her son, Joshua, was in the hands of a maniac. Her mind was snapping. She could feel her mind losing contact with reality. She imagined things out on the blue water. She imagined she saw canoes. She fell to her knees.

"My son, my son," she repeated over and over again, "I leave you for the second time." And then she collapsed in the snow.

When Joshua awoke he found himself stripped and hanging by a rope from the hook that once held Mr. Buttle, the cabin's owner. His back was bleeding from the knife wound and his head throbbed where he had been struck by something. His arms ached and they felt as if they were being pulled from their sockets. His feet could not touch the ground. He moaned in pain.

Jamie came round front to look at him.

"Well, Stevie, look what has happened to you. All trussed up like meat to the market," he laughed. "I could have killed you right off, Stevie, but I didn't. I went looking for Elizabeth. You know, she rode off and left us. She's always doing that, disappearing, leaving you and me to handle things."

"Cut me down, Jamie," Joshua asked.

"No, I couldn't do that. It's a long winter and Mr.

Buttle ain't going to last me through it. Would you like some of him? You must be hungry."

Jamie stuck a bone that he had been gnawing on up to Joshua's face. There was still meat clinging to it. Joshua turned his face away violently, forcing his body to sway on the rope. He felt the vomit creeping up in his throat.

"It's only a leg. It's not like it's liver or kidney. I ate them first. Come on, take a bite. You need to keep up your strength."

He thrust the leg into Joshua's face again. Joshua vomited all over the meat. Some fell on Jamie.

"Christ," Jamie yelled, "you had no call to do that."

He walked outside the barn to clean himself off and finished his dinner in the snow.

Joshua looked about the barn. He tried to grip the rope with his hands so that he might swing forward or backward. But it was hopeless. He could not move. He could only hang on in agony.

Jamie returned to the barn. "Why did you want to kill me, Stevie?" he asked.

Joshua didn't care anymore. Maybe if he antagonized him it would be quicker.

"Maybe, McAlistair, because you are a mad dog. We shoot a mad dog."

"Why do you say that?" Jamie actually looked hurt.

"Your murder indiscriminately. You kill innocent, guilty, it doesn't matter to you. You use your knife, you slit open bellies. You cut off innocent mothers' breasts, you take testicles from young men. You were and you are a fiend. The world cannot tolerate your existence in it any longer. I regret only that I missed you and that maybe I have given you another chance to kill."

"Yes, you have," Jamie said angrily. "You've given me a chance to do all those things one more time—to you. I never made anyone suffer. I killed them clean while they slept, then I took those things that meant something to them. Indians believe that if you got no prick on your body you can't screw around in heaven. Well, I took that pleasure from them. They took my folks from me, my family, and now my wife."

"Elizabeth says that's all lies you made up, Jamie. She says that no Indian ever did any harm to you."

"What about Cree Woman? They killed her."

"If Cree Woman is dead, Jamie, then you killed her. God help you. You killed the only person in the world who cared for you."

"You shut up. You aren't Stevie. Stevie wouldn't say things like that to me. I saved Stevie's life. I saved Elizabeth from the filthy Indian that was going to rape her, that Chris Douglas. I did it good to him." He laughed. "But you ain't Stevie."

"I'm not. I'm Joshua, Elizabeth's son."

"Joshua is a baby. You're nothing but a fucking liar." He backed away from where Joshua was hanging. "I never made anyone suffer before, but you're going to suffer for lying about me to Stevie and Elizabeth."

He grabbed Joshua by the hips and lifted him and then dropped him. The rope stretched but held, jolting the sockets in Joshua's arms. He cried out in pain.

"Now, that's only the beginning. I think I'm going to keep you alive for as long as I can. I'll cut a slice off every once in a while for fresh meat, but I think I'll take my time eating my supply up."

He took out his knife and began to look over the body of his victim. "I need something that will be tender but not vital." He scraped the hairs of Joshua's thigh with the edge of his knife. "Sharp, ain't it? Now, all I have to do is the same motion, just a little more pressure, and I got me a slice of man ham." He laughed insanely at this own joke.

Cold air came rushing into the barn, causing Joshua to shiver.

"Drop the knife, Jamie." The voice sounded vaguely familiar to Joshua.

"Stevie, is that you?" Jamie asked.

"Yup, it's me. Do as I say. Drop the knife."

Jamie continued to hold the blade against Joshua but shifted it from the thigh to the softness of his belly.

"You got my boy and you're hurting him. Now, for old time's sake I'll let you drop your weapon. But if you don't, I'm going to blow your head off."

"I don't want to hurt him, Stevie," Jamie said.

Joshua looked down at his belly, where the edge of the knife rested on his skin. He could see Jamie switching his grip. He was either going to plunge it or throw it.

"Watch out," Joshua screamed.

Jamie twisted to throw but never raised his arm. The bullet entered his eye and crashed through his skull, sending brain matter and blood splattering against Joshua's naked body. Jamie fell to the floor of the barn, his shattered face lying in a puddle of his own blood.

Joshua watched as the gray-bearded man stepped from the shadows and picked up Jamie's knife and cut the rope that held Joshua to the rafters.

Joshua collapsed in the man's arms.

"You've grown to a man since I last saw you, Josh. Here, take the horse blanket. There's some water there for washing yourself off. I'll take care of poor Jamie, here."

He rolled Jamie's body onto its back. "I feel kind of responsible for you, friend," he said softly to the corpse. "I didn't want to have to do it but you gave me no choice. Maybe it is for the best. We couldn't let you go." He wiped his nose on his sleeve. Joshua could see the tears in his eyes.

"My mother?"

"We found her down by the lake. She was in bad shape. That's why it took us so long to get here. Couldn't get the story out of her until she came around."

He lifted Jamie's body and carried it out into the snow behind the barn. Then he returned.

"Is she all right?" Joshua asked with concern.

"My boys are bringing her up now."

The door of the barn opened and Elizabeth entered. She looked around. She saw Joshua wrapped in a blanket. She ran to him and threw her arms around him, kissing him on the cheek. And then she walked back toward Stephen Miller.

They spent the next day preparing to depart. Jamie's grave was placed next to the barn. After they buried him and what was left of Mr. Buttle, they came back to the

237

cabin. Stephen had put out the fire, but it was no longer habitable.

Elizabeth could not pull herself away from Stephen. "Do you know he recognized me lying in the snow? After twenty years of thinking me dead, he finds a strange woman lying in the snow and calls my name. Nearly smothers me and almost lets you die."

Stephen put his arm about her waist. "Well, you ain't grown any bigger," he said to her.

"Too bad the same can't be said of you," she commented, patting his ample belly. "What in God's name brought you back here?"

He laughed. "I was waiting at the junction of the Clearwater and the North Thompson for the boatmen to carry the goods from Cabiney. Well, they came back without the goods. They said this fellow arrived before the snows and says Cabiney has turned back. Now, I've known John Cabiney for many years. We have downed a few together and we've laid—" He looked at Elizabeth and stopped. "We have enjoyed many a good time together," he continued. "One thing John ain't, he ain't no quitter. He sure as hell was not going to turn back. I told my boys we were going back to Moose Lake to find out what's going on."

He could not bring himself to tell her that he knew from LaMotte that she was coming. He had expected to meet her and Joshua at Moose Lake. Then at the Clearwater he had become frightened. He had changed so much. How could he dare to think she would wish to continue where they had left off? He had sunk too low. There was no hope for him. He had stayed behind at the camp on the Clearwater. He had resigned himself to never seeing her again. But then the men had returned empty-handed, with their story about the strange man saying no one could make it to Moose Lake. He had sensed something was wrong. Elizabeth was in trouble. He forgot his fear. He had to go to her.

He sat down at the table, which had remained intact, unscathed by the fire.

"My boys have reached Cabiney's camp. They're bringing the goods over the Divide to the boats. Cabiney's turning around and heading for Edmonton. Wants to know if anyone wants to go with him."

Joshua looked at his mother. At last her arms were around the man she loved.

"I do," he said softly.

Elizabeth nodded in agreement. "There's a girl back on the prairies, a wife and a child he has never seen."

"And you, Mother?"

She looked up at Stephen Miller and smiled. "Your uncle is taking me to an island off the coast in the Pacific that he has become enamored of."

"I can't wait to have you see it, Liz. Mountains, lakes, rivers, fjords, rain forests, and flowers. I don't think it ever gets cold. Not like here."

"Then we go our separate ways again," Joshua said sadly.

"I asked you when we found each other not to leave me alone again. Well, this time when you leave me I will not be alone."

He nodded.

She went to him and kissed him. "Find the girl. Go home to your family."

The schooner slipped between the islands of the straits. Elizabeth stood on deck with Stephen as the ship entered the port.

"We've called the town Fort Victoria. It's nothing but a few shanties right now, not quite grand enough for a queen's name."

"But it is as beautiful here as you claimed, and as warm."

"Compared to a canoe on the North Thompson and Fraser in early December, anything is warm."

His eyes took in not only Victoria Harbor but all the land around it. "It's funny," he said. "Our family stretches back pretty far on this continent. My mother told me how her father was captured as a boy and raised on another island in the sea, only that island was clear across the continent. My grandpa, Stephen Nowell, began there on

239

Cape Breton Island on the Atlantic side, and now this Stephen is prepared to spend his last days with his beautiful wife on this island of Vancouver, thousands of miles away. It was quite a trek." He put his arm around her and together they came to their new home.

XI

Spring 1843

Joshua had to spend the winter in Edmonton. The snows had caught him just as they came to the town. He discovered that LaMotte was right. In winter the saloon was filled day and night. He worked for LaMotte again in order to keep himself in food and stable the black stallion. He had to return his bride price to his father-in-law.

In January the Chinook winds came down from the mountains and melted all the snows. Joshua had wanted to leave Edmonton immediately and strike out for the Minnedosa and Rainbow. He was talked out of it only because the warm air disappeared quickly and new snows swept down into the prairies, piling drifts to great heights.

Finally Joshua had become convinced that spring would never come. In March he said good-bye to LaMotte, but then another storm struck, making travel again unthinkable. Joshua went back to washing dishes and sleeping restlessly in the back room of the saloon. He kept dreaming about her. The last time he heard her voice, she cried out to him in pain. Her voice would call out to him in his dreams and he would wake up crying out and trying to reach her.

Finally in April Joshua mounted the stallion. His saddle-bags were loaded with pemmican for the long trip across the prairies. The horse was anxious to be away after a long winter cooped up in his stall.

Joshua waved to LaMotte and said good-bye to Fort Edmonton. He would retrace his route home along the North Saskatchewan to the South Saskatchewan, along the

241

Qu'Appelle and through the Moose Mountains to the Pipestone, and from there to the Assiniboine.

He traveled warily through the country of the Blackfoot, moving only at night and resting in the day. When he came to the hunting grounds of the Blood, he did the same. He took even more care in the lands of the Peigan. Then finally in late June he came to the Minnedosa. He searched for signs of White Buffalo's encampment. He found them, but they were old—made early in the spring. He followed the trail of the travois as they headed northeast. He found signs of a successful buffalo kill. White Buffalo's Assiniboine were having strong and good medicine. He came to the river called the Whitemud. They had been there as well. They were following the course of the river as it flowed to the east and south. The signs were fresher now, only a few days old.

The stallion seemed to sense that he too was going home after so long a journey. He pranced and stamped his foot when Joshua leaned over the side to read the trail. It was as if the stallion spoke to him: "Give me my head, you fool, I know where they are, I'll lead you to them."

They left the river and headed due east. Now they were very close. Joshua kicked the stallion into a gallop. They rode up a long slope to a bluff. He reined in the horse. Below him and stretching endlessly before him was a great lake. At the shore of the lake, White Buffalo had brought his people to fish.

Joshua kicked the horse into action again. The stallion charged downward, his mane flying in the wind. Joshua called out his greeting in Assiniboine. People came out of their lodges. They recognized the bull calf of Medicine Cow Lady and they sent shrill cries of greeting into the crisp sky.

Joshua halted his charge in the middle of the village, where he expected to find Eagle Face's people.

The old man sat placidly outside his lodge. He did not even rise when he saw Joshua.

"I am happy to see you return my horse," he said in Assiniboine.

Joshua did not understand him but he went to Eagle

Face and kissed him on top of the head. He entered the lodge. Warrior Woman turned around in surprise. Rainbow was sitting on the far side of the lodge. One breast was uncovered as she nursed the baby. Her face went from shock to sublime happiness, all in the space of a second. She stood and slipped the nipple from the baby's mouth and covered herself. The child squinted and wrinkled his face in protest. Rainbow came to Joshua. She handed him the child.

"Your son," she said, "as yet nameless. I waited for the return of his father before I gave him a name."

Joshua held the baby in his arms and he smiled at the wonder of it all. Then he handed the baby to Warrior Woman. He swept Rainbow into his arms and sought her mouth with his own.

Later that day, after Eagle Face and Warrior Woman returned to the lodge, making discreet noises at the entryway to warn the lovers of their return, Joshua took Rainbow and their son down to the edge of the lake.

"What is this sea called?" he asked her.

"We call it Manitoba."

He turned his son's face toward the lake. The baby smiled.

"See this Manitoba," he called out. "This is your water." He turned around and looked at the prairies that stretched as far as the eye could see. "My son, this is your land, this Manitoba. It is not the land of the Assiniboine alone. It is not the land of the white man alone. It belongs to all of us. My son, you carry the blood of the white and the red together. This land, this Manitoba, is a Métis land."

Epilogue

1864

Wilhelmina Brant still looked much younger than her forty-two years. Many people, hearing that Michael Brant had a daughter, mistook his wife for his child. She walked beside her husband, making sure that he did not lose his footing. He complained about having to walk, but actually he enjoyed the stroll through the countryside. The fall colors were in full blaze on the island and on the bluffs across the St. Lawrence. The falls of the Montmorenci soon came into view, framed in the gold, rust, and brilliant reds of the fall leaves and the dark green of the evergreen.

A boy of about twelve years drove a herd of milk cows down the road toward them.

"*Bonjour, monsieur et madame,*" the lad greeted them and doffed his woolen cap in Willie's direction.

"*Bonjour,*" they replied and stepped aside to let the cows pass.

"I wish that Margaret had joined us," Michael complained.

"She said she'd join us later. She and Craig were so excited about seeing Quebec. I could not insist that they spend such a glorious day visiting with stodgy relatives that they don't even know."

"Why do they have to see Quebec? It's not much different from Halifax, and they've seen Halifax."

"And Halifax is no different from Boston and Boston is identical to New York and New York is a small version of London. Honestly, Michael Brant, some day you should remove your nose from your law books and look about at the world around you."

Willie was always at him like this. They shared a deep

affection for each other. He knew that it had never blossomed into a passionate love. Perhaps it was the age difference. He could never seem to get over thinking of her as a child, even now, when she was a middle-aged woman with a twenty-year-old daughter. But he needed her. She took care of him from the time she had found him bleeding at Montgomery's Tavern so many years before. He knew he had replaced her father in her life, but he was a damned sight better father than Donald Mackay had ever been. Margaret, their daughter, had been named in honor of their benefactress in exile, Margaret Nowell Conrad.

His cousin had lived to be present at the child's christening in the Episcopal Church in Boston and to serve as her godmother. Then in 1850 she died, leaving half her fortune— her share of the Nowell estate, all she had received from her mother, Amy Nowell, and the whole of her uncle's, the childless Matthew Nowell's, portion augmented by the proceeds of her share in the vast Ferryman trade and industrial empire in Britain—half of all of this she left to Michael and her goddaughter, her namesake. The rest she left to her son. And Michael Brant, an exiled lawyer unable to practice his profession in the foreign land, became one of Boston's wealthiest men.

He bought his pardon in Canada and returned to British America. The memories in the Canadas were too bitter for him. His mother, Jessica, had died in 1846, and he knew she died of loneliness. They never saw each other again after that bitter cold night in Toronto when he and Willie and the boy Joshua made their escape. He could never forgive Toronto its cruelty. He returned instead to Halifax and Nova Scotia. He built his home in the heart of the town beneath the citadel. It was a showpiece. And who could have thought that the tree-climbing sailor tomboy that he married could become *grande dame* of the province of Nova Scotia?

They had heard little from the rest of the family until two years before, a dark-skinned, black-haired youth from the wilds of the Red River arrived at their front doorstep, carpetbag in hand and bearing a letter from his father, Michael's nephew, Joshua Miller. Joshua asked Michael to house and educate Craig, his son. The boy was soon attending classes at King's College in Windsor. He had survived his first year with difficulty. He was semiliterate and he spoke English in the most convoluted way. His busy father had left his language education to his Assiniboine mother.

No one heard much from Joshua Miller. He almost never wrote. Craig told the Brants that his father farmed a large tract of land on the Red River. The farms that had once belonged to the three families, the McAlistairs, the Rowands, and the Millers, were now one farm. A great house set back on the bluffs over the river had been built. But Joshua and his wife would frequently give up the farm life and ride out onto the prairies in search of the lodges of Rainbow's people.

Strangely enough, Michael heard more from his sister, Elizabeth, Joshua's mother, who lived at Fort Victoria all the way on the other side of the continent. She was widowed now. Her husband, Stephen, had died in 1852. Elizabeth had not revealed the cause, but everyone suspected that Stephen's drinking for most of his adult life had caused a breakdown in his health in the last years.

Elizabeth continued to live in the village that grew about the fort on Vancouver Island, tending her flower garden and occasionally, despite her seventy years, taking one of her three horses on a long ride into the island's interior.

The rest of the family were in Quebec and would be at the Stiegler manor house on the old homestead.

Amy Nowell, a true Schuyler like her mother, Katherine, had lived to see her ninetieth year and had died in 1840. Her younger half brother, Louis Joseph Stiegler, son of the founder of the numerous Stieglers of Quebec and Marc Stiegler's father, died two years later. He and his wife, Marie, were killed in a freak accident as their sled attempted to cross the St. Charles River over ice on their way to Quebec City. But the rest of the Stieglers—Marc, his sisters, and his son, Claud—were very much alive and very influential in the Quebec portion of the Canadian delegation of the conference.

It was Marc Stiegler who had called his family together for a reunion. There were family members present in the city whom Michael would just as soon have avoided, but he was sure he would not be able to.

A carriage came careening down the road, the driver standing in the seat and whipping the horses. Willie looked up in alarm and held tightly to Michael's arm as she gently shoved him off the side of the road. But they need not have moved. The carriage halted with a grinding of metal brakes on metal wheels and the horse reared in its harness. Marc Stiegler, his formerly black hair almost totally white, opened the carriage door and stepped out.

"Pardon, my cousins, my poor imbecile of a nephew failed to inform me that your boat had arrived. Please ride the rest of the way with me."

"Willie, I want you to meet our Quebec cousin, Monsieur Marc Stiegler. Monsieur Stiegler, my wife."

"*Enchanté, madame*," said Marc, bowing and kissing the woman's hand.

Willie blushed, and despite her normally blunt and down-to-earth manner, she was clearly charmed with the almost European mannerisms of this French-Canadian man.

Michael was annoyed with her reaction. He wondered if she could imagine Marc Stiegler as an *avant* for the Northwest Company, a *voyageur* brawling in taverns, sleeping with squaws, carrying furs across half a continent.

The Brants climbed into Stiegler's buggy and the carriage moved foward toward the homestead.

"What do you think of this conference thus far, Michael?" Marc asked.

"As you know, Marc, I have no role in the conference. I am an observer."

"But you do not hesitate to report to Mr. Howe."

"Joseph Howe is Imperial Fisheries commissioner and has nothing to do with the conference."

"And he is the most important politician in Nova Scotia," said Marc, laughing.

"Our premier, Dr. Tupper, would probably take exception to your evaluation."

"Well, who do you work for?"

"No one, Marc."

"What is your opinion on union?"

"I favor union of the Maritime colonies. Nova Scotia, New Brunswick, Prince Edward Island, and even Newfoundland should unite."

"And you find no place for the Canadas in your scheme?"

Michael smiled. "You know I was a Torontonian for most of my early life. I am suspicious of Toronto. I fear my new home would be made subservient to Canadian interests in any but a confederated union."

"Then you share my sentiments. But it is you I do not trust. English Canada, united with the Martime English populations, and the west will soon engulf the French of Quebec. Our language, our church, our customs, our laws are all threatened."

"Then you should oppose unification schemes."

Before Mare could answer, the carriage pulled up before the hip-roofed stone house that had been the seat of the Stieglers in Quebec since the first of them, the Swiss mercenary who fought in the army of the Marquis de Montcalm, received it from the government of Louis XV.

Michael, Willie, and Marc walked up the wooden steps of the house to the porch.

Marc's forty-year old son, Claud, stepped out of the house to greet the guests. He was followed by a strikingly beautiful woman. Her blond hair was piled high on her head to show off the beauty of her neck. Her green eyes searched the newcomers with a kind of haughty interest.

"Allison, I believe, is it not?" Michael asked. "Allison Winslow—I mean, Allison Miller."

"Why, Mr. Brant, I would have known you anywhere. I don't believe you've changed a bit. You've become more distinguished since the last time I saw you. In 1837, wasn't it?"

Willie leaned over and whispered in Michael's ear. "She's as full of shit now as she always was!"

Michael started to choke, trying to suppress his laughter. He knew his wife could be very vulgar, but over the years he had come to understand that her vulgarity was a defense against pomposity and vanity. But most of all, Willie hated a lack of truthfulness.

"Do you remember me, Allison?"

"Why, Willie Mackay, how could anyone ever forget you?"

The door to the house reopened, and an old man, almost totally bald and with only a few wisps of gray hair combed across his head, came out, supported by a young man, a blond, green-eyed replica of Allison Miller.

The old man was bent and walked with a cane. "Michael Brant, you Jewish half-breed. What brings you back here to Canada?"

"I see you are as lovable as ever, Charles."

The old man laughed. "Alex," he yelled at the boy. "Get me a chair. I can't stand here on the porch. And it's cold; get me a shawl."

Claud Stiegler started into the house.

"No, let my worthy son take care of my needs. After all, I won't be around too much longer and he'll have no one bothering him after he inherits all of my money."

Alex Miller sneered at Charles behind his back.

Michael was shocked by the expression. It was a hateful one, and he had seen it so often in the past on the face of Charles Miller.

"Well, Michael?"

"I'm here to advise the Nova Scotia delegation on legal aspects of the talks."

"Lawyers, goddamned lawyers. Save me from lawyers."

Alex returned with his father's shawl and a rocking chair. Claud brought several more chairs out onto the veranda. Charles sat back in his chair and stared across the river at the falls. Allison went to sit next to him, but he looked angrily at her.

"Don't fuss over me, woman," he snapped at her. She ignored his comment but rose from the chair and began to engage Claud in a lively conversation in badly accented schoolgirl French. Claud, however, was enraptured. He could not take his eyes away from her beauty.

"Damn waste," Charles said.

"What is?" Michael responded.

"Not as bad as Niagara because it is not as big. But still a damn waste."

"You mean the falls?"

"They are beautiful," said Willie.

"I say it is a damn waste," Miller interrupted. "I started in boats. Goddamned wind pushed you from one side of the lake to the other. Then I got into steamboats, then trains, power, steam power, energy. The future is about energy. Do you see how much energy is wasted in those falls?"

"You mean the future is about the Grand Trunk Railway, don't you Cousin Miller?" Michael interrupted him.

"It's the same thing."

"And you're a major shareholder in the railroad, which explains why you are at this conference."

A second carriage drove up to the Stiegler house. Craig Miller and Margaret Brant descended from it.

The two young people were presented. Charles looked up at the dark-skinned, handsome boy. "So you're supposed to be my grandson, or so I'm told."

Michael stiffened. He did not wish to rehash ancient arguments of the family.

"Might have known," Charles went on. "The Brants always had more influence than I did on your father. Took up with an Indian woman, didn't he?"

"My mother is an Assiniboine," Craig volunteered.

"I might have known," said Charles sarcastically.

Marc Stiegler joined the other two older men. He produced a decanter of good whiskey and some tumblers and poured a healthy shot for each of them.

"Miller says that the Grand Trunk Railway is the reason he is here in Quebec for the conference."

"I suspected as much," said Stiegler.

"Well, do you want one Canada or don't you?" said Charles. "I am straightforward. I do. It is good for business. And that's what makes this old body of mine continue to function, much to my dear wife's frustration. The future is the west, gentlemen, Rupert's Land and across the mountains to Vancouver Island Colony. The Hudson's Bay Company must give it up, and it must become part of Canada as an area of future development."

"You mean you want to build railroads with government subsidies and make farmers out there all dependent on the railroad and subject to your rates," said Michael.

"Precisely, and that is what America will do with its west just as soon as they get over the idiocy of civil war. They'll kill all the filthy buffalo and the equally filthy Indians and build railroads and towns and churches and farms, and if we are not goddamned careful they'll take over our west too."

Michael glanced over at Craig as Charles spoke. Miller caught the glance.

"Oh, Jesus, I forgot I'm in the presence of a couple of half-breeds. I've got to watch what I say about Indians. It's lucky I've already lost most of my hair." He snickered.

"Fine," said Stiegler, "but let Upper Canada have its way. Let it have its railroads and its west, but leave Quebec be."

"You forget, Marc, that we've been in a legislative union since the rebellions. Upper Canada and Lower Canada are now the United Canadas. We tried to heal old wounds. Why, we even let that old traitor Mackenzie back into the country. We even let him serve in Parliament."

"You also let that old traitor Brant return," Michael laughed.

Charles Miller smiled.

"But really, Marc," Michael interjected, "you might not want a Quebec alone. In your present union with the English you have the protection of your language and your culture. Go it alone and you may fall prey to the Americans. Then what would happen to your French language and culture? Americans take pride that their country is a melting pot. They have very little reverence for differences. And if Quebec is not part of the Union, the Maritimes are isolated from Canada and we fall too. I know the Americans. I have lived there. I love them. But I don't want to be American."

Marc looked at Michael. "So you *do* favor the union of all of the provinces into one nation?"

"I did not say that. I don't want an American master, but as a Nova Scotian I don't want a Canadian one either, be he English or French."

"We've offered to build the intercolonial railroad in the Maritimes," Charles interrupted. "It will tie Nova Scotia and New Brunswick to the rest of British America."

Marc made a snorting sound. "British America."

Willie grew tired of listening to them.

"I think it's wrong that discussions about the future are always left to the old men."

The three men stared at her in disbelief.

"Let's ask the young what they think. Margaret, Craig, Alex, what are your views on the conference?"

Alex looked very uncomfortable with his father staring at him. Allison quickly came to his aid. "You know that Alex acts as his father's secretary. The two of them are almost of one mind. It is incredible how alike they think."

"Truly incredible," sneered Charles.

Alex looked relieved and said nothing.

It was Margaret Brant who spoke.

"I think Mr. Brown of Upper Canada and Mr. Cartier in Quebec and even some of the Maritime leaders, not quite so pigheaded as my father, and now even Mr. Macdonald, the premier of United Canada, have all conceded that a Confederation is essential—a true Confederation that protects the interests of all parties with representation in a House of Commons by population—"

"We will be swamped by the English," Marc Stiegler interrupted her.

"But with the special local interests protected so that language and civil law would be the prerogatives of the constituent members of the Confederation."

Michael was amazed by his daughter's precociousness. He knew she had studied the issues and had questioned him often. But normally she was very shy.

"A Confederation has led to a civil war just south of us," said Michael.

252

"I think that has more to do with slavery—a blight we were fortunate enough to avoid," she responded.

"Yet it was the Confederation idea—states' rights—that made it impossible for the American central government to deal with slavery," her father argued.

"Well, then, you must create a strong central government and give to it all the powers not specifically given to the provinces, while giving the provinces those powers which protect their needs—like language and education. We must learn from the American mistakes."

Charles Miller interrupted her. "I don't give a damn what you give Quebec—just as long as we get the west."

Margaret turned to her cousin, Craig Miller. "You're a quiet one. Speak up. I know you have opinions."

Craig blushed. It was clear he did not wish to speak before these old men who knew so much and spoke so glibly.

"All right, boy," said Stiegler, "what do you see as the answer?"

"I have no idea, sir. I'm not versed in politics."

"My good fellow," said Charles, "that almost makes up for your being part Indian."

Craig blushed. "I don't know," he continued, "if any of you have been in the west."

"I've been to the Lake of the Woods a few times, but not much farther," offered Marc.

Craig smiled. "Excuse me, sir, but the Lake of the Woods is the east."

A look of sudden shock came across Marc Stiegler's face.

"I mean," Craig continued, "if you've never seen the sunset on the prairies, then you have never seen true beauty; if you have never heard the buffalo run the prairies, then you have never heard noise; if you have never seen the antelope dart through the tall grass, then you have no notion of grace; if you have never felt awe for the great mountains as they reach up into the blue sky, then you have never known majesty. That is my land. I have lived in Nova Scotia and I have seen the great ocean. I have seen the might of Quebec's walls. I have seen the

253

St. Lawrence and the inland seas of Upper Canada. They are all magnificent. I want to join them all to my land. I want to be a part of all of it and I want it to be a part of me. I want it all one nation."

Michael actually felt tears come to his eyes as the Métis boy spoke.

Charles cracked a joke. "I thought my wife told me this lad had trouble with English. The only thing he left out was the glory of the railroad stretching from the Atlantic to the Pacific."

Marc rose and put his arm about Craig's shoulder. "I respect your vision, lad," he said. Then he turned to Michael. "I believe it is your daughter, Brant, who really has outlined what it is that the "Fathers" of this nation must do when they sit down together here in Quebec, and in the future conferences that will surely follow. This Dominion of Canada, if it is to be created and survive, must be strong and powerful, yet it must be gentle in its treatment of the peoples who comprise it. I will always be a Quebecker first," said Marc finally, "and I suggest, Miller, if you would just shut up about railroads, you would admit a fondness for Lake Ontario. And you, *mon ami*," he said, looking at Michael, "you are now a Nova Scotian first. But it is the boy who expresses the future of this dominion. He loves the region of his birth, but he tells us he wants all of what he loves to be Canada—one nation. The future lies with the children, gentlemen, and maybe, just maybe, there is a future for a Canada—stretching from sea to sea."

ABOUT THE AUTHOR

A Canadian citizen since 1976, ROBERT E. WALL draws on his love for Canada and his native United States in creating the saga of *THE CANADIANS*. He perceives the histories of the two nations as deeply entwined and, influenced by the writings of Kenneth Roberts, seeks to teach those histories through the historical novel. *Blackrobe*, the first in the series, is Wall's first novel, followed by *Bloodbrothers*, *Birthright*, *Patriots* and *Inheritors*.

Robert Wall is married, has five children (one is an adopted Cree Indian, the most authentic Canadian in the family), and divides his time between New Jersey, where he is provost at Fairleigh Dickinson University, and Montreal, where his family lives.

Adele looked out the front window and turned to Babin. "There is no escape," she said; "you'll never get to the river, the yard is filled with redcoats."

Terror gripped Babin. He turned to his wife. "They'll hang me for sure. I killed one of them."

Just then TiJoe awoke and sat up on his mat rubbing his eyes. He heard the noise of soldiers outside the house and jumped up to go to the window.

"TiJoe, no," Adele called out to him. She stepped forward to block his path to the window. A volley of musket balls rang out tearing through the window pane and splattering glass in all directions. A huge sliver of glass smashed into TiJoe's throat severing an artery. Blood gushed from him and poured all over his front. A look of hurt surprise crossed his face and then he sank to his knees, his life's blood pouring out of him. Adele stared in disbelief at the growing circle of red which stained her skirt just above her navel where the ball had entered her. She too sank to her knees. Odette did nothing but scream and run from one victim to another. Babin stood motionless. He knew without looking that TiJoe would die within seconds and that Adele's belly wound was fatal and he new instinctively that his beloved Dette's mind had snapped. He could never recover from the sight of her baby's blood gushing all over her. Just at that moment Hastings called out or him to surrender. He was numb. There was no use resisting. There was nothing to resist for. He opened the door nd walked out into the yard. He was seized roughly and his rms were tied behind his back. He heard Nina scream out his name. He could not even look at her. He was pulled lmost off his feet by a rope which had been tied around his eck. Twenty-five years before he had planted the maple tree n the front yard. It had grown sturdily. Its roots had sunk eep into the soil of Acadia. The loose end of the rope bout Babin's neck was tossed over a high limb of the maple. 'ive soldiers hauled on the rope walking away from the tree. Babin felt the hemp tighten around his neck and then he was erked off his feet. His legs kicked a gruesome dance in the ir. His face turned red and his eyes bulged. He could not reathe. Finally there was nothing but blackness.

Captain Hastings ordered the corpse to be left hanging rom the maple tree until sundown the next day. He turned o his sergeant and smiled.

"About that girl back at the headquarters, see to it that she ails on the first transport that arrives and that she sails eparately from the rest of her family."

The sergeant didn't like hangings. He had no stomach for it nd he didn't like what the captain suggested about the girl.

"The first ship is likely to be Captain Rofheart's sloop, sir."

"So?"

"He's a bad one. There are few sailors in Boston who will ign on with him and there isn't a whore in any seaport on the tlantic Coast who will sleep with him."

"Luck of the draw, Sergeant."

"I don't like it," the sergeant responded.

"It's not for you to like or dislike, Sergeant. And while ou're at it, add the screaming widow to Rofheart's list as vell. Maybe he can shut her up."

He turned away from the other man and smiled to himself. I guess I am a bit of a cad after all," he said aloud.

They buried the victims of Babin's escape on the next vening at sunset in the chapel yard. Jacques dug a grave for is mother. Lucien stood watching, his shoulders sagging and is eyes seemed to have clouded over. He saw nothing. dele's small body was placed gently into the four-foot-deep grave by her giant son. Then he stood next to his father with his head bowed. The sun's golden rays struck the hills across the bay and then reflected directly into their eyes. They could see no farther than the gravesite. Jacques squinted and held up his hand to shield his eyes. Then he saw them. Three schooners and a sloop lay anchored in Chignecto Bay. He placed his arm about Lucien's shoulders for he was afraid his father was going to collapse. He seemed drained of all strength by the death of his wife. Jacques decided not to mention the transports to him. Nina stood behind Lucien. The British dug a single grave for her father and little brother. Both were placed in it—the boy on top of the man—united in death as they never had been in life. Nina seemed as paralyzed as Lucien. No one had seen her mother or Helene and all questions about them were carefully ignored by the British.

Lucien stepped to the open grave of his wife. There had been no time to build coffins and Jacques had wrapped his mother in the blanket from the bed she had shared with his father for so many years. He stared down into the hole as if staring into an abyss. He picked up a handful of dirt and sprinkled it on top of the still form, then he turned away and allowed himself to be led back to the chapel.